SAVING NOVA

SAVING NOVA

BOOK ONE

LUIS MARTINEZ

SAVING NOVA
BOOK ONE

This is a work of fiction. All of the characters, names, incidents, organizations, and dialogue in this novel are either the products of the author's imagination or are used fictitiously.

iUniverse books may be ordered through booksellers or by contacting:

iUniverse
1663 Liberty Drive
Bloomington, IN 47403
www.iuniverse.com
1-800-Authors (1-800-288-4677)

ISBN: 978-1-5320-5004-6 (sc)
ISBN: 978-1-5320-5006-0 (hc)
ISBN: 978-1-5320-5005-3 (e)

Library of Congress Control Number: 2018906386

Print information available on the last page.

iUniverse rev. date: 05/30/2018

For my father
Who is the bravest man I know
and a better man than I will ever be.

Nearly all men can stand adversity,
but if you want to test a man's character,
give him power.
-Abraham Lincoln

to tribal-painted faces staring down at him with soulless eyes. The faces looked at one another, shouting in an unknown language as they raised their spears toward the sky, set to finish what their leader had started. This might have been a bad start to things, but for Sean, this was a good end. He'd come a long way for this chance, and it was far too personal to let go.

With the spears ready to strike, Sean lifted his hand to shield himself from the final attack. The blood trickling down his arm felt warm, but inside he was cold. The pain no longer seemed unbearable, and the bleeding from his stomach slowed.

Sean clung to every breath he took from that point on. Death was near, and Sean worried what was waiting for him on the other side—some might say heaven, and others might say hell. In a world where there was no law or order, and survival was given to those who were the fittest, a man couldn't be judged if he had killed or stolen. It had to be if he did or didn't do the best he could, and Sean lay there, knowing he'd given it all he had. Accepting his fate, Sean pulled back his hand, deciding to no longer defend himself but to embrace the spears that were readied to strike him down, a mercy that should have befallen him years ago.

That's when it came—the moment, stopping all time while revealing itself. It was his journey. He watched it unravel before him like a movie, starting from the beginning, three very long years ago, the same journey that brought him here because of a promise Sean chose to fulfill, no matter the cost.

The promise wasn't about greed; it wasn't about an unquenchable lust for power. It wasn't for the love of a woman or desperately trying to right a wrong. No, the promise was about one word that needs to be done when there are no rules to break, when there is no justice to protect those or for those to call upon. The promise would be not for him but for all of them. Sean's promise was about one thing and one thing only.

He promised … vengeance.

CHAPTER 1

THE BEGINNING

The fierce sun was high in the air, laying a blanket of heat across its view. Not a tree, plant, rock, or living thing could escape it. Under that blanket lay miles and miles of desert land, stretching without end. To the naked eye, it was barren. Nothing could or would exist within its emptiness except for four walls of metal, none of which were the same. Their length and shape all depended upon the items available. Stop signs, stripped cars, street posts, bed frames, whatever survived the fall of humankind and would continue to survive was used. Within the emptiness was its greatest strength and weakness. Nothing would ever venture this far into thinking there was precious life or food to be found. There was safety in the isolation but also inevitable hardships. Food lay far from their grasp, needing days to search for it. But life carried on inside these walls, and they named it Nova.

From inside its metal walls, tanned faces glanced at the sun with contempt, exhausted with its presence. Many were beginning their daily jobs, while others started to rest after working all morning. The sea of people scattered about like a colony of ants, all working except for one. Sleeping on his bed, Sean awakened in his room as the candles neared their end. They wouldn't last another night and needed to be replaced to keep his baby sister, Lucy, from crying. She was having trouble sleeping, and Sean's mother hoped that leaving lit candles near her bed would do the trick. Luckily for Sean, it did. Lucy slept sprawled on her back for hours on end, even snoring a few times, allowing more sleep-filled nights. Sean struggled out of bed, battling the grogginess of oversleeping. Having tossed his clothes on the floor, Sean grabbed them from where he'd left them, ignoring the shower bucket as he slipped on the jeans and T-shirt. Water was scarce around the land and had to be used sparingly. Once dressed, Sean gave the door handle a hard counterclockwise turn and pushed forward. Loud moans bellowed from rusty hinges that hadn't been greased in over a hundred years. A burst of sunlight from behind the metal door engulfed the entire home.

Sean blocked as much of the sunlight as he could and watched laughing children scurry across his home. He waved at them as their mothers gossiped together, washing dishes. Shoulder to shoulder they stood, blabbing away over a bathtub filled with dirty pots and plates. On a few occasions, the gossip they traded back and forth was about their misbehaved kids and good-for-nothing husbands before fantasying about Nova's hunter, Alex. The sex-starved wives took turns glancing over at Alex, trying not to look suspicious. Thoughts of the black-haired, blue-eyed heartthrob being the father of their children made their knees weak.

Alex stood tall behind the grill in his black boots and tan overalls, without a shirt. Thick white smoke rose from burning meat and stretched to the sky. The heat from the grill caused sweat to pour over Alex's shoulders and chest, adding better definition to his already toned body. Alex didn't need help defining his muscles; the man seemed to be carved out of stone and belonged on a calendar that firefighters did for charity.

While waving away the smoke, he stabbed a slab of meat with his barbecue fork, giving it to the next person in line, Stacey Parson, but not before giving her a playful wink. Having a body that women lusted for and the prestige of being a hunter did come at a price. The job was very demanding, both physically and mentally. Most hunts required hunters to sprint long distances, carry heavy weapons, and hide for long periods of time. Because of this, Alex loved to show off his well-defined muscles earned from the hunts like badges of honor. Sean even caught his very own mother blushing a few times around Alex's broad shoulders and big arms. He also loved telling stories about his hunts for cattleworm, a species that emerged in the new world.

Cattleworm did not have any feet; they dragged their bodies like snails on the surface. Catching them was easy; the real challenge occurred when they dug tunnels to travel underground. Hunters needed to be extremely careful. Some tunnels were so close to the surface that the ground would collapse if they stepped on that spot. Those who were fortunate walked away with a few bumps and bruises. The unlucky ones received broken legs or arms or even fell to their deaths. Cattleworms had sharp teeth and thick hairy sides to pull or push dirt as they moved underground, making their way to the top. They stayed underground until it was time to feed. That was the only chance for anyone to see them and pick up their trail. Before Alex killed a cattleworm, he would milk it and then store the milk in jugs deep underground to keep it cold.

More smoke filled the air, carrying with it the smell of roasting meat seasoned with garlic (Alex's signature ingredient). Sean's stomach growled, and his mouth watered with anticipation. He walked over to the already long line of hungry children and took a spot in back. The kids who had run by earlier made their way back now, playing with a soccer ball that had been patched over the years. After waiting a short while in line, it was Sean's turn for a slab of meat. Alex smiled and wished him good morning as he threw a solid pound of meat on a plate.

"Rise and shine, Sean. Heard you slept through the early part of the day," Alex said.

"Yeah, Lucy had a bad night and kept me up," Sean said.

"Candles didn't work this time?"

Sean shook his head and waited for the plate of food.

"What could it be this time, Sean?"

Sean bit his lip, fighting back the urge to be rude. Alex, unfortunately, was the talkative type, a bad habit learned from the Lin twins, which made it hard for people to get on with their day.

At first, Alex wasn't the one yapping away without end. It started when he found the courage to talk to the Lin sisters, Ashley and Kira, who were chatting near him. There was no beating the Lin sisters in gossip or regular banter. Their conversations easily lasted for hours. Sean recalled a day when some folks swore they'd heard Ashley and Kira talking outside their home from sunup until sundown without so much as a break.

Sean needed to be careful; the conversation didn't start bad, but he could be trapped talking until sundown, leaving a juicy plate to get cold. Hungry and dying for food, Sean tried to end the conversation by sounding exhausted and hinting for the plate of food in Alex's hands.

"I really don't know what's been bugging her. I think she is growing in some teeth. It keeps her up at night, screaming," Sean said.

To Sean's surprise, it worked. Alex nodded his head and handed him the plate. Without hesitation, Sean left the line and found a seat. It took him all of five minutes to scarf down the thick chunk of cattleworm meat. Somewhere in between the second and third mouthful, he noticed the meat's texture was juicier and softer than usual. There was no mistaking that the piece came from the belly—hands down the best part of the cattleworm, with the most flavor. Alex's generosity helped peel away the grogginess and added a kick-start of energy. Sean handed the empty plate to the sex-starved wives and prepared to plan his day.

A hand reached over and grabbed him by the shoulder, turning him around. "There you are, sleepyhead," Diane said, poking around Sean's eyes, rubbing the sleep away.

"Hey, Mom, good morning," Sean said, pulling back, embarrassed that his mom still treated him like a baby.

"Good morning, sweetie. Are you going to see Mr. Davis today?" She looked for the truth in his eyes.

Mr. Davis taught all the children how to read and write, as well as other everyday skills. Two years ago, at the age of sixteen, Sean had finished the final lesson that Mr. Davis could offer. But Diane still expected Sean to go every day, even though he had passed every language, writing, and history test that Mr. Davis had given. For Sean, still attending the class was uneventful and a huge waste of time. He rarely cared to listen anymore about the old world and how it died. Even helping students cheat on tests lost interest for him after a while, no matter how much it angered Mr. Davis. Despite the accurate and logical response that Sean spent hours putting together for a moment like this, he still failed to convince Diane that he should skip class, as she refused to listen.

"I'm sorry, Sean, but you probably missed a lot already." It was a lie Sean always heard when Diane caught him skipping class. As he stared into his mother's blue eyes, he knew there was no use in arguing anymore. The look was determined to make him attend the rest of the lesson. Without delay, Diane escorted Sean across Nova and into Mr. Davis's classroom.

CHAPTER 2

HOW THE OLD
WORLD DIED

T wo refrigerator doors were used as an entrance to the classroom. Sean reluctantly gripped their handles and swung them open, revealing small sections of broken benches organized into rows around Mr. Davis. A dozen children sat crossed legged, writing with chalk on small pieces of broken chalkboards. Anyone who didn't have a board wrote on the ground. Mr. Davis gave a polite smile as he caught Sean taking a seat in the back row. He waited for Sean to get comfortable in his seat and then rocked back and forth on his heels.

"So glad you could join us, Mr. Anders," he said.

Sean nodded and remained silent.

Mr. Davis placed his left arm on a podium. Sean's frequent constant skipping of class was a pet peeve for Mr. Davis, and he wasn't going to let Sean off the hook so easily. "Before I continue, can you answer a question?"

Sean readied himself for Mr. Davis's overused style of "punishment."

"How many years has it been since the end of the old world?" Mr. Davis asked.

Sean tried to remember the answer over the snickering children down in the front row. Mr. Davis was going to get his revenge as Sean answered incorrectly. "Around ninety-four years."

Mr. Davis shook his head and frowned behind his thick, groomed white beard. The younger kids, including Sean, made fun of Mr. Davis for how he resembled the old wizard Merlin in the books he made them read.

"Sorry, Mr. Anders, the correct answer is 103 years ago. You may have exceeded the age to attend my class, yet you failed to retain its knowledge."

The other children dragged out an *ooh* sound at the way Mr. Davis had burned Sean. Sean watched the old wizard turn to his desk behind the podium and grab a thick brown textbook with a drawing of the earth on the cover. Mr. Davis held the book high for everyone to see. "This here, ladies and gentlemen, is the old world." He pointed over to Sean. "Since our dear Mr. Anders had forgotten all about it, let me refresh his memory."

A negative stir broke out inside the classroom. The children rolled their eyes as they moaned and grumbled, a few turning to give Sean an evil glare from across the room.

Mr. Davis happily smiled, ready to refresh everyone's memory through an hour-long history lesson that would extend the class well past its period. He placed the giant book on his podium. He grabbed a piece of chalk and wrote a few words on the blackboard, being careful around the edges. For the children's sake, the blackboard was severely damaged when it was salvaged, missing a few sections. The edges and the upper right portion were broken off when one of Nova's explorers found it in the north. It had been surrounded by broken tree limbs, rocks, and random salvage, suggesting that a powerful sandstorm had carried it there. Since the blackboard's size was now only half of what it had been, Mr. Davis could only write a few portions of the day's lesson at a time. If the mad wizard had been given a full-size blackboard, class time would have been three times as long.

Mr. Davis turned and spoke. His words were dull and slow, exhausting everyone's minds. The kids leaned back, fighting the urge to fall asleep. Mr. Davis continued on, pacing back and forth. "All right class, 103 years ago humankind's way of life came crashing down on everyone's head. Human greed and corruption would lead to the fall of civilization. Gas and oil prices came to an all-time high. At seven dollars seventy-eight cents, it crippled much of Earth's population."

A brown-haired, freckle-faced girl held her hand in the air, interrupting Mr. Davis. "Uh … Mr. Davis, what are dollars and cents?"

"You see, Mandy, that is what people used to buy items. They used dollars and cents, called currency, to purchase items or services. The old world didn't live like we do. We care for each other and share our food. The old world only cared about these dollars and cents. They worked, killed, stole, and cheated for it. It was already falling apart, but the rise in gas prices was just the final push to their demise."

Sean rolled his eyes and looked away. He hated the way Mr. Davis talked about how the old world died. He always spoke in that way, as if he knew the old world would have ended in chaos and even sounding happy that it did. Sean wished he'd had a chance to see the old world and to experience the things he imagined and read in Mr. Davis's books. So many wonderful things were held within those pages—animals he would never see, buildings stretching high into the heavens, with cars carrying people to distant places. In spite of Mr. Davis's biased take on the old world, Sean closed his eyes, imagining what it would be to like to stare up at the massive buildings of downtown Chicago.

Meanwhile, Mr. Davis continued on faintly in the background. "When the poor became the homeless and the middle class became the poor, an uprising began. Streets filled with people fighting, looting, and killing each other for anything and everything. The riots moved across America's land and all the way to the White House."

Sean smiled, picturing how amazing it was that a house, no bigger than Nova, had led a nation of over three hundred million people. He wondered how America's leader, called the president, had dealt with all their problems, when Nova's leader, Mayor Reyes, seemed to have his hands full with only a village of a 133 people. Still picturing downtown Chicago, Sean no longer needed to listen to Mr. Davis, as he knew all too well the tragic tale of the old world.

It continued as the American people carried on suffering, while the rich tried to stay rich. With gas and oil reserves coming to an end, America resorted to buying oil from other countries. The supply was in high demand, forcing prices well above people's incomes. Those who could afford the steep prices had only a little time to enjoy it. Eventually, that supply ended as well. Other countries, such as Iraq, Canada, Korea, China, and Mexico, no longer offered the option to sell oil to America or to each other. The world came to a standstill. As the resulting chaos broke out over the remaining available resources, all of America's government grouped together and discussed a way to fix this struggle. Weeks and then months went by until one day, America appeared to have a plan.

With no room for conversing or trying to agree to terms, the final option for America to save its people from the crisis was to take the remaining reserves by force. War brewed, with threats frightening each and every country. No one was to be trusted. Russia fought with America. North Korea planned attacks on both Russia and America. Canada threatened China, as China planned attacks against both Canada and Korea. Tensions increased as nations stopped communicating with each other and planned for World War III.

No one felt safe, and the talk of nuclear war weighed on America, along with the other nations. People all across the States built fallout shelters underneath their homes and backyards. Water and foods with the longest shelf lives filled the shelves inside, using as much space as possible. Farmers built homes for their cattle and crops to continue growing underground. At the same time, America decided that they would not sit back and watch riots break out and people loot in the streets. With another broadcast to every nation and television set, America's president held no other solution to save its people but to declare war.

The image of the broadcast faded in Sean's head as Mandy raised her hand, asking another question.

"Uh … Mr. Davis what is a television?"

The moans and mumbles that had stirred against Sean earlier now were directed toward Mandy, leaving her ashamed. She vowed to never ask another question ever again. Mr. Davis went to his podium and took a swig of water from his canteen.

"Please, no more interruptions. If you have any questions, please save them for after the class. Now where was I? Oh yeah, World War III. So America, the first to act, sent fleets to Iraq and Russia …"

Right on cue, Sean drifted away to where he'd been earlier. Mr. Davis's voice faded in Sean's ears as the tragic tale continued. Russia sent troops to Canada and America. Korea went after China. Within three days, all nations were at war, spilling blood across the world. For three weeks war wreaked havoc across the globe until the worst possible outcome occurred.

A nuke launched into the sky and headed for its target. All the nations were in panic, and everyone accused each other. The nuke landed in the Pacific Ocean near Mexico. No one was sure if the nuke was intended for Canada, the United States, or Mexico. It was a matter of minutes before every nation placed their fingers on their respective launch buttons. Beyond terrified, the American people ran inside their fallout shelters and shut them closed.

Russian president Nikolai Rudin received evidence that the nuclear warhead had come from Brazil. Despite the treaties made and announcing themselves a nation free from weapons of mass destruction, it was found to be true. Brazilian president Diego da Costa declared it a possible act of sabotage for the misfired nuke and conducted internal investigations to find how such a thing could have happened. In fear of being attacked and under heavy pressure from the Russian prime minister, Nikolai Rudin took a desperate measure. With the intention of protecting his people and land, Russia launched their nuke into the air, which landed and destroyed most of Brazil. The result was horrifying; in seconds, innocent people vanished without a trace. America, no longer waiting for a nuke to fall on their land, acted and gave a final warning over a national broadcast.

America announced they held fifty nuclear warheads and had calibrated them around the world to effectively destroy the other nations, using this information as a threat to end the war. Unafraid of the US president's claims, Nikolai called his bluff, saying it was a weak attempt to avoid surrendering. Rudin sent more troops to America, determined to take it over. Mass panic forced all nations to arm as many warheads as possible to eradicate their enemies.

On March 4, 2023, the world ended. Every nation filled the sky with nuclear warheads that spanned the entire globe. Altogether over a hundred warheads filled the sky, killing billions in a matter of minutes. Twenty-seven warheads fell on America, leaving millions dead. With the war ending, and every nation destroyed beyond repair, the worst was still to come.

CHAPTER 3

HOW WE LIVED

Humankind's battle for survival was just beginning. Radiation left by warheads became the new threat for the world. Any life that survived such horror now faced radiation poisoning. Those who were in the fallout shelters had to finish their lives underground, not knowing when it would be safe to return. Through the years, a full generation lived without ever seeing the sun or sky. Sixty-five years passed, and people eventually ran out of food. Survivors with cattle and crops to harvest sustained themselves a little longer, but others abandoned their shelters and ventured out to scavenge for food and water long before that. Starvation killed over half of the fallout survivors, while a few never returned from the surface.

Not until eighty years had passed since the bombs fell did humans build again. Forty survivors built Nova, using salvaged pieces of metal, plastic, and iron. Nova now held over fifty families and thirty livestock that continued to grow.

Sean snapped back into reality as Mr. Davis pointed his chalk, half of its size now, to each student in his class.

"We have survived this terrible lesson, and we must learn from it, so we will never make the same mistake again."

Sean rubbed his hands over his face, wanting to rip out every strand of hair on his head. The boredom was too much for him. Everyone in Nova sat through this lesson, just as Sean did, and listened to the mad wizard tell it over and over again. But different versions of the story also were told from different parents, which Sean thought was odd.

From the Savannah family, Sean heard that America was the evil country that destroyed the world. The Cole family blamed the Russians, calling them insane and power-hungry. Mandy's mother mentioned that the Koreans and the Chinese were at fault for the entire thing. Sean even listened to the Leonards accuse the Mexicans while hosting a friendly book-reading club. There were times when even Sean didn't know whether the story he memorized from Mr. Davis was true. It didn't matter which one was, though; Sean believed everyone should have been held responsible. Their actions left a world no longer filled with trees, birds, or wildlife. All that was left was sun, sand, sky, and metal.

Mr. Davis turned to scribble on the last blank space on the blackboard. Sean saw his opportunity to leave his chair and creep outside into Nova. Above him, the sun dangled closer to the horizon, not casting its deadly heat as it prepped for sunset. Sean grew impatient and found himself trapped in the late part of the day with nothing to do and needing to escape. He needed adventure, which he found in scavenging. Out there beyond Nova's walls, far into the open desert, Sean found his escape. Discovering metal, toys, books, clothes, statues, and many more lost items buried in the sand filled Sean with an incredible rush. There were endless miles of freedom to be walked, countless mysteries buried under the sand, and Sean wanted to experience it all. One mystery Sean would never forget was when he discovered a crashed airplane two months ago.

The airplane was military by the design and a day's walk north of Nova. Knee-deep in sand, Sean stared at the B-52 bomber with a smile so wide it hurt his jaw. A piece of the old world lay at his fingertips. Close to a century old, the B-52 bomber's fame remained intact. The nose end lay buried deep underground, leaving just the back half of the plane exposed. Half of the bomber's side door poked from underneath, preventing Sean from opening it and getting inside the cockpit. From the tail end, he could see a few sections had received severe damage, and the left wing was missing. Sean made his way around, wiping a section covered in sand and then tracing the words "Pretty Lilly" painted underneath. He stepped back and stared at the massive size of the plane. His nerves shivered with amazement under the scalding sun. There were no books or writing lessons that ever took Sean's breath away as the B-52 had done. It was a relic of his history, a memento of the lives lost and soon changed forever.

Sean wanted to continue his search, hoping to find something new and better than the B-52. With the day nearly over, Sean knew he wouldn't be ready in time before nightfall. Leaving Nova walls during the night was extremely dangerous and insane. Any campfires or lights could draw creatures from every direction that killed without mercy. The fields of radiation from nuclear bombs falling on America had killed most species, but a few had survived and were evolving across the land. As a result, humans no longer reigned at the top of the food chain. Dangerous predators and unexplainable monsters roamed the desert, looking for food. Death fell upon even the strongest and well-trained hunters if they left at night, and Sean wasn't either one. In fear of death, Sean bit his lip and accepted waiting for tomorrow to explore.

CHAPTER 4

FAMILY, FRIENDS, AND ONE TOUGH SOB

On his way home, Sean passed by Old Harrison's stand near the water well. Old Harrison had spent nights and days scrapping for metal and copper to build it. His deathly skinny frame held a hammer twice the average size, pounding away and sweating in the intense heat. Whenever Old Harrison smiled, which rarely happened, he showed a giant gap of missing teeth that he'd lost years ago. Back when Old Harrison wasn't so old and skinny, he helped build Nova with the others. During Nova's construction, Old Harrison hammered away, just as he'd done many times before, but he pulled back his hammer just a little too far, knocking out his front two teeth. Old Harrison did not yell or scream in pain. He stopped for a second to spit out a mouthful of blood, along with his teeth, and then continued to work as if nothing had happened.

The event became legendary of how tough and crazy Old Harrison was. When Sean was growing up, he had watched Old Harrison from a distance and had been fascinated. Old Harrison never could fit in with the others around him in Nova, despite being a part of its creation. Everyone associated his quiet nature with wanting to be left alone and assumed his constant hammering was a release of his uncontrollable anger. A mystery surrounded Old Harrison, and Sean soon discovered the truth—that Old Harrison wasn't crazy after all but was a soul filled with sorrow who needed something more.

It all boiled down to the fact that Old Harrison had been born in the wrong world. He belonged somewhere else—among the skyscrapers with the men sitting on top of the metal beams, eating lunch high in the air without fear of falling. Or even mining dangerous tunnels while breathing hazardous waste into his lungs, only to take a moment to expel the waste by spitting through his teeth, and then tunnel farther. Old Harrison belonged in a world that was changed not by computers but by the blood and sweat of men themselves. In the end, Old Harrison had no world to change with his hammer, no men to call brothers, so he sat trapped in a desolate world, waiting for a reason to pick up his hammer and get back to work. Three years would pass after Nova's completion before Old Harrison found a reason to pick up his hammer once again, and as a result, Nova would be indebted to him once more.

Old Harrison began a new project and worked on it without end, showcasing his undying will not to take a break until its completion. Many became angry with Old Harrison's hammering, and Diane feared it would wake Sean in his crib. Neighbors asked Old Harrison to stop the hammering at night, but he stared back in silence for a moment and then continued. One day, everything fell silent, and people ventured out from their homes to see a massive metal device. The obscure hunk of metal jutted outward and high into the sky from the middle of Nova. No one knew what Old Harrison had finished building, but by the end of the week, Old Harrison fell to the floor, shouting and laughing. It was the last time he ever smiled. He shouted slurred words, unrecognizable except for one—*moonshine*. Nobody understood what it meant until Old Harrison blacked out and fell face first onto the ground.

Diane and the others thought Old Harrison had died, but at a closer look, he was alive and deep in a drunken slumber. Sean didn't understand why Old Harrison became a village hero for it or that moonshine had existed during the old world. He thought it lost with the other fine drops of alcohol for over half a century.

Sean passed the stand and waved to Old Harrison, who stared back in silence. Sean carried on, smiling, as he understood that this was Old Harrison's way of saying hi, goodbye, thank you, sorry, and many other responses. Along the middle of the street, right next to Old Harrison's moonshine still, stood the six-foot-tall bulletin board. The red board held announcements from Mayor Reyes and other information, including upcoming birthdays, the date, and awards ceremonies. All of these were posted by John Campbell.

John served as the librarian who maintained a great collection of novels and textbooks found throughout the desert from scavenging runs. He was changing the time cards to display that is was the late part of the day when Sean walked by, nodding his head in hello. Sean glanced over and read that the day was Tuesday, and he sighed in relief for not missing Uncle Junior's poker night on Thursday. Every week Junior held a local game at his house and invited his friends. Junior had learned the game of poker from his father, who played underground after the bombs fell.

His father spoke of grand tournaments each year, with prizes of vast amounts of money, rare valuables, and fame to the best players from around the world. At one point Junior's father saved enough money to attend one for the tournaments, but the war created panic, and all future tournaments were canceled. With currency having no meaning anymore, Junior only played for fun and laughs, but thanks to Old Harrison, moonshine became an item to play for and win, which meant Old Harrison prepped a giant batch right before Thursday night every week. At first Old Harrison grimaced at the annoying work to be done, but Junior gave extra food, metal, and scavenged parts as tips for the hard work.

Sean proceeded farther down, passing more homes. A soft glow of light peeked under Junior's home. Sean approached the rusted green metal door and gave a hard knock. Junior wasn't just Sean's uncle; he quickly became a second father to Sean. He watched over Sean, raising him as a son after Sean's father died, scavenging for food and metal nine years ago. Life never returned to normal for Sean after that. Diane suffered a broken heart and cried every night. She was in no shape to raise a nine-year-old boy, Diane accepted Junior's help to take Sean in while she dealt with her pain.

At nine years old, Sean didn't understand his dad dying, but deep inside there was dark pain in his heart that grew as time went on. Death was common and should be expected for everyone in Nova. Sean was too young to fall apart and cry like Diane did. Life was still new to him, and Junior was by his side the entire time to help him through it.

When the door opened, Junior gave a warm smile, along with a hug. He patted Sean on the back and welcomed him inside.

"How's it going kid?" he said.

"It's been okay. Mom forced me to attend Mr. Davis's class again, but I ditched toward the end."

Junior couldn't help but laugh. His acceptance was predictable. Even though he'd become a parent himself, he never forgot he too was a kid at one time. Junior pointed Sean to sit as he closed the pan's lid, sealing the bubbling contents. The aroma in the air gave away the mystery of what boiled inside. There were always two sure things about Junior: one, he made a mean pot of chili; and two, he always had a poker deck on him at all times. His daughter Nicole sat on the floor playing with her dolls. When she noticed Sean had paid a visit, she smiled, mirroring the image of Junior subtly underneath. The two waved hello to each other, and in her excitement, she showed a missing tooth; she'd lost it earlier in the day.

"You remind me of myself when I was your age. I never really grabbed the whole books thing. But I didn't have a good teacher like your Mr. Davis either. So what's up?" Junior asked.

"Nothing much; just wanted to stop by to say hello. It's been boring all day and I overslept. Not used to having quiet nights again, thanks to Lucy and the candles," Sean said.

Junior rose from the table and blew out the oven's flame. Nicole disappeared into another room, lost in her imagination with her dolls. Junior shouted, his voice booming throughout the house, saying that the food was ready. Nicole ran out, jumping in joy for the chili waiting to be poured. Sean couldn't believe that Nicole had grown up so fast. He remembered when Nicole stood only at his hip and now she neared his chest. *Where did the time go?* Sean thought. Unfortunately, Junior suffered greatly while raising Nicole after the loss of his wife from childbirth. He made sure to never cry in front of Nicole or even lash out in anger. He became the rock that both Nicole and Sean needed to hold on to. Junior loved and missed his wife, Tammy, more than anything. She was his world before Nicole. Sean cherished the brief time he'd known Tammy. He became a big brother to Nicole before Diane gave birth to Lucy.

Junior set a bowl for Nicole, who scarfed down the hot chili. His left hand rested on Sean's shoulder. The heavy palm and fingers displayed many years of long and grueling labor. Pain from his knees reminded Junior that he wasn't getting any younger and that he needed to put more hours into playing cards than in repairing Nova. "I have been meaning to tell you, kid. I'm so proud of you and how you look after Lucy. I know that she's your half sister, and the way you love her takes great strength and responsibility."

Sean's face struggled to accept being reminded that he had a stepfather. He still held resentment towards his mother for finding someone new. He never wanted his father to be replaced, but Sean didn't want to see his mother cry every night either. In time, Sean accepted Diane's new husband, Eric Nole. Eric displayed kindness and a funny personality, and he never raised his voice toward Sean or Diane, but he wasn't Sean's father. And that's how Eric remained to Sean. With tears gathering in the back of his eyes, Sean fought hard not to cry at the memory of his father's death. He scratched the table with his index finger, hoping to hold back the tears.

"Yeah, I know. It's not Lucy's fault. I just wish that ..." The words didn't come out; they didn't need to.

Junior felt the same way. He wanted his brother back for Sean as well.

Sean's heart was an empty shell deep inside, and it didn't heal over the years. Sean wished for the pain to go away, but it still lingered, waiting for a memory or a name to trigger overwhelming emotions. Even the thrill and happiness from scavenging in the desert could not erase the feeling. For Junior, Tammy's death created a greater bond of understanding between him and Sean. He experienced Sean's pain and understood what he was going through. Out there in the open desert, scavenging for new wonders, a part of Sean hoped that the same fate would fall on him as it had his father. Nights enticed Sean to sneak out from Nova's walls and walk blind into the dark and never come back. Junior reached out his hand and patted Sean's back.

"I know, kid. I know."

Sean's tears were on the verge of spilling out. Every muscle tightened in an attempt to hold back the tide of tears. Sean changed the conversation as fast as he could. "So Junior, how much did you win last week?"

Junior walked over and opened a wooden box full of moonshine. "Around eight bottles." Junior losing at poker became a rarity. Every Thursday he sent his friends out the door with their heads down and pockets empty. Many husbands and neighbors occasionally stopped by to play, but Barry, Matthew, Isaac, and Andy played every week. Barry Walter was the cunning one, always having a trick up his sleeve. He loved deceiving others, which later earned him the nickname Satan. Matthew was the hopeful one, clinging to the last possible card to save him; many times it did, causing Barry to scream in anger. His friends just called him by his last name, Morton. Another man, Isaac Moore, had the gunslinger persona, calling a bet no matter what the cost and recklessly raising without worry. Isaac ended a couple of Junior's winning streaks over the years. They called him Doody, a name that Sean still didn't understand, even to this day. Then there was Andy Wick, nicknamed the Rat. Sean watched the guys yell it as Andy laughed and gathered his bottles. Andy was sneaky; when he appeared to be losing a hand, he somehow avoided terrible losses by recognizing trapped bets and lucking out on the river card.

Junior's success over his closest friends didn't come from luck, as many assumed. Sean realized this when Junior taught him how to play at the age of thirteen. A few players were busy working around the town when Junior needed a seat filled. Sean didn't expect to play. He enjoyed just watching. Then Junior pulled out a seat for Sean and told him to play. Junior vouched for Sean's bets and had plenty of moonshine to back it up. Sean tried to play the best poker hands possible. At the end, Sean had lost his share of moonshine from all the folding he'd done. Only three times had he held a good hand before running out of chips.

When Sean had nothing left, Junior leaned in, telling Sean, "Play the players, not the hand." Sean didn't understand what Junior meant until everyone finished playing. While Sean was cleaning around the house and sorting the bottles of moonshine, Junior explained. "Poker is a game of three important things: your hand, your tell, and your luck.

"With your hand, play the best five cards you have. Your tell means an unknowing gesture that indicts the value of your hand, which could be exploited if caught. Every player has one, and it's your responsibility to hide it. Barry's tell is his eyes. Every time he gets a good hand, he turns his head to talk or stare elsewhere. Matthew's tell is nervous fingers; he fiddles with his chips, restacking them over and over again. Isaac moves his eyes toward his chips to bet or raise, but he does it in quick fashion, making it hard to catch at times. Andy's is the easiest."

Sean nodded; he'd caught it on his own. "Andy shakes his hands in excitement and doesn't make eye contact with anyone at all," he said.

Junior was proud and impressed. "Right. There are more tells but I'm still working on them. Last, there's your luck, and nothing can beat it. Your hand is the weakest because it isn't dependable. Your tell is important because it could win you tons of moonshine or cost you as much. And your luck is the Holy Grail." Even though Junior seemed unbeatable, having luck always beat skill.

Sean smiled at Junior's moonshine pile. "That's great, Junior. I just wanted to stop by to say hello. I guess I'll be going now." The two hugged, and Sean walked out the front door. Nicole waved goodbye. Her mouth filled with chili muffled the words she tried to speak.

Junior shouted as Sean walked away, "Say hi to Diane for me when you get home, okay, kid?"

Sean shouted that he would. Continuing on, with his hands in his pockets, Sean made his way home.

CHAPTER 5

THE BAD BOY

Billy Rose leaned back in his chair, propping his biker boots on the watchtower railing. It was a calm night so far, and the sky was crystal clear. The stars shined bright enough to see far into the open desert. No signs of predators or cattleworm. Billy drummed on his thighs to a beat in his head. He stopped as he caught Sean walking home.

"Hey, Sean! Come here, dude!" Billy shouted.

Sean stopped and turned toward the watchtower. Billy placed his right foot on the railing and positioned himself for an air guitar solo. More loud noises came as Billy rocked out and finished with his hands in the air to an invisible crowd worshipping him. Sean laughed and looked over to Old Harrison, who stared at both Sean and Billy in silence. Sean continued toward the ladder and made his way up to the tower.

"Hey, Billy, what's up?" Sean said, high-fiving him.

"Same ol' stuff, dude; still keeping the rock legacy going, you know," Billy said.

"I see you changed a few things," Sean said, pointing to Billy's Mohawk.

"Yeah, some new stuff came in a couple of days ago from a local run." Billy pulled off his leather jacket, showing off the new studs and patches he'd added.

"That's awesome, Billy, but the Mohawk is going to freak out a few people. You know there some parents who won't let their children near you."

Billy shrugged his shoulders, popping the collar of his jacket. "Who cares anyway? If trouble comes my way, it will know I'm one bad dude!"

Billy shadowed-boxed an invisible raider, showing the few moves he had waiting for them. "Anyway, dude, you should go up top and catch the view. It's already pretty amazing from here. Can't even imagine what it would be like up top."

"All right … Bad Boy Bill. Looks like his friends showed up." Sean pointed to three invisible raiders behind Billy, who began throwing more kicks and punches. Sean pulled himself over to the roof of the watchtower and found Casey Clarke, a childhood friend, waiting for him.

She'd laid a blanket down with a jug of cold milk. She smiled and patted the seat next to her. "Here. I saved you a spot."

"So you're the reason why Billy woke half the village and brought me here, huh?"

"Yup." Casey laughed. "He needs to be more discreet next time."

Sean shook his head. "There is nothing discreet about Billy. Did you see his new haircut? I can't wait to hear what everyone is going to say now."

"It's all a look. Billy is one of the nicest guys I know, and he wouldn't even hurt a fly," Casey said.

Sean pointed down below. "Oh yeah, you should see what he did to those three raiders down there. It wasn't pretty. The raiders didn't even know what hit them."

The two stared at each other, listening to Billy still shadow-box, and they burst into laughter.

"How was Mr. Davis's class today?" Casey smiled ear to ear.

Sean fell on his back and shifted his eyes. "Oh, not you too. How did you find out?" Sean asked.

"Your mom. She and I had a talk as I dropped by a few candles for Lucy."

"Yeah, you're lucky that your mom doesn't make you go. I keep being forced to hear the same old useless babble out of that mad wizard's mouth."

"You know that useless babble is true," Casey said.

Sean pulled himself up and looked over at Casey. Her blue eyes stared down, wishing she could be lucky to attend Mr. Davis's class. With the death of her father from a heart attack, the chores around the house became too difficult for her mother to do alone. Casey was forced to help out. Later, the chores increased, and Sean saw less of Casey in class as the years went on.

"I guess, but how many times do I have to hear the same speech from the mad wizard? This whole day sucked. I wanted to explore, but I woke up late."

Casey leaned over and placed a glass of milk on Sean's lap. "The day is not completely over, so cheer up." She smiled.

"I guess you're right," Sean said.

An hour passed, and the two didn't say a word. They finished the milk, and Casey began to fall asleep. Her blonde hair dangled over his chest as she laid her head on his shoulder. The moon beamed bright overhead, with stars sparkling all around. Sean shivered as the air grew cold, but Casey's warm body made it bearable. He looked at Casey's white, soft skin in the moonlight. He pictured her blue eyes again while imagining her lips on his. Sean wasn't blind to the fact that Casey liked him from the moment they met. The other kids even teased that Casey wouldn't notice anyone else but Sean.

He bit his lip in frustration, wondering how he could wander the dangerous deserts without worry or fear, but asking Casey for a date or for a kiss left him scared beyond reason. Sean leaned back, embracing Casey as she readjusted on top of him. She placed her leg over his and laid her head back on his chest. Casey's fingertips shined black from nail polish. Sean was surprised to see that Casey had used it. Nail polish was rare and hard to find; it must have been saved throughout generations. Her nails were painted his favorite color. He rubbed the black nail of her thumb with a smile and hurried off to sleep, for the night was soon coming to an end. An hour later, Sean awoke to Billy switching shifts. He closed his eyes again and felt Casey's heartbeat on his chest. Morning came as Sean and Casey were awakened not by the sun but by a bell.

CHAPTER 6

A RINGING OF A BELL

The bell gave a booming ring pulling everyone from their homes to the center of Nova. Paul Clarke gave another swing toward the bell, striking it even harder. The second ring woke Casey and Sean from their sleep. Casey rose, rubbing her eyes. She looked over and smiled.

"I wonder what's going on, Sean." She pulled Sean to his feet.

Sean didn't care, but Casey already had swung herself into the watchtower. The sun's glare grew stronger as Sean blocked as much as he could with his hand. He bent over, feeling the tower's metal roof becoming hotter. Without delay, he swung after Casey. She stood waiting for him with her hands on her hips. Sean quickened his pace and slid down the ladder. He pulled closer to Casey as they made their way into the crowd of people.

Different words scattered around from so many faces. Sean tried to hear, but it was no use. Too many people stood shoulder to shoulder, talking all at once. There was something strange about the whole thing; Sean could feel it. No one looked happy or delighted.

"I hope it's a new baby," Casey blurted. "They are so cute to look at. What do you think, Sean? Do you think it's a new baby?"

Sean looked through the crowd and shook his head. "I don't think so." His eyes scanned around and found Junior carrying Nicole near his mother's house. Diane came outside holding Lucy, who sucked away on her pacifier and played with a toy. Sean heard Casey whispering as she grabbed his hand, clutching it close to her stomach. Her breasts gently pressed against his upper arm.

"I think you're right. Something is wrong here. I can feel it," she said.

"Yeah, me too," Sean said.

The bell rang one final time as Mayor Reyes emerged behind a podium, stopping to gaze around the crowd that stared back with worry. His fragile body quivered in the heat. He took his time placing his hands on the podium. The look of worry no longer just rested on the crowd but found its way to Reyes as well. The crowd grew silent as Reyes opened his mouth and spoke.

"People of Nova, I have proudly served as your mayor for forty-three years. With the death of my father, I took his place to finish his term. I was young and carried so much responsibility. When I finished the remaining four years of his term, I experienced the many wonders and the many troubles that came with this responsibility." His voice did not reflect his aging body; it was strong and powerful, easily heard over the crowd. "Now another sacrifice has to be made. It is the hardest one yet. Before I can tell you, I need to tell you why."

Reyes walked over toward a group of hunters standing near Alex. "I asked our hunters to keep track of the local cattleworm population because of several rumors that frightened me. A month ago, the average tracks found revealed fifty to sixty cattleworms near here. Now there are only fifteen. Soon, there will be none left for us, thus bringing the terrible rumor to life. So I asked David to venture farther … toward the outer desert."

A burst of chatter erupted. Mention of the outer desert had the village shaking. It was forbidden to venture near it. The dangers it brought were unimaginable. Beasts and the endless miles of hot scorching sand were enough to scare anyone away. Then add the deadly sandstorms that could leave any expert navigator lost forever or force a hungry predator to enter new territory such as Nova. The crowd became louder. Venturing near the outer desert was shocking enough, let alone it being approved by the mayor.

"I know, I know, please, please calm down, everyone." Mayor Reyes held his hands above him, trying to reach the crowd. "I am aware of the rules and that we forbid wandering near or in the outer desert. But I wouldn't ask this from David if it wasn't important. Last night when he returned, he gave me the news I hoped to find. The cattleworm are not dying out; they are migrating into the outer desert." Reye's eyes appeared hopeful as he continued with his speech.

"We are guessing they found a new home or food source. This can bring us new land to live on that we did not know existed. Nova can expand or discover another village to join us."

Another village? Sean took a moment to think. Nova hadn't seen any trace of outside survivors. The scouts, hunters, and salvagers found no piece of evidence that proved that survivors were near them somewhere.

"I understand the possibilities are extremely rare, but we cannot ignore the inevitable. There will be no cattleworm left to sustain our population. With over a hundred people, we will run out of food within two months."

Casey's hands squeezed Sean's, turning the tips of his fingers red. Commotion from the crowd overlapped the mayor's voice. Casey spilled tears all over her face. She trembled in Sean's arms, and he didn't know what to do. He continued to hold her and tried to listen to the rest of Reyes's speech.

"It is with the greatest suffering and pain that I have to do this."

Do what? The crowd roared again. Diane struggled to keep Lucy calm. Sean looked over at his baby sister. Her brown eyes matched his but had become red from crying. She dangled in Diane's arms, reaching for Sean, wanting her big brother. Sean couldn't move with Casey holding him, and he needed to listen to what Reyes had to say.

"I decided on four people to venture out and search for the cattleworm or a place to trade. One of the four will go north from here. The other will go south. The third will go west and the fourth east. They will have thirty days to return with news. We placed the names of men that are of age in a bucket."

Casey screamed "Oh my God!" and placed her hand over her mouth. Fathers and sons held each other close, and a few started to cry. At that very moment, the world was about to end again. There was no doubt it would be a death sentence for those who were chosen. Reyes could feel the tension in the air, as if he'd just betrayed the very village he claimed to love.

"Everyone, please calm down. I am aware how difficult this can be. We have no choice."

A man screamed "Why not?" to Reyes from deep within the crowd.

Reyes replied, "Picking four random people might not make sense to you, but we cannot afford to send four of our best hunters to wander the desert."

The same man now screamed "Bullshit," causing a rise of agreement in the crowd.

Reyes didn't back down. "The cattleworms are already hard enough to find, even with our best hunters. What chance do we have if we are left to depend on men without experience to keep Nova fed?"

Casey tugged on Sean's arm and shouted back at Reyes. "But you would send the same men to their death?"

A point well made with the crowd that left Reyes speechless. He froze for only a second and then walked over to the bucket. Sean's heart slowly began to beat faster. Reyes's hand stretched in and grabbed a name.

Somewhere deep inside the bucket, Sean's name swirled around Reyes's fingertips. Sweat formed on Sean's forehead and neck. With a pull, Reyes held and then opened the piece of paper.

Sean's eyes fell to the ground he didn't want to hear his name. Scavenging was a passion of his, but this meant suicide. He knew that the names Reyes would soon call out weren't coming back in thirty days. They would be lucky to last thirty hours. Reyes looked toward the crowd and shouted out the first name.

"The one who will head north is Henry, father of the Collins family."

Henry stood still as the air in his lungs vanished. Sean couldn't believe it. Henry made weapons and repaired broken metal. He wasn't close to being a hunter or scavenger. He didn't have even the faintest idea of how to survive in the open desert. Sean watched as Henry remained silent and hugged his wife, who screamed in agony. She fought and kicked him in rage. They both fell to their knees. Henry no longer could hold back the tears of fear inside. Soon Henry would be leaving his wife and three children behind. Sean struggled with how this was reasonable. He understood the town was in trouble, but there had to be another way. Again the Mayor's hand reached in the bucket as Sean stared at the ground. Reyes's voice shouted out the next name.

"The one who will head south is Jason, son of the Matthews family."

More moments of agony and despair swarmed throughout the crowd. Jason was a twenty-three-year-old with high hopes; he held his mother close. His long frame helped his field-running abilities, and he was in the middle of training to be a hunter. There was a good chance he could survive.

"This isn't right at all. We should go against it. Whether chosen or not, we shouldn't leave, no matter what," Casey said, staring at Sean, who disagreed. It was for the same reason that Henry and Jason weren't going to do what Casey suggested. They would go out there, no matter if it was suicidal. In the end, it was simple.

"It's for the Nova," Sean said.

"What?" Casey asked.

"Even if we decided not to go, Reyes said Nova would run out of food. Then everyone would starve, including you." Sean looked away and stared as Reyes reached in. With another grab, another name was called.

"The one who will head west is Sam, oldest brother of the Uffner family."

Sam ran to his mother in tears. He cried uncontrollably. Sam was an assistant to Carl, the farming hand. He helped tend to the cattleworms and milked them when they were ready. His mother nearly engulfed his five-foot-eight body that weighed only 110 pounds. Sam's eyes closed in terror. He didn't speak, but he reacted as if he wished this was all a bad dream.

Casey squeezed Sean's arm even harder, hurting him.

Reyes pulled the final name. Sean closed his eyes and swallowed hard.

"The one who will head east is Sean, son of the Anders family."

Sean's heart sank deep down into his chest. He felt it keep falling without end. Fear soaked his veins and made his breath weak. Pain now squeezed his heart while it fell. There was no sound, no screams, just the words *Sean, son of the Anders family* echoing in his head. He heard a scream break through from the right. Diane fell to the ground, crying hysterically. Lucy cried as well, nearly being dropped to the ground and scared to death. Her eyes were even more red than before as she now reached for anyone to take her from Diane. Thick strong arms reached over and grabbed her. Junior now held and calmed Lucy with kisses. Eric wrapped his arms around Diane, impossibly trying to comfort her. Sean tried to grab a hold of himself but couldn't. He felt hands touch his face, and blue eyes stared into his.

"Sean. No … this can't be," Casey said.

Each word faded from him. Sean fell to his knees. The ground moved from under him. The crowd blurred and mixed into each other, and the sun's heat choked the air around him. Voices were drowned out from a loud ringing inside his ears. His tongue tasted of rotten food and sweat; he closed his eyes and crashed to the ground.

CHAPTER 7

WAKING UP

C overed in sweat, Sean awoke on his bed. Diane had left the door cracked for fresh air. The room was dark, and so was the sky. Casey's and Sean's faces were only visible from the two candles lit by their sides. Sean didn't notice Casey at first. She'd sat there the entire day only leaving to replace the candles before sunset.

"Hey, are you okay?" she said with a gentle, soothing voice.

"I think so." Sean took time to gather himself. Eventually, he asked, "What happened?"

Casey's face still showed signs of disbelief and concern. She too wanted to ask that question. One moment they were having a special night on the tower, and in the next moment the world fell apart.

"Reyes pulled your name from the bucket, and you fainted," she said.

Sean took a deep breath. Embarrassed, he shifted his eyes away from Casey's.

"I still can't believe it myself," she said, covering her mouth and fighting back the tears again. She already had cried enough for both of them hours before. She shook her head. "You can't do this. Your mom is falling apart, and who will help raise Lucy? We have to change this. We can talk to Reyes, and maybe we can have him pick another—"

"I don't have a choice," Sean said. Despite not wanting to go, Sean didn't want Casey to change it either. He knew the consequences of leaving. All the selected did. None of it was fair, but it was reality. Sean didn't want Lucy or Diane to starve to death. He didn't want Junior or Casey to starve either. Saying no meant sitting back and watching Nova die off before starving himself. For Sean, saying yes was a lot better than saying no. At least there was chance to save his friends and family. It was a small chance but he had to try. "Casey, what happened when I fainted?" He already felt like a fool for fainting. He didn't want to add to the embarrassment by forgetting something important.

"Junior and your mom picked you up and carried you to your bed. Reyes went on talking about holding a ceremonial dinner, which you missed. He also thanked you all for your sacrifice and wished the travelers the best of luck."

The low-lit candles help hide the shame Sean felt inside. He'd became one of the four chosen to save Nova, and he'd responded by fainting. *What kind of hero am I?* He rose to his feet; the old bed hurt his back. The mattress was made before the bombs fell, and somewhere in its being passed through the generations, it left its comfort behind.

Sean told Casey he needed some fresh air. He pulled the metal door wider, expecting Diane to grab him and cry in his arms, but she was gone. No signs of Eric or Lucy either. Sean proceeded right and farther into Nova. He was going to see the one man he always consulted when in need of advice. Along the way, Sean fought the swirling emotions and questions in his head. For every question that popped up, Sean paired it with a way to die.

Nova was empty except for a few late-night stragglers. Everyone else had gone back to their homes. The stragglers gathered near the bulletin board, talking and keeping their voices low, as if it was impolite to mention anything about the chosen. Their eyes watched Sean approach them. Three of them pitied him for being chosen, and the other remaining five were angry that their lives dangled on the shoulders of the kid who had fainted; the other three selected didn't look so promising either. It didn't take long for their looks to make Sean feel like an outsider. Sean quickened his pace and hurried past them. He made it to Junior's home and banged on the door as hard as he could.

"Junior, it's me—Sean. Please open up." *Thud, thud, thud.* Sean's fist punched the door again even harder. He continued pounding like a fugitive running from the law. Sean needed Junior to hurry up. He felt Nova slowly beginning to disown him, and he couldn't bear it.

Finally, Junior opened the door. His giant arms weren't ready as Sean slammed into him, squeezing as hard as he could. The force nearly knocked Junior over. He wrapped his arms around Sean and embraced him.

"Hey, kid, how are you holding up?" Junior's words were weakened by the tears that had fallen earlier.

"Okay, I guess. I need to talk."

"Of course."

Nicole was asleep in her room, tucked under her blanket in a corner. She was so deeply lost in her dreams that Sean's loud banging didn't pull her from her trusty pink pony, riding to the giant chocolate castle.

Junior pointed for Sean to sit. He pulled out two bottles of moonshine and placed them on the table. The smell of alcohol filled the air as soon as the lids popped open. The aroma nearly made Sean faint for a second time.

"Here, kid. Enjoy." Junior pushed the bottle into Sean's hands and patiently waited for him to grab it.

Sean stared at the moonshine as if it was poison. He hesitated but then pulled back his hands. "Ah, Junior … I think I shouldn't."

"Well, why the hell not?" he barked. "If you're old enough to have your name in a bucket, then you're old enough to drink." He leaned back to see if he'd woken Nicole.

Sean reached for the glass and pictured himself dead within forty-eight hours. He lifted the bottle off the table and pressed his lips on the rim. The moonshine swirled inside and spilled into his mouth. Sean grimaced and then coughed several times before slamming the glass back down.

Junior laughed and gave Sean a pat on the back that almost broke a rib. "Be a little less noisy next time," he reminded Sean.

Sean braved another sip to impress Junior. "Junior, I don't know what to do. How am I supposed to survive? No one has ever crossed the outer desert and returned. I'm scared that I won't come back."

Junior lifted his glass and took a swig before answering. When the glass came down, a quarter of the moonshine was gone. Sean looked at his glass, which still looked untouched.

"Don't say that, Sean. You can't think like that, or you will not come back." Junior lifted the glass again. Now half was left. "I'm so sorry about this, kid. I can't imagine what you're feeling, and I know you're scared. Hell, I'm scared, and that's okay." He raised the glass again. Now only a quarter of the liquid was left. "Don't think that Henry and the others aren't scared either. Henry doesn't know a single thing about survival." Junior emptied the glass. "You at least scavenge, Sean, and have spent a day away from Nova alone."

Sean felt a small sense of confidence. "That's true, but that was just a day. We're talking about thirty days, out in the middle of nowhere, and if I do manage to trek across safely, I will be heading into the outer desert. Junior, there is no way to prepare for something like this."

"I know, Sean. I didn't say it was going to be easy. They are going to give you plenty of food and some items to trade if you encounter anyone else out there. If you can't find anything within thirty days, head back home right away."

Junior tried to calm Sean, but his words weren't helping.

"The sandstorms, Junior. What happens if I get lost?" The more Sean thought about the situation, the more it seemed impossible.

"I was just thinking about that too," Junior said. He rose from his seat and went into the bedroom. He pulled a green chest from under his bed. It was military and very old. The word *Army* stretched across it in giant yellow letters. A lock held the contents secure. Junior snatched a key hidden behind a picture of Tammy. With a quick turn of the key, the chest opened. Inside were toys and magazines from the old world—and pictures of women in bikinis posing on vehicles. It took a minute before Junior lifted a knife from the chest and handed it to Sean.

"Here. I want you to have this. It's a survival knife. My grandfather used it and his grandfather before him. I would never trade it for the world, but you will need it more than me."

Sean held the rare antique in awe. It was by far the coolest thing he had seen since the B-52 bomber. "Wow, thanks, Junior. It's amazing, and I can't thank you enough."

The nine-inch blade was still clean and sharp, but the handle was a little worn. Sean examined the knife three times over until Junior pointed at the handle.

"The bottom screws off, and there are more items inside."

Sean screwed the cap off and poured the contents onto the table. Inside were a needle, thread, and fish hooks, and the cap served as a compass.

"That's the solution to your worries, kid. If you get lost, you can use the compass to help keep you on track. It's pretty rare and valuable, so don't go breaking it." Sean didn't know if it was the moonshine that Junior chugged down, but Junior was in tears in front of him in a matter of seconds. "God, kid, I'm so sorry that you have to do this. If I could trade places with you I would. It's just that I can't leave Nicole behind."

There was no way Sean could ever be angry at Junior. He knew Junior loved him, and it was killing him inside that Sean was leaving. The two made their way outside to a table, fearing their conversation would wake Nicole.

Casey overheard Sean and Junior talking and made her way over to them.

Diane carried a freshly made stew in her hands, which explained her disappearance earlier. With tears in her eyes, Diane surprised all them with the dinner that Sean had missed. They all ate together and shared past times. Diane brought up a few baby stories that embarrassed Sean, while Casey held his hand under the table the entire night. Junior and Diane disappeared back into their homes, saying goodbye, giving Sean and Casey some privacy.

After they left, Casey whispered into Sean's ear, "Watchtower. Now."

Both ran as fast as they could and didn't waste time. Billy was on duty and was a little quieter than usual. He didn't say a thing except for an apology to Sean on hearing the news. When Sean pulled himself over, he was greeted with a blanket for them to lie on and several snacks for the night. Casey hoped Sean would be pleased, and he was. Above him, the stars shined along with the moon, as they had the night before. Casey asked Sean what he was going to do when he was out there. He truly didn't know. Her face showed a little worry, in spite of her smile. All Sean could do was stare back at her and return the same smile.

Billy moved a few things around below, breaking up the hour-long silence that Casey and Sean enjoyed. They lay cuddled together, basking in the peace and quiet. Not long after Billy interrupted, Casey rose and kissed Sean. She kept kissing him over and over again. The kisses were fast and hard. Her lips began to quiver as tears splashed onto his face.

Her body laid flat on top of him as her hands tugged on Sean's shirt, pulling it in every direction. She kept at it, somehow trying to merge inside him. Suddenly, Casey stopped kissing him and began to erratically punch his chest in anger. Her head fell to his chest, exhausted, with tears still pouring from her eyes.

Sean was in shock. He had no idea what had happened, and he certainly didn't know what to do. He lay there, staring at the stars as if they held the answer. He continued to listen to Casey cry, hating himself for not knowing what to do.

After several minutes, she stopped crying and knelt over him. She pulled her black tank top slowly over her head until it was free from her body. Her soft, delicate fingers ran across the black bra, releasing the hooks. Casey sat exposed, staring at Sean. She reached over and grabbed his hand, holding it and then kissing it. She wanted to sit on the tower forever and have the moon and the stars all to themselves.

Sean nervously allowed Casey to move his hand above her heart and then place his hand on her. There would be no more crying. Casey and Sean continued kissing and wishing for time to stop forever.

CHAPTER 8

A LAST MEAL

The sun rose across the desert, reflecting off the metal surfaces of Nova's walls. The silence from last night carried over to the morning. Old Harrison sat watching the heat rise from the ground. Even in the shade, there was no escaping the heat. Beads of sweat trickled down his forehead and neck. His sunburned shoulders from last week were now beginning to peel. Lifting his glass, Old Harrison took a swig of moonshine. He swirled the cool liquid around his tongue and closed his eyes as he swallowed.

Loud bangs broke the silence as doors opened and then closed. Four villagers appeared from different homes and greeted one another. They exchanged hugs and then waved at the stand, shouting good morning to Old Harrison. He remained still, except for raising his hand for another sip of moonshine. His eyes traveled and caught Sean, sitting on a bench by himself. Sean was never up this early for anything, but today was understandable. Taking another swig, Old Harrison watched from afar.

In the last hour of the night, Sean and Casey snuck back home to catch whatever rest they could. For Sean, there wouldn't be any rest. He walked in and found a backpack on his bed. The sheer size and weight of it broke any lingering effects of his time with Casey that he called heaven. He pulled the backpack outside with him, plopping it down. Sean glanced at the bag a few times as he watched the stars disappear and the sun break the horizon. Each time he glanced at it, he hesitated, not ready to see what it held. Finally, Sean grabbed the backpack and placed it in front of his feet. He ran his fingers over the smooth hide—a parting gift from Nova for the sacrifice he was going to make. It teetered a bit as Sean loosened the top. Overly packed items squeezed and pressed from the inside, distorting the backpack. It looked like it held a dead body. He flicked back the top flap and peered inside. No dead body.

Alex and Reyes had worked through several nights, prepping the bags. Inside they had crammed twenty-five pounds of dried meat and three gallons of water (divided into twelve glass jars). Reyes averaged out the rations to less than a pound of dried meat and twelve ounces of water a day (if the chosen didn't find a water source).

Among the food supply Sean also found four bottles. They were bound together with a thick yellow string and had a note attached, written by Junior.

Hey, kid, the note read. *I told your mother to pack this in the bag for you. It's moonshine from my last winnings of poker. The yellow string should help indicate which jars are which.* Do not drink this if thirsty! *It will only dehydrate you. I gave this to you so you could have more to trade besides food. Be careful out there, kid.*

Sean tucked the note back in the backpack and fastened the top flap closed. He tightened the string, wanting to close the bag forever. Testing the weight, Sean lifted the bag from his seat and then leaned back, pressing his back against the wall of his home. Sean gazed at the backpack, picturing hauling the fifty pounds of contents across the endless terrain. The morning heat rising from the ground sucked out everyone's enjoyment of the fresh air, and now it seeped into Sean's thoughts.

More of the villagers poured from the homes, greeting each other as kids now began to play. Mothers gathered around the pit area, grabbing plates and utensils to set tables. Among them, Alex chatted away casually while starting the pit's fire. He proceeded to clean the cattleworm meat and added garlic. Today was like any other day for them. The only families that didn't leave their homes to help were those of the four chosen. Their day wouldn't be the same. Loud sizzling of meat filled the air; the aroma of meat and garlic broke Sean's trance. He left his bag on the ground. There was no need to keep an eye on it. No one in their right mind would grab the fifty-pound burden or trade places with him. It would sit there, untouched and unwanted.

Sean made his way toward the line and stood patiently. The smell of garlic and burning meat grew stronger with each step closer to Alex. Laughter and cheers spurted from in front of and behind Sean, but he had no reaction; inside, Sean was numb. He had the backpack to thank for that. But Sean did react to a hand that reached out toward him in line, pushing people away. Someone in front noticed Sean and allowed him the pleasure of cutting in front. The gesture stopped everyone. Sean nodded and said thanks. The word barely made a sound. Then another hand reached out, grabbing Sean by the wrist pulling him up in front.

One by one, man, woman, and child stepped aside, allowing Sean to cut in front. Cheers began to stir from the line as Sean moved closer to Alex. Pats on the back joined in as Sean passed by; he was halfway to Alex. He could see their faces of appreciation and their eyes full of hope. This wasn't like the night before.

Now in front of the line, Sean grabbed a plate. A large rectangle pan held fresh scrambled eggs, ready to serve with a wooden spoon. Sean piled heaps of eggs onto his plate and didn't stop. Thick yellow chunks created a mound that filled three-quarters of his plate and kept rising. Sean planned to eat the biggest meal of his life, pushing his stomach to the brink of exploding. Overeating would be a better death than the kind that waited outside the walls. Sean finally stopped scooping more onto the over five pounds of eggs. He handed the spoon to Andre King, the last man to allow Sean to cut in line while patting him on the back. Andre smiled behind his scruffy black beard and gave a nod of approval to Sean's plate full of eggs. Being a good eater, Andre wasn't shy about stuffing himself; in fact, he took Sean's plate as a new challenge—or better yet, a new goal.

Alex swatted away the giant white puff of smoke in his face. His back still ached from the previous work he done with the hundred pounds of cattleworm meat. He sported a giant necklace of sweat from the collar of his white T-shirt, and it was spreading farther every ten minutes.

"Hi, Sean," Alex said, fanning his shirt, trying to cool himself. The effort failed.

"Hi, Alex," Sean's eyes reluctantly lifted from his plate.

Alex didn't break into conversation. He didn't want talk at all; the urge to gossip vanished somewhere in the smoke he'd just swatted away. Alex simply stared at Sean for a while. An uneasy feeling fell over the two. The time was drawing closer to say goodbye, and they both knew it. Turning his head around to see if anyone was watching, Alex poked his knife into two large pieces of meat behind him that weren't on the table. His secret stash, the juiciest pieces Alex had ever seen, which made him pour more effort into the prepping—a perfect ratio of succulent meat and fat, seasoned in garlic. Alex plopped his masterpiece onto Sean's plate.

"Thanks, Alex. I appreciate it," Sean said.

More white smoke rose from the pit, disguising the tears on Alex's face. Maybe it was the smoke that made Alex cry, or maybe he was just going to miss his friend.

On the way to a table, Sean quickened his pace as he smelled his food.

If his stomach had hands, it would have been rubbing them at this very moment. The plate flopped on the nearest table Sean could find. His mouth watered to the smell of Alex's masterpiece and fresh eggs. Without delay, he began stuffing himself. For ten minutes, Sean was a human vacuum, devouring every last piece of egg and meat in sight. Sean wiped away the scraps of eggs around his lips and then exhaled slowly. It was the best meal of his life, and he savored every bite he took.

A satisfying sigh spewed from Sean's bulging stomach as he pushed the plate away. He was one bite away from exploding. It hurt like hell to breathe or move an inch. He let the food settle for a bit before even thinking of getting up. From behind him, two soft hands rolled down his shoulders, and a quick kiss landed on his cheek.

It was Casey. She sat next to him with her legs crossed and her back to the table. "Hey, I got to make this quick. Junior and your mom are gathering a few things for you to take, and I'm helping. So here," Casey reached in her jeans pocket and took out a bracelet that she placed in Sean's palm. "I made it from a few strands of my hair and torn pieces from the tank top during our night on the tower."

Sean didn't say a word. He stared at Casey's bracelet and stroked the weave of hair and cloth with his index finger.

She smiled. "I know it's a little corny, but … now I'll always be with you in a way."

Sean pulled on both ends of the bracelet testing for durability.

"So do you like it? You can tell me the truth."

"Yeah, I like it," Sean said, and he meant it.

Casey planted another kiss on Sean's cheek before running off to help Diane and Junior. The bracelet itself would be pretty stupid to most, but for a scavenger, it served a purpose. While away from Nova, isolation could be the worst for those who weren't used to it. Any type of mementos from loved ones kept the drive to stay alive going. If he was to die out there in the open desert, he would like to think that someone was with him, at least. And now he did.

CHAPTER 9

DEPARTURE

Reyes called a final meeting with the four chosen to thank them for their great sacrifice. Jason, Sean, Henry, and Sam stood shoulder to shoulder next to Reyes's podium as the crowd stared at them. Henry held his head high, never taking his eyes off his darling wife and beautiful kids. No one in the crowd could see, but Henry's right hand trembled in fear. Horrible dreams kept him tossing and turning all through the night. The youngest child, Mary, wiped the tears with her stitched teddy bear as she looked at her father, only to cry some more. The teddy bear's stomach had been ripped opened during Mary's crying fit when Reyes pulled Henry's name out of the bucket. Henry later stitched it back together when he couldn't sleep anymore.

Sean glanced toward Sam, who stood quietly staring at the crowd. He wore a similar white T-shirt to Alex's, with a ring of sweat from the heat, but instead of two thick, muscular arms jutting out to his sides, there were only two puny limbs. Sam's arms were a fifth the width of Alex's and resembled two toothpicks poking out from the sleeves. Sean realized a horrifying fact. Last night he'd found his parting gift from Nova, which meant Sam had to have one as well. The damn thing weighed over fifty pounds. Sam would be lucky to weigh a hundred pounds himself, soaking wet. For Sam, it meant carrying around half his weight across desert land. Out there, the sand might be soft, but it wasn't your friend. Without finding solid ground to walk on, the give of the sand killed your legs, making each step feel like five. The terrible truth sunk in Sean's mind. No matter how he looked at it, Sam had it worse than anyone. Sean bit his lip in guilt for feeling a little better in knowing it.

Jason shouted toward the crowd that he was going to save Nova. His voice and posture beamed with confidence, which riled the crowd, and they shouted back with cheers and praise. Confetti flew into the air from Jason's family; oddly enough, they seemed happy and proud that their son was chosen. Among the crowd, Diane, Junior, and Casey blended in with the families that cried hysterically for their loved ones. Holding each other's hands, they fought the thoughts of not seeing Sean again. Over and over, they told themselves that he was coming back. The people of Nova needed to be saved, and Sean would save them.

Far back, Reyes watched as the crowd cheered, shouted, cried, and praised with sadness and joy. Emotions blended together, getting lost in translation. Words were smothered by more shouts and clapping.

Henry ran off the podium toward his grieving wife, trying to console her. His lips moved to her ear. He told her not to worry because he was coming back. He also told her that he loved her. But she didn't listen. She pried herself from his arms and then slapped him across the face. There wasn't anything he could have said that would make things better. More cheers filled the air as people pushed and shoved their way toward Jason, swallowing Henry and his family in the crowd.

Sean lowered his head and saw he'd been rubbing Casey's bracelet the entire time. The bracelet dampened the fear; slowing its intentions of shaking Sean or even breaking him. Everyone left the podium and returned to their families, hugging each one. Diane continued to cry. Junior reached over to hug Sean and kiss the top of his head. Sean lifted Lucy from Diane's arms and held her tight. Her soft skin and silky hair rubbed against his face. She too cried and flailed her arms, somehow knowing what was going on. Her brother was leaving, and it hurt. Sean wiped away the tears of his sister's first heartache. Eric patted Sean on the shoulder and wanted to say a few words of comfort, but he looked away instead. Casey was the last one to hug him and it would be the longest. She whispered to Sean that she would sit on top of the tower and watch until he disappeared.

All the families said their final goodbyes and waited for the doors to open.

"You better comeback, kid!" Junior shouted as he stood with Nicole, who ran over to Sean for a hug.

"I will. I promise," Sean said. It was a promise he hoped to keep.

Loud scraping and grinding roared from behind him. Sean turned around and watched the doors begin to slide open. Alex and Billy cranked the wheels from each side of the door. With each sliding inch, the image of death became clearer. The sun was going to be their misery; thirst would be their punisher; hunger would be their pain; and the sand at their feet would be their grave. If the universe was merciful, it would call the monsters that lurked about to bring death before sunrise.

The doors were a quarter open when Diane snuck up behind Sean. "Here," she said. Her hands were holding a circular object. The sun reflected off its gold color. "It's your—"

"My father's pocket watch." Sean grabbed it, having immediately recognized it.

"As a baby, you would play with it all the time. He would give it to you so you would stop crying when he had to leave. When your father disappeared several years ago, that's all they found. It was lying on the sands near the outer desert." Her fingers flipped the watch open, revealing its face and hands, still moving. "I took care of it while you grew up, cleaning it and winding it when necessary."

"Why didn't you tell me you had this?" Sean said.

"I wanted him to give it to you himself when he came back. I always thought that he would walk through those doors and give that smile of his that I loved. I wanted him to kneel down and hand it to you, but he never came back."

Sean turned back to the doors that only had a quarter left to go. His father's pocket watch triggered memories and tears. Taking deep breaths, Sean controlled the tears that were already at the back of his eyes, waiting to come out. He swallowed. "Thanks, Mom." Squeezing the watch, his eyes fell upon the desert yet again, and he watched the heat rise from the ground. Alex and Billy gave the final turn of the wheel, and the door was fully open.

Alex looked back at the chosen and then walked over to Sean. He noticed that Sean wasn't carrying a weapon and asked why. Sean didn't dare tell him that he had one from Junior in his backpack. He said he hoped Alex might have a spare for him to take. A lie to a friend would normally bother Sean, but the odds were against him, and he needed all the help he could get. Alex nodded and handed Sean his walking stick. The staff had both ends sharpened to a deadly point, good for keeping a distance from any dangerous animal or foe. It could also be thrown as a spear, if properly trained.

"Thank you, Alex," Sean said.

"Don't mention it." Alex pulled Sean in tight, and then he slowly walked with him. Their talk wasn't over yet. "Last night I talked with the others during the dinner that you missed. When you're out there, Sean, you need to watch out for yourself. You can't be so trusting. Out there is a whole different world from what you have here. Unspeakable things await you—bandits, sandstorms, poisonous snakes, beasts, and—most of all—mimics."

Sean couldn't believe he hadn't thought of mimics. The fear of venturing out into the outer desert was nothing compared to confronting mimics. Sean grew up listening to his father and Alex talk about their travels. They would talk of tracking cattleworms, where they were headed, and items they scavenged or found. The tales were exciting—until one day Sean's father mentioned mimics. He said that he had seen one while hunting for cattleworms near Nova.

He came across a trail left by a baby cattleworm. It was alone and must have been separated from its pack. He approached a northern hill and reached its top. The baby cattleworm was only fifty yards away. Sean's father had said there was something different about the sand to the far left—it seemed to move slowly; its true shape was hidden. Slowly, it crept toward the cattleworm as Sean's father watched. As it crept closer, the cattleworm showed no signs of being startled or aware of its presence. Then, in a split second, the mimic lunged and magically appeared, ripping the cattleworm apart.

His father had told of the screams that filled his ears as the cattleworm's body was severed and ripped open. He told everyone that the mimic's fur was pitch black, and somehow it was able to camouflage itself with its surroundings, turning it nearly invisible. Its eyes were yellow, and its claws were the size of full-grown bear. A five-hundred-pound man-killer would look at Sean as a mere snack to eat.

The stories didn't end there. Others claimed to have seen it too. One man saw it kill his brother. His tale explained something new about the creature. He claimed that there was somebody calling out to them. The brothers said it was probably someone who fell into a sinkhole and needed help. The calling didn't stop; it grew louder until it was too late. One of the brothers ran forward, right into the creature as it snatched him away.

Not only could mimics camouflage themselves, but they could mimic their prey's sounds as well. That's why Nova started calling the creatures *mimics*. Sean didn't know why he'd forgotten the possibility of mimics, but they were real, and they were waiting. Billy walked over as Alex left.

"Sean, I want you to have this. It's my favorite one." Billy placed a black pin in the palm of Sean's hand. Sean flipped the pin over and rubbed the image with his thumb, removing a small layer of dirt. It was an eagle holding a leaf and a baseball bat in its talons. Under the eagle, the word read "The Ram," but the other letters to it had faded a while back. There also was a ribbon in the eagle's mouth with words "Hey Ho Lets Go." The pin was weird but so was Billy.

Sean thanked Billy and pinned the button on his duster jacket. After the two shook hands, Sean put on his goggles to protect his eyes from the sun and dirt. He began walking toward the open doors. With every step he took, his mind begged him to stop. Sean passed the doors, and his mind went quiet. Loud screeching sounds gave way as the gate began to close behind him. Henry, Jason, Sam, and Sean were finally beginning their journey.

CHAPTER 10

SO IT BEGINS

The four chosen wished each other good luck. They positioned themselves on each wall of Nova and prepared for their walks. Casey climbed the tower, as she said she would, and looked at Sean, while Billy returned to his post underneath. Sean stared at both of them from behind his goggles. Tears began to fall from his eyes. Luckily for Sean, the goggles hid his tears. He rubbed Casey's bracelet, soothing his tears and fear. Billy broke the silence with a shout. He raised his hand and gave Sean what he called the rock 'n' roll sign. Sean returned the sign and faced east.

Endless miles of sand and sky were all that stood before Sean. No signs of life, water, food, or hope. The desert lay at his feet. His black boots, which had belonged to his grandfather, were becoming hot. Sean wiggled his toes in the hot air trapped inside. He was already tired and wanted to turn back. With great hesitation, Sean took his first step. *East—my way is east.* Clutching the staff and backpack, Sean took a step and then another to begin the journey.

Sean never had ventured outside before with fifty pounds strapped to his back. The weight pulled at his shoulders, and his lower back throbbed slightly. Sean glanced over his shoulder and saw Nova a mile away. Marching forward, Sean moved to a rhythm in his head. Left, right, left, right, left, right—he was making good progress. A mile back, thirst found him, but Sean continued on for another mile before stopping to drink. As the backpack slid off, Sean heard a crack in his back, which felt good. He dug inside the backpack for water and was careful not to spill any. The water was still cold as it swirled around his tongue. Clinging to the taste,

Sean's eyes closed for a moment, embracing the small break from walking before placing the water back into his backpack.

Sean checked his father's pocket watch. Based on the time, he knew he'd be nearing the outer desert soon. He turned around and saw Nova was gone. Its walls and tower were no longer visible. Casey could no longer see him. If Sean were to die now, no one would see or hear him scream for help. He was truly alone, but he had to keep going. The sand at his feet started to cool down, which was good and bad for Sean. No longer would he keep walking on what felt like hot coals, but with the sun almost gone, the night was approaching, along with the unknown creatures. After walking another mile, Sean could see that he was closer to the outer desert. Caution signs lined the perimeter to warn Nova not to venture farther. Sean's pace quickened. It was easier with the cooler sand and air. The sweat on his back became uncomfortable and annoying. His shirt was soaked in it, and the throbbing in his back grew almost intolerable. Sean bit down hard and pressed forward, blocking his mind from the pain.

He thought about Nova and what his family was doing. Had the village continued its routine as if nothing had happened? Were they still mourning? Sean's mind began to fill with doubt. He shook his head, wiping his mind free from such things. Twenty yards away, the outer desert waited, just past a small hill. A small stir of pain and adrenaline coursed through him, manifesting into a voice that told him not to go around but over the hill. Sean readied himself and accepted the challenge. He placed the staff at the base of the hill and lunged forward, sinking a little with every step. Shouts filled the air with every other step as his thighs burned from the inside. Closer and closer, Sean neared the top and then finally reached it. His hands thrust into the air as he conquered the hill in triumph. Winded and exhausted, Sean misplaced a step and lost his balance. His foot slid down the hill, spreading his legs apart. Sean tried to regain his balance, but the backpack pulled him down. There was no saving him.

His arms fought to regain balance while his body hurled down like a rock. With a thud, Sean's back slammed against the ground. The throbbing from his lower back now spread to his entire body. Clutching his side, Sean endured the sharp pain. Sand covered his mouth; it felt as if it was in his lungs. Sean coughed, becoming hysterical, which then turned to a growing laughter. He had been walking for only five miles and nearly had died—that would have been embarrassing. Now the time for worry began. The fall was a rough one, and he wondered about the contents inside his backpack.

He flipped the top flap back and checked to see if any items were broken. To his relief, Sean caught a break; all was intact. Sunlight flickered off the unbroken glass and clear water still inside. He reached for the same mug he'd used before and wrapped his lips around the rim, taking slow sips. The remaining sand on his lips and tongue made the water taste terrible. But the rationing that Reyes had determined left Sean no choice. There was no room for being wasteful. Sean lay on the hill, resting his tired muscles and back. He watched the sky grow a shade darker and decided to camp for the night.

The walking was over, but Sean needed to keep guard for any approaching threats. He shifted through the backpack, grabbing food. He pulled Junior's knife free from the sheath and cut several pieces of jerky for dinner. Sean handled the knife with care, not wanting the smell of blood to lure any starving animals from a careless cut. After eating his fill, Sean put the remaining jerky back and double-checked for any damage to his supplies that he hadn't found earlier. With a full stomach and a cool breeze blowing, Sean relaxed his guard and enjoyed the view.

The sky turned darker and darker until the sun vanished below the horizon. Far and soft sounds surrounded Sean, coercing his mind into thinking they were approaching closer. Sean continued to lie against the hill, gripping Alex's staff. His eyes grew heavy, begging to be shut. Sean's heart raced from his vulnerability, out in the open. His mind flooded with open questions. How could he sleep, not knowing what was out there? What if he awoke and found himself being eaten alive? Or even that he was trapped inside some animal's stomach? The questions kept Sean awake for only an hour; then his eyes fell shut without his permission.

Before finding out what would become of him in the morning, Sean dreamed. However, it wasn't of him saving Nova or random nonsense blended together; rather, it was of a memory—a memory when Sean was ten, playing with Casey in her house. Casey held an empty pot over a table, pretending to be cooking. She smiled at Sean as she turned the large wooden spoon. Casey loved to cook. She would make stews, soups, cakes, and pies. Sean ate every pretend meal, giving Casey the thumbs-up routine, never wanting to make her cry. While waiting for Casey's dessert, Sean sharpened a thick branch that his father had brought back for him. Sean wanted to create a sturdy knife, a project that he worked on for weeks later. He wanted to use it while scavenging outside when he turned fourteen. No children were allowed outside the walls until their fourteenth birthdays. His father even promised to take him on a scavenging run too. Three weeks before Sean turned eleven, his father disappeared.

The scouts in the watchtower didn't see what happened. One minute Sean's father was out there in the distance, just a speck in the sand, and the next minute he was gone. Nova sent a search party but came back empty-handed. No signs of animals tracks, clothing, or any of his possessions, except for a small gold pocket watch. Many theories spread though Nova. Some said it was a mimic attack. Others suggest he'd fallen into a cattleworm hole that collapsed on him. There was even speculation that he went mad and never stopped walking. But it all ended with him dead or gone.

Sean would later throw the wooden dagger down Nova's well in tears of rage, never to see it again. The pain was too much and a constant reminder of a broken promise. He knew it wasn't his father fault for disappearing, but a broken promise was still a broken promise. Days were spent wondering how life would have been, had his father never vanished out there. How would the day have been on their very first scavenging trip? Would the bond between them have grown or weakened. Would his father have encouraged him to venture farther, or would he have babied him like an overprotective parent. How would his father have reacted to hearing his son's name pulled from a bucket? Would his father have traded places with him and be out in the desert now? That day—that one day, just like any other in Nova—changed his destiny. Had his father just stayed home that day, he would still be alive.

The dream now shifted the memory of what was to what if. The dream reacted to Sean, almost to the very will of his mind. Sean created a world where his father still existed and briefly saw what life would have been like. Sean's father was no longer dead but alive, appearing out of nowhere after all these years, like a ghost. He stood in front of Diane, heartbroken and forgotten. There was a new child that wasn't his, with a father who had replaced him, and a world that moved on without him. He stared at Sean with tears in his eyes. So many words would have to be said. So many stories needed to be explained. But the dream longer responded; it didn't form or bend anymore to Sean's will. It just opened a door to the possibility, but it didn't allow Sean to go through it.

Sean felt himself cry. Whatever cruel punishment this was, Sean didn't deserve it. The old wound held too much pain to mend. All Sean could do was fight back, ignore it, and hope he could forget it. He stared back at his heartbroken father, knowing it was time to wake up. But he couldn't move his arms or turn his head. Everything stopped all at once. Sean's father's face froze before him and then began to fade. Everything began to fade, including Sean. He felt the clothes on his body grow lighter. The entire village vanished, and then his father, and then him.

CHAPTER 11

THE OUTER DESERT

Morning arrived, with the sun beating down over Sean. He slowly opened his eyes to find himself still alive. The goggles were off his face and lying on the ground beside him. Sore muscles hesitated to move as Sean stretched and grabbed the goggles, slipping them on. The clear sky lay open for the sun to begin its torture. Sean was relieved to have survived his first day, but the feeling vanished in the miles of walking still ahead. Sean readjusted the goggles to a more comfortable fit. He pulled on the straps, tightening them further around the head. Thick beads of sweat rolled down, curving around his cheek and chin. It hurt just to breathe, and the heat slowly started to sap his energy. Sean checked his father's pocket watch for the time. He had twelve hours of daylight left. Sean figured that another thirty more minutes of rest wouldn't hurt. His body relaxed as he closed his eyes.

His right leg itched near the thigh, but Sean ignored it. Then the shirt tugged near his waist, applying small pressure against his stomach. Sean opened his eyes in terror. Something was alive in the desert with him. His heart banged against his chest, wanting to break free and run away as fast it could. It wasn't the fact that there was something else alive that scared Sean so deeply. He knew it wasn't a mimic or any beastly creature that could swallow him whole. What scared him the most was that this thing was on his chest and slowly moving closer to him. Tiny feet pressed against his stomach and crawled toward his sternum. Sean remained paralyzed, staring at the blue sky, not daring to move his eyes down.

He feared any movement would startle the creature, moving it closer to him. Pinned down and trapped, Sean rolled his eyes, knowing he had to see what it was. He needed to plan his next move very carefully. The goggles shifted as his head rose. His eyes adjusted to the bright light, and he saw what crawled on his chest—a four-inch yellow scorpion with claws wide open.

"Oh God," Sean said.

The words slipped from his mouth, floating onto the scorpion. The scorpion leaned back, moving into to a striking stance. The claws twitched and crawled closer to Sean, while lifting its stinger higher. Sean clutched the sand and held his breath. Closer and closer, the scorpion crawled toward his face. Scorpions were nothing new in Nova. Sean even had smashed a few with the bottom of his shoe, but never had he faced one this close. The tiny legs were now pressing against the bottom of Sean's neck. Sean closed his eyes, feeling the claws run along his chin. Prayers swirled about; he was begging not to be stung. The scorpion lifted its body onto his chin, crawling higher. Sean hated himself for not swatting it away when he had the chance.

Please. Please. Shit. The prayer went on.

The prayers were whispers; he did not want to agitate the scorpion in anyway. The scorpion's legs stopped and then shifted toward his left ear. Slowly, it moved across his nose. Sean could see sweat slither down his goggles. Still squeezing the sand, Sean's veins bulged from the blood rushing through his body.

Oh no.

Sweat piled over the brim of the goggles' lens. It dribbled down, but one bead ignored the rest and was headed straight for the scorpion's stinger. Sean's heart sank at the thought of the renegade bead of sweat catapulting the scorpion's stinger deep into his face. Inch by deadly inch, the bead stretched for the scorpion. His heart lay still no longer; it was trying to burst free from within. No prayers were spoken in Sean's head, and no veins bulged under the skin. The bead lay a centimeter away from making contact—and then time seem to stop. Sean feared the worst; he was stung, and the venom must be making his heart stop beating. Then time regained control, bringing back Sean's heartbeat, his prayers, and the blood rushing back into his veins. The scorpion's feet sputtered toward the ground and onto the sand.

In the blink of an eye, Sean jumped to his feet and moved backward away from the yellow scorpion. The scorpion stopped and stared with jet-black eyes, raising its stinger. It continued to watch Sean step away, unaware of the backpack behind him. Sean fell backward, landing on his aching back. Air rushed out of his lungs on impact. The scorpion rushed forward with claws and stinger ready to strike.

"No, you don't!" Sean screamed.

Bits of sand flew into the air as Sean rolled onto to his feet. The scorpion drew closer, preparing for an attack. Within seconds, Sean slammed his foot down, stomping on the scorpion. He heard a loud crunching noise from under his boot. Blue liquid splattered across and oozed into the thread of Sean's right boot. Sean lifted his foot, staring at the scorpion's blood that stretched from the crushed corpse to him like hot melted cheese.

Sean patted all around his body, shaking madly left and right, looking for anything else crawling on him. He searched around the ground for any more scorpions that were ready to avenge their fallen comrade. When he felt it was finally safe enough to relax, Sean grabbed his backpack and took a swig of water. Before him was the outer desert, with its warning flag staring him right in the face.

If it weren't for the flag, the outer desert would have looked no different from what Sean had walked through already. He stared at miles of empty land, no different from his side. Yet Sean felt a change the moment he crossed over. A strange chill surged through him. This place was not safe for anyone. Sean was not ready for this. His stomach tightened, and his heart pounded away in his chest again. This was real. This was a different world indeed. A few steps in, Sean gripped the straps of the backpack as hard as he could and kept a sharp eye about.

The goggles gave a thin filter of yellow over the desert. They sat heavy around his eyes, and the strap pulled a few hairs out from the sides of his head. Thirty minutes of walking passed without any signs of life or trouble. Sean's encounter with the scorpion made him lose any appetite for food, but he found it gain after the first mile. Sean glanced around, making sure nothing was near. He grabbed a handful of jerky and water from the backpack. Near the end of his break Sean grabbed Junior's knife and unscrewed the cap of the handle. He checked the compass and drew a line in the sand in the exact direction of east.

A few more miles had passed and still nothing. Empty land stood before Sean. No signs of food or water and not even a single tree. A small breeze cooled Sean's body. He closed his eyes and embraced the wonderful feeling. The heat was getting to him, but now Sean could bear it a little while longer, thanks to the wind's mercy. After two more hours, Sean decided to stop and make camp. He was still tired from yesterday and couldn't continue any longer. The gold pocket watch read one o'clock; there were only a few more hours before nightfall. Sean drank more water and ate a more of the jerky. He had only a few more pieces in the small bag; then he'd have to open a new one.

As Sean stuffed the remaining food into his backpack, he discovered something unusual. Among the supplies he found small pieces of paper and half of a pencil, bundled together with string and tied to a small note.

Dear Sean,

I want you to write and tell me everything you see on your journey. I can't wait to read it when you come back.

Miss you,

Casey

Sean smiled at the note. Casey wanted him to keep a journal. The note made Sean feel that he would make it back and be a hero—but only for a second. He grabbed the pencil and scribbled a few lines.

I have made it to the outer desert with no signs of life or water. There aren't even signs that life once lived here. All I can see is empty land and an endless sea of sand. I have survived for a day, and now I must camp again to rest.

He wasn't going to write any more about the journey. It was stupid and pointless. Sean needed to be realistic and know that this wasn't going to end well. So far, he'd nearly died twice, only to discover more miles of endless sand. He was simply going to die alone, hundreds of miles away from Nova. That was the truth. That was what waited for him. At least maybe there was a chance to come back as a ghost and haunt Mayor Reyes. Sean placed the pencil and paper back into the backpack—all but one piece. He stared at the blank paper for a few minutes and then reached for the pencil.

My name is Sean Anders. If you are reading this, I am dead. Please know that I have wandered here for the sake of my people. We will soon starve and need your help. I do not know how far I have traveled, but my home is to the west, beyond the miles that you see before you. There lies the village Nova. Please send help before it's too late.

Please tell my mother that I love her and that I tried my
hardest to make it back alive.

Sean folded the piece of paper and placed it inside his duster. He
returned everything to his backpack and sat on the ground with his legs
crossed. For now, he would rest as he waited for the night to come and
pass. Time seemed to drag as thoughts filled his head of people and places.
Henry, Jason, and Sam all had been traveling for more than a day, as he had.
He wondered what they had seen. Had they come across any food, or did
they find a place where they could trade? What if one of them had found
a new place for food or to trade? How was he supposed to know? Was he
supposed to keep venturing out here for a month? He almost got stung by
a scorpion on the first day. Rubbing the sole of his boot, Sean focused on
driving the thoughts out. His mind worked against him again, and hope
started to dwindle. For the next hour, he stared across open land as the
temperature fell. The cold night made sleeping hard for Sean, and tonight
was no different. Sean had trouble using the backpack for support. He tried
to lean against it with his head and then his back, but nothing worked.

Sean gave up and plopped himself on the ground, staring up at the night
sky. The stars hung overheard, stretching far and wide. They sparkled in
the moon's light, creating a view better than that on the tower. Casey would
have loved it. His fingers rubbed the bracelet and hoped she was thinking
of him too. Sean closed his eyes, picturing her and hoping he could dream
about her again. This time he wanted to dream of her and no one else. Sean
pictured her face and blue eyes; he pictured her kissing him on the tower's
roof that night. He drifted away from the outer desert, with his fingers on
Casey's bracelet. Casey never appeared in the dream, nor did anyone from
Nova. There was no dream at all, just darkness and complete silence.

The night passed. To Sean, it seemed like only minutes. The sun
beamed, warming his stomach and face. Sean quickly ate and finished the
second bottle of water. He tossed it on the ground. Each day the backpack
became lighter as his resources were depleted. The water had not been
cold since yesterday. Now it was lukewarm. Sean changed his mind about
not keeping a journal for Casey. He grabbed the same piece of paper and
jotted a few words on it.

I fell asleep staring at the night sky. The stars were brighter
than before, and the moon was bigger. I didn't dream at all
last night, and it's now morning. I will continue to walk
more and more. I hope I will find something very soon.

Exhausted and mentally drained, Sean walked another hour deeper into the outer desert. His body ached, and he had a sore back and legs, despite a full night's sleep. Along with battling the heat and sand, his eyes kept seeing more empty land and it became too depressing to deal with. Three days of walking and nothing—still nothing at all—could be found. Sean's hope faded with every amount of food he ate, coming closer to starvation. Empty land and heat bore down without mercy, forcing Sean to stare at his feet. He watched them move left and right and saw that a shoestring somehow had come undone. Winds swirled about like a small tornado, tossing the sand around. It resembled the thoughts that ran in circles in his head. Sean took a moment to stop and rehydrate. It would help to clear his thoughts and give him time to add another couple of lines to the journal. He pulled what he needed from the backpack. The paper and pencil were now ready in his hand.

CHAPTER 12

THE ONE THAT
HEADED WEST

Sam Uffner had not stopped walking west since leaving Nova. Step by step, his boots left their imprints across the sand. His jeans held a trail of blood down his leg. The blotches dripped on the footprints that he made. For sixteen hours straight, Sam covered fifty miles of sandy terrain. Now his feet walked on small dried rocks of dirt and barren soil. The amount of sweat that soaked his shirt and pants reflected the unbearable heat that the sun poured over him. Sam's thighs became chafed and inflamed. Every step hurt like hell, but he wasn't going to stop. He couldn't stop. Not until he found a place to rest.

Ahead, a change in the flat terrain caught Sam's eye. Sam changed his course for the distant rocky hill to the northwest that could provide shelter. It was only half a mile from his current location in the middle of nowhere. Small trees began to appear around him, scattered across the miles. Without any leaves sprouting from the branches, it was difficult tell if the trees were alive or dead. There wasn't any time to check either; his feet quickened toward the hill. As he increased his speed, so did the pain in his thighs. Sam managed to last for only a few minutes before bending over on his knees, trying to catch his breath.

The wound on his arm looked worse, as more blood slithered across his forearm, dripping from his elbow. He placed his left hand over the wound and applied pressure as he walked. Squinting in pain, he could see that the hill was very close now, only a few more yards away. Beads of sweat dripped from his forehead and into his eyes. Sam wiped his forehead, smearing blood all across his face, while keeping his eyes focused on the hill. His skinny legs and shoulders quivered under the backpack, the muscles fatigued beyond repair and unable to keep Sam upright any longer. Stumbling forward, he saw he was only a few steps away from the hill. Sam crawled the rest of the way and struggled to climb onto the boulder.

Taking a deep breath, Sam finally rested for the first time. His tiny arms stretched backward to roll the backpack off his shoulders and onto the ground. He opened the top flap and reached for a clean shirt and water. Wasting little time, Sam spun the cap off and chugged the bottle of water without stopping. Every muscle in Sam's body slowly loosened and relaxed on the boulder. Sam would need more than twenty-four hours to properly recover. He then wrapped the clean shirt tightly around the large teeth marks on his forearm. He felt the blood soak the shirt but eventually stopped as he tightened it further. Grimacing in pain, Sam tried to relax and rest as he thought of what had happened last night.

A mountain lion was looking for food. It likely had wandered the desert for days without finding anything. Sam would have walked right into it, had it not growled as he approached. Fear forced Sam's heart to skip a beat, turning his complexion pale in the pitch-black night. Reaching to his right, he grabbed the new self-winding flashlight, a gift from his parents. All it required was to be shaken for a few seconds, and it would work. Sam heard the growl come closer. The light came on, and Sam scanned the area in front of him until the light fell on a pair of eyes.

Stepping back from the lion only made things worse. The lion bared its teeth. Sam held his breath, hoping to cause the lion to lose interest in him. The two stared at each other, not moving or making any sounds. Sam scanned the area, trying to find a way out, but it was impossible to see anything in the dark. If the lion didn't lose interest, Sam would have to make a decision on what he would do. Seconds later, Sam watched in sheer and utter terror as the mountain lion darted straight for him.

Tackling Sam to the ground, the lion snarled and bit Sam's forearm. Sam shouted in pain, whacking the lion with the butt of his flashlight as hard as he could. The lion didn't let go of Sam's forearm, so Sam began to hit the animal with his fist and feet. Every kick and punch landed with some force, but the lion refused the let go. Sam yelled in great pain as the lion pulled and shook him with its mouth. Sam felt his skin rip and tear under his clothes. The lion's right foot scraped at Sam's belt, revealing a small wooden dagger. It was the dagger that Alex had given him for the journey; Alex had given every traveler a special weapon to use in the desert.

Sam reached for the dagger and pulled it from his waist, slamming it as hard as he could into the lion's neck. Blood squirted into Sam's eyes as it yelped in pain. Leaping off his chest, the lion disappeared into the night. Sam grabbed his flashlight and scanned the area for the lion. It was nowhere to be seen. There was no way that Sam was going to stop and rest now. He had to keep moving and create as much distance between him and the lion as possible. Without stopping at all, Sam continued to walk well into the morning. Dawn came, and Sam felt the temperature rise with the sun. He could now see where he was going, but the beads of sweat poured down his face faster and faster.

Everything had been the same since leaving Nova. There still was an endless amount of sand everywhere, and nothing was in sight. With his forearm in pain, Sam kept an eye out for the lion, not seeing that he passed a rusted, bent sign sticking out from the sand to the right. It showed a man holding a pick ax and staring out toward the open land. There were silhouettes of mountains in the background, with the lightly faded words, "Welcome to Nevada."

Now resting on the hill, Sam tried to forget about that terrible night. His muscles began to ache as soon as he started to rise from the rock; he didn't want to move. Accepting that he had no choice but to make camp at the hill, Sam closed his eyes and tried to get some sleep. Sounds of whirling winds and rocks falling off the hill filled his ears, but it was a calming sensation.

I'm so tired, he thought, over and over again. Leaning farther back, he made room to fully lie down. A few seconds were all it took for Sam to fall asleep. Now comfortable, he stayed that way, catching three full hours of sleep before he was awakened by a familiar sound.

Grrrr.

The lion had returned and was staring straight at him; it stood several yards away. Sam lifted himself from the rock's ledge as fast as he could and began to search his backpack. Pulling handfuls of clothes and food from his bag, Sam tried desperately to find anything to use for a weapon besides his flashlight. His arms and legs were beyond exhausted; they felt ten times heavier than usual. Sam eventually turned the backpack upside down, spilling all the contents on the rock. Food and water bottles rolled, fell off the rock's bed, and broke on the ground. His father had given him a hatchet to use for protection, but Sam couldn't find it—it wasn't in his backpack. He couldn't believe it. He could have sworn he'd placed the hatchet in his pack because he didn't like holding weapons.

It wasn't there. Sam was defenseless. The dagger he'd used to stab the lion earlier was no longer in its neck. The lion watched from a distance but seemed to not want to approach; it didn't come any closer to Sam—and he soon realized why. The lion had been an outcast, a wanderer, as a pack of lions now appeared and stared at both Sam and the outcast. Growls came from every direction, surrounding Sam. Hanging his head in defeat, Sam began to slowly cry. He knew what was going to happen. Without a weapon to defend him or the energy to use it, there was no happy ending in sight.

Two lions slowly stepped cautiously closer to him. The lion to his right reached him first. Sam's teary eyes stared directly at the starving predator. In a split second, two-inch teeth struck Sam, ripping a chunk off his face. Sam screamed as he struggled to fight off the lion. He fell from the rock ledge and crashed to the ground. Two, three, four, now five lions all leaped on him, ripping chunks of flesh off his skinny body. The outcast didn't move from its spot. It dared not try to join the feast, or it would risk becoming dinner as well. It remained still, watching the lions feast on Sam. Four minutes went by, and Sam was still screaming as the lions ate him alive.

CHAPTER 13

REMNANTS OF THE OLD WORLD

The pencil scratched the surface of the paper. Sean's words created a scribbling sound, which was the first thing he'd heard all day.

I have been walking all morning. Still no signs of anything at all, just the same stupid, endless miles of desert in front of me. I miss you, Casey, and I rub your bracelet to help me know you're with me somehow. Nothing exciting has happened or probably will happen. I guess it might be a good thing. I wonder at night what you are thinking and doing. It is about time for me to start heading off again. As always, I miss you every day.

Sean neared the bottom of the page and would need to write on the back if he decided to continue. Thoughts were all he had, nothing else. Hope was fading slowly, and death ran around his mind every moment that he stared at the desolate land. Finding motivation to keep going was a struggle. Reyes's mission was failing and soon would cost Sean his life. Casey's bracelet kept the fear and madness at bay, but for how long? Something had to be done. Sean had walked the desert for miles and had found nothing. Changing direction would cost Sean several days; it might lead him to Nova's salvation, or it could just kill him faster. Sean hit his leg in frustration, burying his knuckles into his upper thigh while he walked. More thoughts crept in, keeping Sean's mind busy.

Left, right, left, right. His legs moved, but his heels dragged, leaving a trail in the sand. Exhaustion reemerged, slowing Sean down. He hadn't eaten all day, and it was past two o'clock. Anger rose from the heat and endless walking. It pushed Sean to keep going, even with limbs begging him to stop. He ignored the tired muscles and continued on. He walked and walked, shutting out the sounds from his stomach. Pain soon followed, adding fuel to the anger inside.

Ravenously hungry, Sean closed his eyes, hoping that when he opened them, he would find food or salvation. It would be a dream come true. Everyone would cheer his name for saving Nova, and Casey would kiss him like she did on the tower that night. Family and friends would hold a celebration in his honor. Sean pictured the giant cookout with savory cattleworm meat, and he felt his mouth water and stomach hurt. Sweat poured around the goggles and wet the dry skin on his face. The pain seemed to subside, as if it knew it wasn't going to win, but eventually it would shift toward Sean's back and shoulders.

"Ugh," Sean moaned. Grinding his teeth, he moved his shoulders up and down, trying to shift the backpack so the pain would go away. Sean's foot tripped over something jutting from the ground, sending him tumbling face first. The ground gave a hard smack as it greeted Sean; it wasn't sand but a hard surface. The slam squeezed the air out of his lungs with ease. Several coughs spewed before Sean crawled to his hands and knees. His palms pressed against the ground, feeling for strength to pull him back up. His fingers felt the ground's texture, leaving Sean confused. Never before had he felt anything like it.

Bits of sand and dirt rolled away as Sean lifted his hands. Something underneath was black and broken. Slowly pushing the remaining dirt away, Sean revealed what he'd landed on. He'd learned in Davis's class that this object was a road—a long, black, broken road. Cracks scattered the surface, intersecting with each other and allowing pieces of dead grass to break free. After exploring, Sean saw that the strip of road was no longer than two-thirds of a mile. The rest had disappeared long ago. Goosebumps rose on his neck and spine from the excitement.

"Old world," Sean whispered.

Motivation filled him, convincing Sean to eat and build more strength for the journey ahead. While sitting on the broken road, Sean stared at the relic of the past. Broken, forgotten, and a shadow of itself, the road left more questions than the cracks in it.

Sean ate mouthfuls of jerky, washing it down with water. He ran his fingers along the asphalt. *What was it doing here? Where did it come from? Where was it going?* As he brushed away more dirt and sand, he found faded yellow paint, dividing the road in half equally. The scene was exactly like the pictures from the books in Mr. Davis's class; Sean never thought he'd see one with his own eyes. He grabbed the pencil and paper to begin writing.

> Casey, I can't believe what I found—a road from the old world, like the pictures we saw in class. It's broken apart, but it's still here. I tripped over a thick broken root sticking out from the side of the road. I'm writing to you now as I eat, sitting in the middle of it. I do not know where it came from. I just know that it is here in the east somewhere. It is truly incredible.

Sean shoved the paper back in the backpack, along with the leftover food. He took a final moment to stare at the road before continuing. Sean desperately wanted to follow the road and see where it would take him but decided against it. There wasn't a clear sign to follow in either direction. Both the north and sound ends were broken off, leading to nothing. Sean checked for any more objects, but the road was all that was left. There was no need to waste any more time. His stomach was filled, and the muscles in his legs no longer hurt. Sharp pain still lingered in his back, but it was bearable for now.

Junior's compass pointed east as Sean headed toward more endless miles, though now the terrain changed. To Sean's relief, the ground no longer gave with seeping hot sand but now supported each step with hard, stable soil. He hoped it would be interrupted with more of the old world, but for now Sean was happy to leave the sand behind. After an hour, Sean had covered more land on soil than he did on sand. He also left the road behind, as he did Nova. *Am I the only one to have seen it after so many years? Who knows?* He hoped that he wasn't going to be the last one. Sean threw away the road from his thoughts and focused on walking a little farther. Since the beginning of his journey, the sun had remained the same, cruel and unforgiving. Sean wiped his neck, feeling the entire area was sunburned and covered with sweat.

Another hill approached ahead. Sean's legs quivered at the base of the hill. Walking around it would be the obvious move, but if he climbed, the elevation would give him a clear view of anything within a mile. The common pattern suggested more emptiness, but then, he hadn't expected the road, and that had given him hope where there had been none. Sean imagined the burden on his tired thighs as he carried the backpack uphill. He swallowed, shaking away the choice of taking the easier path, and pressed on. His unwilling legs resisted with every step he climbed.

As Sean climbed higher and higher, he thought more about the old world, and he pictured the people walking and driving, like in the books, on that very road. Mr. Davis spoke of big metal vehicles moving at great speeds on roads like the one he had found, covering long distances in little time. They connected people to cities, towns, stores, homes, and food. Sean's mouth watered as Mr. Davis talked about buildings called restaurants that someone could walk into and ask for food. There was no hunting for it or growing it. *Were their same buildings like the restaurants along the side of road?* Sean hadn't seen any on either side of the road.

Maybe he'd find another road that led to a restaurant. Sean lifted his head to check on how far it was to the top. Several more steps, and he would be there. It was ridiculous to think there would be a restaurant in the middle of the desert, waiting for someone to walk inside. But Sean didn't care how foolish it might be. He was glad that his mind was thinking of something other than pain or death.

CHAPTER 14

A STORM IS COMING

At the top of the hill, Sean scanned the land. He slowly turned, examining every inch. There were still no signs of a town to trade with and no water or food to hunt for. The broken road lay far behind now, a mere black dot in the distance. Sean carefully trekked down the hill, not wanting to trip again. He made his way down safely, only losing his balance briefly but regaining it before falling.

After reaching the bottom Sean grabbed his father's watch from his jacket and checked the time. The watch read five minutes after four. Two more solid hours were all he had before the sun vanished from the sky. As he moved forward, Sean's palms were sweaty, and the blisters that had developed made it difficult to hold the walking stick. A gust of cool air swirled around Sean, delivering a sweet moment of mercy on his hot skin. Then it soared, giving a strong push, lifting dirt into the air. Strangely, the sound of the wind was louder than usual. Sean came to a halt, with a worry deep in his stomach. He furrowed his brow in confusion of what was before him. Somehow, the treacherous land vanished without a trace.

The sky straight ahead became smothered with sand and dirt. It didn't make sense at all. Sean struggled to understand what was happening. How could a sky disappear? His mind raced through the possibilities. He could be hallucinating from the low rationing of food and water, but having eaten several hours before, he ruled that out. The other possibility was the goggles. They were likely layered with sand and needed to be cleaned. Sean hadn't taken the time to adjust them, let alone clean them since leaving Nova. He pulled the goggles from his face and began to wipe the lenses with his shirt. A sense of relief fell over him; he was right about the goggles being dirty, and he removed a thick layer of dirt from the lenses. With the goggles now clean and off his face, Sean's eyes adjusted to the light and searched for the lost sky.

"Oh no," he muttered.

Sean was wrong about the goggles being the problem. There was a third possibility that he'd forgotten—the possibility of a sandstorm heading straight for him. Sean slipped the goggles across his eyes as fast as he could. Moving in any direction proved useless without there being any shelter. Sean was trapped and in deep trouble. The sandstorm hurled its way forward, creating a giant, thick wall several hundred feet high. He was running out of time and needed to come up with a plan quickly. The heavy winds created a thunderous sound from a hundred feet away and closing in fast.

Sean took a deep breath to gather his strength. He lifted the walking stick over his head and then drove it repeatedly into the ground, piercing the soil several inches deep. He kneeled and braced for the storm squeezing the walking stick as hard as he could. All he could hope for was that the storm wouldn't blow him off the ground. There was a small chance that the stick would hold through, but he didn't have much of a choice. Sean lifted his shirt collar over his face so he wouldn't inhale too much sand or other flying debris. Sandstorms were no laughing matter. According to Mr. Davis's books, they were reported to have winds reaching above twenty miles per hour. Many would leave their victims with severe coughs and completely lost or separated from groups.

The winds grew louder, blocking out all thought. Sean held the walking stick to his chest more tightly and readied himself for impact. The storm struck Sean with a heavy pounding to the chest, pushing him steadily away from the stick. It took all the strength not to let go. His palms burned from the blisters ripping open as he clung for dear life. Sean couldn't hear himself scream while the scratching of hurtling sand pierced the exposed skin. They were like paper cuts all across his hands and face. The winds felt faster than twenty miles per hour. Sean screamed again as the wind nearly lifted him off the ground. The duster jacket whipped violently in the air trying to pull free from Sean. Sean stared at his stick worried that it would break free and send him flying backwards. What felt like hours were only mere seconds that the horror the storm brought forth. Small, dark, black shadows whizzed behind with incredible speed. Sean squinted and tried to see what sped past, and one of the shadows almost struck his face.

Rocks.

Sean ducked just in time to see a flying rock whirl right through where his head had been seconds earlier. The storm was taking everything it found with it into the air. More shadows whirled toward him from a distance. They were increasing in size, almost equal to his chest. Without proper cover, Sean couldn't avoid the rocks by kneeling any longer. He rose to his feet fighting back against the wind with all his strength. His wounded hands loosened their grip from the stick as he pressed forward into the storm, dodging any debris he could. A small bird unfortunately was caught in the wake and flapped its wings wildly in the storm, but it was useless. The storm had its grip on the poor bird and wasn't letting go. As it chirped loudly, Sean could only guess it was screaming for help.

The bird soon faded away into the cloud. Sean looked away and saw a small child's chair rolling across the ground, pieces of its legs breaking apart as it skidded by. Sean was in shock to see more evidence of possible life. He was getting close; there had to be something near. Lost in a daze, Sean forgot the reality of flying debris that hurled past him with malicious intent. His shoulders relaxed, and so did his guard. Sean followed the rolling chair, never taking his gaze off it. As wildly as the chair spun, so did his thoughts of finding more life and saving Nova. From the corner of his eye, another shadow appeared. Sean snapped back into reality within seconds and instantly tried to catch a glimpse of the shadow, but it was too late. The flying black circle was a rock the size of a baseball, and it struck Sean at full speed. If it weren't for his goggles, Sean would have been killed. The right lens shattered into pieces that were blown away into the sandstorm.

Sean stumbled backward, stunned. Pain pierced his forehead while the wind kept pushing. Every muscle fought hard trying to keep him level but failed. Another strong burst from the wind lifted Sean into air. He would mirror the bird, helpless and screaming for help. Sean knew what came next, and he waited for the impact. He readied himself to hit the ground, but the piercing pain on his forehead intensified. Sean would not feel the ground on his back or the howling winds. Darkness engulfed him completely. His mind left, seeking a memory from long ago. Unconscious, Sean's body slammed into the ground and was slowly dragged away by the storm.

CHAPTER 15

A FACE FROM LONG AGO

Darkness fell, blanketing all sound and perception around Sean. As his body fell, so did his mind. Memories, a dream, a nightmare— whatever it was, it would all be revealed soon. A small cloud of light broke through the pitch-blackness, reaching for him. Words were muffled; Sean couldn't hear them clearly. The light grew as it drew closer, and Sean felt himself reach for it. He didn't know why, but he wanted to. The light was safe and kind, and he wouldn't stop until it fully embraced him. He felt the warmth of the sun on his face as an image formed of a man from long ago—a man whose features could be seen subtly within Sean's face. He shared the same nose, eyes, and crooked smile that would drive Diane crazy. Sean was reaching for his father. He stood a great deal taller than before, almost giant like. Sean's hands could only reach the right thigh on his father's jeans.

Sean squeezed the pant leg with short, stubby fingers. Sean shouted with joy, but the words held no form or structure. Speaking and walking seemed new to Sean, and he almost fell when making his way over to his father. Sean's legs were chubby, and his feet were bare. The ragged jeans he usually wore had been replaced with a cloth diaper. More screams of excitement burst from Sean's mouth; he begged for attention. His father knelt to shorten the distance to only an arm's length away. Dark brown eyes glistened with a smile, naturally inclining Sean to smile back in delight. He could see why Diane had a difficult time staying mad at his father. Sean hated him for disappearing, but he couldn't hate him for too long with a smile like that.

Sean grabbed his father's nose and squeezed as hard as his tiny muscles let him. His father reached over and kissed Sean on the cheek. Thick prickly hairs from his father's beard either tickled or hurt Sean when he gave kisses. This time they tickled Sean, and he laughed as his father lifted him off the ground with two thick arms. His father tossed him high into the air and then caught him as he fell. Sean dangled above his father's shoulders; Sean was the giant now, looking down. His small, short arms jabbed recklessly in every direction with quick thrusts. Sean's father made little quirky sounds as he drew Sean closer to him, tickling Sean's stomach with his nose and mouth.

"Be careful, dear," a voice said.

Both Sean and his father turned toward the loving voice. Diane walked out and stood near them. Her green eyes watched the two of them. Her lips stretched into a warm smile. Sean cheered and reached over to grab her. Diane continued the tickling that his father had stopped. Her hands were softer and the skin smelled of jasmine.

"I wouldn't think of dropping him," his father said.

She turned and shook her head gently. "I'm not worried about you; I'm worried about Sean giving you one of his strong punches."

He balanced Sean on his hip, holding out an open palm. Sean touched the palm with his tiny fingers.

"C'mon, champ, give me a hard punch," his father said.

Sean stared at the open palm, then at his mother, and then back to the palm again. There was no chance that Sean could have understood what his father wanted him to do, but Sean did indeed throw a punch. The punch was not to the open palm but to the face. Sean swung his arms rapidly in every direction until a backhand landed cleanly on his father's left cheek.

"Wow. That's some punch you got there, kiddo."

Diane laughed innocently and gave a look of approval to Sean. "Ha. I told you he would get you. It was only a matter of time." Her fingers stretched wide, grabbing Sean as he reached for her as well. Tired and out of breath, Sean rested on Diane's chest, burying his face in her neck. The smell of jasmine eased Sean's heart rate, calming him down. Diane kissed Sean on the head several times, rocking him up and down.

"How long do you plan on being out there this time?" Her voice was subtly worried.

"Only a couple of days at the most. I should be back soon and with more cattleworm." His father reached over, ruffling Sean's hair.

"Can't they find someone else?"

"Diane, you always ask me that every time I have to leave. You know it's my turn to head out. You don't have to worry about me. I'll be fine."

Diane's face expressed worry and disappointment. She hoped that it would be enough to convince him to stay. She knew the rules about Nova as well as anyone else—everyone had to contribute in some way. Sean felt Diane's heartbeat increase as it pounded against his cheek. Her worry never ceased throughout the years. Some nights she would wake completely drenched in sweat from nightmares of the horrible dangers that waited those who ventured out. A few of the nightmares were so bad she couldn't help but cry. Sean would never know how much Diane loved his father, but he did know how many tears it cost her.

A few children emerged from the other side of Nova, running about, playing tag. Sean followed with his eyes, eventually turning away as they disappeared. The screams and shouts startled Sean, and he began to squirm impatiently. Sean plunged his face deeper into Diane's chest, seeking comfort. His father leaned in, stroking the back of Sean's head.

"Keep an extra eye on Sean. He seems angry, Diane."

"He's angry to see you leave," Diane said, hoping that the guilt would work.

Diane shifted Sean just above her shoulders as she soothed him with more rubbing. Sean was getting more difficult to carry. He was growing up fast, and his weight was becoming a problem for her. From a distance, Sean could see other children playing with their toys on the ground, Casey's parents were across the road. Unlike Sean's parents, they were happy at the moment. Her dad held her mom gently, and they kissed each other in the joy of having a child. Casey stirred in their arms, and then her mother began to breastfeed her. The older children played with balls crafted of leather. Running and screaming, they kicked, caught, and threw the balls off walls and tables. An object would break once in a while, and everyone would flee and hide. Parents would gather and argue who had done it and who would have to fix it.

These events proved useful for Sean, years later. He seemed to always be in the right place at the right time, witnessing the guilty child who broke something. Sean would blackmail the kids into doing his chores in exchange for his silence. It created extra time for him to explore, eventually leading to the discovery of the B-52 bomber buried under the sand.

A few times on his way to explore, Sean would catch Billy playing air guitar while humming and dancing to a song in his head. Billy would stop in the middle of the road, head banging radically and taking applause from a crowd that wasn't there.

Nova was filled with love and happiness then. Reyes wasn't worried about the amount of food they had or needing to find any. Families weren't being torn apart or watching their loved ones disappear into the desert.

Sean's father placed his hand on Sean's head, kissing the top of it one last time before his departure and gave another kiss for Diane. Sean moved to face the giant and grab his nose again. He waved his hand up and down as he softly said goodbye. Sean began to cry like any other baby would when seeing his parents do the same. Unfortunately for Sean, it foreshadowed an event that would cause more tears later on and would continue to haunt him to this day. Sean's screams roared as he tried to break free from Diane. She held on tightly as Sean reached desperately for his father, wanting him to take Sean with him, but he didn't.

"It's okay, Sean. Take care of your mother, and I will be back in no time. I love you, Sean."

The doors began to open, as they later did for Sean. His steps moved away from them, and Sean's cries were filled with tears that fell on Diane. She too began to cry, holding Sean as he buried his face again.

The lucid memory began to weaken, and Sean felt himself more aware and in control. Sean tried to shout for his father, but the words were muffled in sobbing noises. He was trapped in a baby's body, and all he could do was cry and cry. His father lifted his hand and gave a small wave, never looking back. The doors began to close slowly behind him, limiting their view.

This was how they lived for several more years. Sean felt the memory weaken even more as the blackness covered his eyes again, like before. Everything was fading. Sean was slipping back into consciousness. Sean didn't want to go back. It had been years since he'd seen his father's face or felt his comfort. There was nothing Sean could do; the fading grew stronger, and he could no longer feel Diane holding him.

The smell of jasmine was all Sean could still hold on to, but soon that too began to weaken and slip from him. There was something still in the darkness, though not yet lost. Sean focused as hard as he could on what was left. He heard Diane whisper to her husband. It was impossible for his father to hear her, but there wasn't a day that passed that he wouldn't believe that. Her words softly echoed in Sean's head as he felt the hot wind and the sunlight through his eyes. Sean was about to wake up. The words would soon be left in the darkness behind him.

Sean tried to hold on to her voice as long as he could. His heartbeat returned, pounding inside. Sean felt the warm air slip into his lungs. Sensations filled his arms and legs. Sean's body twitched, pulling him faster from the memory. With one final effort, Sean held his breath, trying to hear Diane's voice one last time. The echo was faint, but he could hear her voice as she said four words that she always meant: "I love you, Jacob."

CHAPTER 16

THE ONE THAT HEADED SOUTH

Jason Matthews stood tall, looking out into the southern desert. His six-foot-two frame made the young girls of Nova huddle around, gaping at and ogling his body. With broad shoulders, defined muscles, and rock-hard abs, he had started to give Alex some competition. If it wasn't his body, then it was his face, rough blond hair, wide jaw, and hazel eyes. The girls called him a heart throb.

Taking a quick sip from his new water bottle, Jason clipped the bottle's cap to his belt, holding it in place. Fully rested from his nap, Jason continued down the path to the south. He had come across several giant gaps that forced him to walk around, killing his time and progress. The journey so far had given no worries to him. For days now, he had not come across any type of dangerous animals or cattleworms. Jason was becoming impatient as the days passed. He promised Nova that he would be their hero and bring salvation to them. He needed to hurry; any one of the others could beat him to it. There was no room for sharing the glory on this one.

The backpack gave little resistance as it barely felt heavy at all. Out here, Jason applied all the lessons that Alex had taught him while growing up. He scanned the ground for any signs of animal tracks and trees with scratch marks or urine deposits on them. Every tree and every bit of ground he covered had no signs of anything living. Jason kicked a puff of dirt into the air. It would have been easier to spot something in the sand, but he had passed that several hours ago.

So the journey went on as Jason headed south, keeping an eye out for anything that might give him a sign. A little farther ahead was a giant mountain, blocking his path. Staring at its massive size, Jason realized there was no way in hell he would be able to climb over it. Even though, as he looked straight to the top, its height would give him a great view of what was around him.

Damn. Jason bit his tongue and turned right, walking around the mountain.

An hour passed, and Jason still hadn't even begun to circle around it.

You're a big son of a bitch, aren't ya? Jason thought as he placed his hands on his waist, shaking his head in disappointment. Finally, Jason was pleased to come around the side of the mountain, but soon he was caught by surprise.

Two men were sitting inside a little cave in the mountain, watching Jason. They looked at each other and rose to their feet. Jason lifted the newest pair of goggles off his face in case, making sure he wasn't seeing things that weren't there. With his hazel eyes free from the goggles, he still saw the two men standing in front of him.

The one on the left was a faired-skin man. Jason could see that he had suffered severe sunburn on his shoulders, arms, and face. His red hair was barely visible under the caked layer of dirt on top of it. He was tall and muscular, unlike his dark-skinned friend on the right.

"Hey guys, over here!" Jason shouted. Waving his arms over his head, he rushed toward them, quickening each step. "Man, am I glad to see you." Jason finally stopped a few feet short of the men and began to take off his backpack.

"Oh, really?" the faired skinned man said, giving a curious look to his friend.

"Yes, I am, sir," Jason replied.

"Sir?" The man gave a loud laugh, showing his dirty yellow teeth with a few missing. "You hear that, Darrius? This polite young man called me *sir.*" He watched Jason place his large backpack on the ground then slowly open the top flap for some water. The bottle he had earlier had run dry and needed to be refilled.

"Yes, I heard, Jack." Darrius nodded his head, leaning forward trying to catch a glimpse of what was inside the backpack. Darrius was a foot shorter than Jack and half his size. He walked a little closer to the bag. Jason kept smiling as Jack too slowly walked toward him. The stench of bodies not bathed for weeks—even months—was almost unbearable, and Jason fought the urge to cover his nose, for fear of offending the strangers.

These two men gave Jason an eerie feeling; he sensed they couldn't be trusted. Jason knew he had to proceed carefully with what he mentioned about Nova or himself.

"Can you guys help me?" Jason asked, pulling a new jar of water out to fill his bottle.

The two spread outward until they stood on either side of Jason.

Darrius shrugged his skinny shoulders. "That depends on what you need."

"I'm looking for some food or even a town where I can stay for the night," Jason replied.

"Looks like you're a little lost here, boy. Where are your friends?" Jack laughed, tucking his hands in his belt.

"It's only me here, and I was just passing on through, sir." Jason finished filling his bottle and placed the remaining jar of water into his backpack.

"Well, there ain't no town or food around here, boy," Jack said.

"Well, then, I thank you for your time, gentlemen. I will just keep on walking." Jason began to flip the top flap closed when Darius interrupted him.

"Whoa, whoa, now. Where are we headed off to in such a hurry?" Darrius stuck his hand out as he spoke.

Jason now felt a little on edge. He didn't like how the men seemed to be circling him to prevent him from backing away or moving on. Jason tried to calmly talk his way through while keeping an eye on his weapon inside his bag. "Please, guys, I don't want any trouble. I'm just looking for some food and a place to stay; that's all. So if you don't know anything, then I would like to keep on moving."

"Okay, okay, so what's your name anyway, boy?" Jack asked.

"My name is Jason."

"You see, Jason, Jack and I are also looking for food and shelter. My poor friend here has been badly burned by the sun, and we have been hungry for some time," Darrius said.

Jason kept the two men in his sights as he said, "I don't understand what you guys are getting at."

Jack shook his head, as if in disappointment. "You see, boy, you come around here flashing that good-looking water and not even offering us some."

"Yeah, now that's rude," Darrius joined in.

Jason nodded his head. "You're absolutely right, fellas. Here—you can finish one off." Jason reached inside his pack and grabbed the jar of water that he'd used to fill his bottle. He tossed it to Darrius. "Now that you have some water, I'll be on my way."

Jason was interrupted for the second time as he tried to close the bag.

"Thanks, but me and Darrius are still hungry, and judging by that big bag of yours, we think you might have some food in there as well." Jack thrust his hand out, palm up, expecting Jason to hand him something.

"I don't have any food for anyone. I used it all up last night," Jason said firmly, trying to convince them.

Darrius shook his head in disbelief and came within an arm's length of Jason. "How about we take a look and see if you're telling us the truth."

Jason knelt down, sticking his hand in the bag and grabbing the handle of his weapon, although he did not yet wield it; he waited to see if the men would back off. "No, I don't think so."

Both Jack and Darrius reached behind their backs and pulled out two blunt clubs.

"We weren't asking," Darrius said in a menacing tone.

Jason looked both men in the eyes and waited for Jack to approach. When he did, Jason lunged backward, pulling free his weapon and firmly wielding it at both men.

The weapon was a hatchet—Sam's hatchet, to be exact. Well into the night, Jason snuck in Sam's room and had stolen the hatchet, leaving no signs that he had been there. Now facing the two men, Jason shouted with great force, trying to scare the two away. "Get back! Step back before one of you gets hurt!"

"Oooo, our boy Jason, here, has himself a weapon now," Jack teased.

"The only one about to get hurt here is you," Darrius said, threatening Jason.

Jason swung his hatchet toward Darrius, who blocked the attack with his club. The two were locked together as the hatchet dug itself into the club's wood. Jack swiftly attacked and hit Jason in the back, sending Jason falling to his knees. Jack struck again with a great blow to the side, cracking one of Jason's ribs. Wincing in pain, Jason let go of the hatchet and held his wounded ribs.

Darrius pulled the hatchet free from his club and threw it down to the ground. Jack reached around Jason from behind, holding him in place. Darrius used his club to lift Jason's chin and look into his eyes. "Looks like we will be taking that bag of yours and whatever else you got." Gripping the club's handle tighter, Darrius pulled back and swung as hard as he could. The hard hit sent Jason falling face first onto the ground. Blood spewed all across the dirt surrounding Jason's face. His nose had been broken and a tooth had been jarred loose. The tooth was on the ground in front of him, still connected with a trail of saliva from his mouth as blood slowly pooled around it.

Jack and Darrius celebrated with cheers and laughter, enjoying their new possessions. The two men pulled out jars of water, jerky, clothes, and letters from his family telling him how much they loved him. Jason, hearing the men cheer, began to crawl away. Inch by inch, he pulled himself across the desert until he could muster enough strength to rise to his feet.

Jack was first to notice Jason walking in the opposite direction.

"Hey! Where do you think you're going?" he shouted. Jack lifted his club from the ground and rushed toward Jason. Jack wildly swung the club in the air and slammed the head into Jason's shin, shattering the tibia into three places.

"Aaahhhh!" Jason screamed as he crashed to the ground, holding his broken leg. Darrius and Jack both lifted their clubs and viciously took turns beating Jason. The attack lasted nearly two minutes, leaving Jason with a swollen left eye, broken right hand, dislocated left shoulder, and a ruptured spleen.

Darrius bent over to catch his breath. Sweat poured from his face and onto his clothes. Jack stood still over Jason, watching him moan and mutter in pain. His sunburned face smiled as he saw tears mixed with blood fall down Jason's cheeks. Jack's eyes scanned the area around him, looking for a place to leave Jason. Turning to Darrius, who had finally caught his breath, he asked him to grab their shovel. Jack stripped Jason clean of his clothes to prepare him for what was about to happen next.

They threw Jason into the hole that took them an hour to dig. His broken body and swollen face lay still, soaked in blood. Jason's only movement was his mouth that begged for his mom as he continued to sob. Piles of dirt began to fall on his chest and mix with his blood. More and more, the dirt rose slowly, covering his legs and waist, waiting to consume him. He couldn't move his feet or legs, and now his left arm was buried as well.

"Stop, please stop," Jason pleaded but heard only mockery and laughter. Dirt cupped around his chin, and Jason felt a huge amount of pressure on his chest. The dirt caved around him every time he exhaled, causing there to be less and less air to breathe. His pleas became weaker and weaker.

Jack waited until Jason's face was all that was left exposed. He knelt down by the hole and placed his ear on Jason's lips as Jason barely whispered a single word: "Why?"

Jack reached for Jason's swollen eye, spreading the eyelid open as tears of pain fell over his thumb.

"Because we can," Jack said.

He nodded to Darrius, who threw a pile of dirt on top of Jason's face;

it spilled into his mouth. Jason's coughs threw dirt into the air, even as another pile fell on top of him, shutting all light from his eyes. There was no air, no sunlight, and no breeze. There was only the sound of dirt still falling on him. After several thuds, Jack threw the last of the dirt, sealing Jason's fate forever.

CHAPTER 17

MIMIC

Wind, sand, and sunlight fell over Sean, pulling him from the memory. Puffs of sand flew into air, and Sean coughed, leaning over to his side. Pain stretched all over his body and pulsated from the head wound. Sean rubbed his upper right forehead where the rock had hit, removing some of the clotted blood. The wound reopened, and a trickle of fresh blood seeped down his eyebrow and onto his cheek.

"No. No. No! *No!*" Sean screamed. He pounded his fists on the ground. "Take me back! I don't want to be here anymore. Take me back!"

The words began to break apart as he cried. Chunks of red dirt and sand crumbled away between his fingertips. Sean rocked back and forth. His anger blended with nausea. Sean spread his hands apart and plunged his face forward nearly kissing the ground as vomit sprayed everywhere. Drained and helpless, Sean continued to lie on the ground in a fetal position, crying away the remaining tears. He closed his eyes, trying to find a way back to his father.

Sean was tired of being alone and afraid. The loneliness was becoming worse than death. It crippled his mind and slowly crushed his will. Sean knew he was breaking but didn't know how long he could last. Seeing his father again made the whole world disappear. Sean had forgotten about Nova and that its fate was on the shoulders of four men. The endless miles of barren land, the scorching heat from the blistering sun, and the tired muscles that refused to move another inch were gone. All of it was gone. There was nothing more in this world that Sean wanted more than for all of it to be gone and for him to be back with his dad.

An hour went by with Sean still lying on the ground in failure. He wasn't going to see his father again. Not in this life, at least. Sean unwillingly accepted the reality of it being over. Even if he did dream or fall unconscious, there wasn't a guarantee that he would see his father again. Sean took his time to get on his feet. He dusted off his jeans and jacket. Near his feet was a small trail from his being dragged across the ground by the storm. The trail wasn't long—only thirty feet—but it had created small rips in the back of his jeans and left small scratches on his calves. Sean felt the air flow through the torn jeans, soothing his aching legs while irritating the scratches.

His tried to gather his bearings as he followed the trail he'd left behind. It was good news that he'd been dragged only thirty feet, but now his walking staff was nowhere to be seen. Out here, losing a weapon was just as bad as losing water or food. The journey was becoming harder as the days passed. Sean stretched back, letting the backpack slide off his shoulders. He was sore and hungry, and the backpack's weight doubled the pain to the muscles on Sean's back. As if losing his walking staff wasn't bad enough, Sean discovered more bad news. A couple of jars filled with water had broken when he'd fallen and were seeping through the backpack and onto the ground. Some clothes and jerky were soaked in the water; thankfully only a few splashes had fallen on the pieces of paper. Sean took off his jacket and changed shirts. He proceeded to remove all the broken glass as carefully as possibly then began to calculate his losses.

Sean lost a half gallon of water and had only than two gallons left. He now hesitated in grabbing a new jar of water. He needed to drastically ration the portions now. This changed everything. With less water to drink, Sean would reach dehydration faster, and his traveling needed to be cut shorter to conserve energy. Sean reflected on how long he had left out here. His mind and body were getting beaten to hell, but Sean was still fighting on. He ripped a few strips of cloth from the T-shirt he replaced and then wrapped them around the scratches on his calves. They were small but many. Tiny lines ran down his left and right legs, and small dots of blood were visible. The scratches needed to be cleaned and cared for. Sean cursed himself for wasting water, but he had no choice.

Wincing in pain, Sean tied the strips tightly around his calves and prepared for more walking. He checked the compass to find east one more time. Everything was back in place as Sean began to walk again. Left, right, left, right—his feet pressed on like a brainless zombie, walking endlessly to the unknown. For now, the walk was all Sean had, and in return, it gave him time to think.

Keep walking. Keep walking. Don't stop. Left … right, left … right. It's so hot.

This damn sun just won't let up. I'm so tired. There's nothing but sand and sky. Keep walking. Keep walking. Don't stop now.

Sean checked his father's watch. He had been walking for five hours and rambling on about the same thing, over and over in his head, before he saw it. All depression, hopelessness, isolation, and exhaustion vanished with a single glance.

Twenty feet ahead was a small patch of grass. Dark green blades pulled from the ground and reached for the sky. Sean slowly approached it and gently placed the backpack on the ground. He fell to his knees, laughing. He touched the grass between his fingers. It was there, not a figment of his imagination. The blades of grass moved with the wind and pressed against his hands. Sean pulled himself closer to the grassy patch and took the strongest whiff he could muster. What he smelled was fresh, moist, and strong with life. Hope retuned, and a small bit of it filled his soul. Sean's mind rattled a million thoughts back and forth. There was no mistaking that he'd found life, but he needed more than just a patch. Water had to be nearby. If Sean could find water, not only would he extend his time before dehydration, but it would lead him to wildlife or even a town. Sean was sure of it. He grabbed his backpack and continued on.

Sean's eyes were keen on finding more grass or possibly water. He scanned left and right while walking for another thirty minutes—and then he found more good news. Sean stared upon grass yet again, but this time instead of a small patch by itself, there were forty patches spread across the ground. All the patches were dark green and healthy. The blades looked fertile and growing. Still pushing forward, with determination surging through his body, the misery of the backpack chained to his body disappeared. The weight no longer dragged him or his energy down. At that moment, Sean was invincible; his energy became endless, and his will was unrelenting with every patch of grass he found. More patches of green filled his eyes until he finally reached the source. Sean entered a small field of grass. It spread across the desert, and within it were tree stumps scattered about, their roots crawling out to the surface. The trees were dead, but the wood would provide a fire and warm food. Everything began to turn for the better. Sean didn't know how or from where he'd drawn luck, and he wasn't going to ask. He picked the nearest tree stump and began to make camp. He flipped open his backpack and neatly placed everything on the ground before him. He picked up the survival knife, along with the box of matches.

He ran the survival knife up the surface of a root and toward the bark. Sean began to laugh with joy that this was real, and a sense of accomplishment swirled inside him. He slammed his survival knife into the dead wood, working a piece free and throwing it near the belongings. Sean continued hacking away until two more pieces were cut free, but he needed to find more for a good fire. Ignoring the heat and sweat, Sean continued to search for more wood and found a small dead tree. The tree stood nearly to his chest and was more than enough wood for a fire. Sean chopped the tree free from the ground and dragged it back to camp. It was sunset when Sean finished chopping the tree into logs, leaving him with enough firewood to last through the night. Now Sean just needed to start a fire. He grabbed one of the pieces of paper left in the pack and crumbled it. Sean placed three pieces of firewood together and then tossed the piece of paper. He rattled the box of matches he pulled from his pocket and heard only a few inside.

Sean realized that he'd never counted how many matches were rationed to him before his departure. The heartache, cries from families, and the fear caused him to forget to check everything. Sean never thought he would actually survive this long or even a single night. He slid the box open, counting six matches—six possible nights with warm food, light, and protection. Sean needed to be careful and make them count. Holding the shaft of the match, Sean snapped the end against the striking strip, igniting it. The fire hissed with glory and then sputtered, almost going out. Sean's heart stopped, but he felt it beat again as he carefully moved to light the crumpled paper. Small flames crawled across the paper, slowly increasing their speed. Sean waved his arms and blew air, feeding the flame.

"C'mon, burn, baby," he said softly.

Sean kept blowing and waving his hand. Smoke spurted from the center as the fire reached higher to the sky, touching the wood. Sean stared in anticipation and worry. He crossed his fingers, hoping that the flame was strong enough to catch the wood. The flame wrapped itself around the pieces of the dead wood like a snake but then retracted. The crumbled piece of paper was soon nothing but ash, and he knew the fire would eventually die out. White smoke rose from the center again but into Sean's face. He placed his hands over his mouth as he coughed, making sure not to blow out the flame. Tears lined his eyelids from the smoke as Sean's struggles continued.

"C'mon, please, please." Sean pressed his hands together, pleading to the flame not to burn out. The pleas quickly turned to wishes and prayers to the fire god that Sean created in his head. The flame shrunk to nearly half its size and was on the verge of going out. Sean's prayers turned into an open letter to any god in the universe who would listen and answer him.

With the last section of paper consumed by the flame, there was a final burst that finally gripped the wood. A surge of heat flushed Sean's face, surprising him.

"Yes!" he screamed. Over and over, Sean continued to shout out *yes*, following it with a dance. Jumping up and down, he shifted on his feet, left then right and around the fire. He waved his hands through the thick white smoke that rose into the night sky. A giant cloud of smoke collided with Sean. A sharp taste of bitterness from the burning wood filled his lungs. Sean fell to his knees, choking, still laughing with excitement. Everything was coming to together, piece by piece. He'd found patches of grass, dead trees, a field of grass, and now he was making fire. This was a huge turning point for him in his journey.

Sean lay on the ground, basking in the celebration, as he thanked all the gods he could—the fire god, water god, wind god, Almighty God, and the universe's God; one of them had answered his prayer. Now he thought of Casey and the journal she wanted him to keep. Sean reached over to the supplies, grabbing what he needed. He continued from where he'd left off.

> I found it. I found life, Casey. In what seems to be impossible here in this barren desert, there is actual life. I had to survive a sandstorm earlier today that nearly killed me. Some of my supplies were lost from the storm. Things have always been bad since leaving, but they became worse after the storm. Just when I thought all was lost, I found grass and then trees. There were small and scarce at first. But pressing on, I found a whole field in the distance. Even the ground felt different. No longer was it hard and sandy. It seemed softer than before; the ground changed, with more dirt and clay than sand. Now, as I write to you, I'm wondering how close I am getting. How close can I be to water or to people? I am wondering how long of a walk I have left. I hope that this journey ends soon, and I can hurry back to you. Tonight I will sleep with a fire and look up at the stars, hoping you are doing the same.

The pencil's tip was worn to the end, worsening the neatness of the words. Before preparing dinner, Sean had sharpened the pencil with the army knife and placed it back with the supplies, along with the pieces of paper. Staring at the food, he jokingly said out loud, "What should I eat for dinner? I can eat cattleworm jerky or more cattleworm jerky."

The choice was easy; he ate the jerky while looking into the fire. Orange, yellow, and red flames swayed left to right. They created a trancelike state, stretching higher and then breaking apart at the end. Sean always loved staring at fires. He stared for over an hour, never breaking his eyes away while eating. The wood was nearly ash, and the flames began to dwindle. Sean still had some pieces left from the tree he'd dragged back earlier. Sean tossed more firewood into the fire. He had enough to last him through the night. After the final piece of wood was added, Sean sat down, grabbing a jar of water.

The water seemed colder than usual on his lips. Each swallow blissfully traveled into his stomach. Sean drank a whole jar of water, forgetting to ration his supply. He even ate the jerky well beyond the planned potions. This was his celebration, and Sean wasn't going to let anything ruin it, especially hunger or dehydration. He lay back near the fire, feeling the warmth of the flames on his side. The air was beginning to cool, and the sun had vanished a while ago beneath the horizon. Pitch black surrounded him, except for the stars above. The moon hung overhead, shining as it always did. It was a little bigger than usual tonight, and with the stars glistening, the view became amazing. Sean took in the sight the best he could, but it still wasn't the same without someone to share it with. He rubbed the bracelet that Casey made him, hoping to somehow summon her like a genie. Sean lifted the bracelet under his nose; he could still smell her, even through the sweat-soaked strands. As he slowly drifted to sleep, Sean softly spoke out loud to the stars. "I miss you, Casey."

Sean closed his eyes, picturing the words flying through the air and falling into her ear. He pictured her hearing him and running to the tower's roof to stare at the night sky as well. It was a wonderful idea. Sean needed to dream of something that could take him away from here—something that could help him forget the long journey and the countless brushes with death. Sean needed to dream of Casey. Sean rolled over, nestling himself, with the fire soothing his back. Each minute that passed eased the pain and soreness he felt. The fire crackled and spurted soothing sounds. Sean dared not wiggle around. He found the perfect spot for the night.

"I miss you, Casey." Sean smiled. Those were the exact words he wanted her to hear and feel. There wasn't a day out there that he didn't miss her or need her. Sean was scared to admit the truth that everyone knew. He loved her. There was no denying it.

Suddenly, Sean rose to his hands and knees as fast as he could. His heart pounded in his chest. The tiredness disappeared in an instant and was replaced with sheer terror. The endless walks that Sean had taken held whirling winds that created distinct sounds that could deceive any wanderer. Distant shouts, muffled words, or even cries would make anyone think that someone was near when there was no one. The years of exploring allowed Sean to learn how to filter these sounds. He knew when to ignore them.

This time was different. Sean clearly heard words spoken that no wind could ever create. The words were spoken exactly in his own voice, except Sean didn't say them. Sean had closed his eyes for less than a minute. This wasn't a dream or a nightmare. This was real; it was happening. Sean tried to think on what was going on.

He heard the words a second time. He swore he hadn't spoken, but the voice was his. *How?*

Fear poured from the surrounding darkness straight into Sean. His entire body shook. He had never been this scared. His mind couldn't think anymore. The thoughts that tried to rationalize what was going on disappeared. Instinct took over, and Sean lunged for the knife near the fire.

"I miss you, Casey." He heard the words again from within the darkness.

They were closer than before, this time to his right. Sean gripped the handle of the knife tighter and tighter with each passing second. His breath quickened with a thought that emerged from the darkness. It was the answer he had feared.

Mimic.

There was no denying it. It was real, and it had found him. The mimic lurked behind the darkness as the sound of its footsteps circled around, trying to find the perfect time to attack. Sean became paralyzed with fear. He didn't know what to do. His hands shook with intensity, and his legs were too tired to even hold him up. Sean not in fighting condition. Tears started to pour down his face. There was no way Sean was going to survive this. Every encounter that man had faced against a mimic had ended in a brutal and painful death. Sean faced the reality of it. The outer desert had come to take his life. Sean now thought of his father.

All the panic and fear disappeared in a blink of an eye. A spark of rage flowed from his heart through his veins. It grew with every beat, giving him strength. The monster probably had taken his father and now it had come for him. All the tears of heartache he'd spilled those years ago were because of this creature that had taken his father's life. This was Sean's chance for revenge. The only thing he could do now was to make the mimic work for its dinner. Sean promised himself that he wasn't going to die easily. For his father, Sean would make this beast remember him forever. The footsteps circled around even faster and heavier, turning Sean around and around. Sean's eyes were now consumed with rage.

"C'mon, you bastard!" Sean screamed, staring into darkness.

Suddenly, two bright yellow eyes appeared. They floated in the air, swaying left and right. They moved gracefully, studying Sean, trying to strategize their next move. The eyes shook Sean's confidence but for only a moment. The mimic paced around again a few more times before it growled. The deep noise stirred with anger and strength. Sean shook with rage again. With the darkness blanketing the mimic, there was no way Sean could tell the size of the creature. The flames only gave a small circle of light around the fire. Sean kept close to the fire as much as possible, keeping it between him and the mimic. The eyes drew closer and closer to Sean. Finally, an image of the beast came to view as the creature's paw poked from the darkness. The paw was nearly as big as Sean's chest. The fur was as black as the night, and the claws stretched out six inches long. They were beyond lethal and stained with the blood of its prey.

The mimic knocked Sean's backpack over like a rag doll as it circled around again. The supplies spilled out, tumbling closer to the fire. Sean made his way to the backpack while still keeping his eyes on the beast. He found a jar of water and opened the top. Sean poured half of the jar over a piece of wood on the ground. The mimic still waited in the darkness, watching Sean's every move. Sean placed the dry end of the wood into the fire creating a torch. He now had another weapon to defend himself.

The yellow eyes kept circling, moving with Sean, trying to pull him away from the fire. Sean screamed again, waving the torch back and forth like a madman, hoping to scare away the mimic. The yellow eyes began to retreat, step by step. Sean pressed forward into the darkness without stopping. Each wave of the torch pushed the mimic away.

"That's right, you bastard! C'mon! You want me? I'm right here!" Sean lunged forward, hacking away with the torch. The smile on Sean's face disappeared. His rage could no longer fight back the fear that clutched his body. The growling started again, louder than ever, with the eyes closer to the ground. Sean wasn't winning the battle against the mimic. The torch wasn't scaring the mimic away; it only wanted Sean to move away from the campfire. Sean didn't notice until he was eight feet from the fire—plenty of room for an attack. Sean's grip tightened as he spread his feet to keep his balance.

There was nothing left to do now; Sean had fallen into the mimic's trap. The momentum reversed in the mimic's favor, and the attack was about to begin. Sean readied himself to fight. He readied himself to die.

In the blink of an eye, the beast leaped straight toward Sean. It was the size of a male lion. Sean fell backwards, swinging the torch and knife, striking the beast as it landed on him. The mimic's weight nearly crushed Sean's chest. It snarled wide, revealing the teeth that were about to rip his flesh apart. Sean pulled the knife from the mimic's upper shoulder and slammed it as hard as he could into the beast's rib cage.

Sean heard a loud yelp from the mimic as it leaped off him. The beast's claws scraped Sean's stomach in the process. Blood gushed from the wound and soaked his shirt within seconds. Sean screamed in agony, clutching at his stomach. His face turned as red as his blood from the pain. If it hadn't been for the dust jacket and T-shirt, the mimic's claws would have ripped farther in, possibly tearing out Sean's intestines. Sean rose to his feet as fast as possible. The fight wasn't over; instinct kicked back in. Sean needed to find Junior's knife—fast. He could see that he wasn't the only one injured. The mimic's blood was on his dust jacket and around Junior's knife, leaving a trail for Sean to follow. There was no way for Sean to mistake the blood as his own. The color was something he had never seen before. It was a luminescent blue that glowed in the night. Sean quickly gathered himself and searched for the mimic. His breath was short, as the breathing became difficult from the wound; it hurt with every breath. The yellow eyes appeared again in the darkness.

Another attack was coming. The eyes lowered to the ground again. The mimic leaped and tackled Sean the ground. The force of the slam knocked Junior's knife free from Sean's grip. A bloodthirsty growl deafened Sean as the mimic's jaws snapped toward his face. Sean grabbed the side of the mimic's neck, keeping the jaws away from his throat. The mimic kept growling and snapping away at Sean. Its razor-sharp teeth were four inches away from him. Sean's eyes locked with the beast's. Its yellow eyes tore through his heart, shredding it as the mimic would do to him if Sean lost his grip. So close the death, Sean could feel his arms shake and muscles begin to tire. He didn't have much left in him. Sean didn't want to look into the eyes of the beast anymore. With every second that passed, Sean's grip lessened, and the mimic grew closer.

Jacob's face flashed in Sean's mind once again.

I'll make you proud, Dad.

The mimic jerked free from Sean's grip and clamped its jaws on his shoulder. Sean screamed in agony, trying to break free, but he couldn't. He swung his hands wildly, making contact with the backpack, pushing it sideways. The flap opened, and out came the small pencil that Sean had sharpened earlier. Sean reached for it, feeling the jaws press harder into his shoulder. With one final ounce of strength, Sean grabbed the pencil and jammed it right into the mimic's bright yellow eye. It yelped again as its teeth came free from Sean's shoulder, and it jumped back into the darkness.

Blue blood dribbled down Sean's hand and onto the ground beneath him. There was no strength left in him. Sean stared at the sky above, too weak to move. He hoped he had a few more minutes to see the sky and stars before the mimic returned to finish the job. Sean began to slow his breathing and finally closed his eyes. The fire's crackles weren't there anymore, and its warmth had faded.

Sean felt his body being moved. There was no pain, no suffering; he accepted death. He felt the mimic touch his chest and stomach. It was probably already ripping out his organs with its claws and sharp teeth. Not wanting to open his eyes to the horror of being eaten alive, Sean kept them closed. In his mind, he held the image of his father, Jacob, with arms wide open, waiting to embrace his son.

I got him good for you, Dad. I made him pay. I'll be seeing you soon.

CHAPTER 18

GOOD SAMARITAN

I t was morning, and the sun returned, pouring its heat back across the desert. The campfire had burned out, leaving only ashes and smoke. Sean lay still in a deep sleep. His body was padded several times. Sean's dry chapped lips spread open, releasing a small moan.

"Oh my," a voice said from above, sounding surprised to find Sean still alive. A pair of hands grabbed Sean, pulling him to his feet. Pain shot out from Sean's stomach and shoulder, sending him falling to his knees. Sean cupped the wounds on his stomach, wincing in pain. He focused on breathing as the pain began to subside. Then the voice spoke again.

"Mister, are you okay? What's your name?" The words were sincere and full of worry. "Here—take this. You need to drink it."

Sean felt a bottle pressed against his lips. Warm water cleansed his dry mouth and throat. Sean spoke his first words to the stranger, coughing in between. "My name is Sean. Sean Anders. What happened?"

"Mr. Sean"—from what Sean could hear, the voice belonged to a man—"I found you lying on the ground. I called to you, but you did not answer. I tried waking you, but you didn't move. After seeing all this blood here on the ground, I thought you were dead."

Sean stared at the ground for few seconds before his mind brought back the events that had taken place last night. Both the fear and adrenaline returned as Sean pushed the man away in panic. Sean grabbed Junior's knife from the ground and jumped to his feet, ignoring the pain that burned from his stomach and shoulder. His heart raced as Sean circled around, searching for the mimic. He found nothing—no sounds, no eyes—but that didn't mean it wasn't there. Within seconds, Sean fell to one knee. He was still too weak and tired. The pain crippled his mind, and his body needed rest and food.

Sean turned to find the stranger's wide-open eyes watching him from underneath a small baseball cap with the letters S-O-X embroidered on the front. Wearing the cap—and a layer of dust and dirt—was a Korean man. His eyebrows stretched upward, as if he was confused by what was happening.

"Who are you?" Sean asked.

The stranger stood, still looking at Sean and then at the knife before speaking. "My name is Han." He slowly stepped forward with his hands held high. Sean struggled to determine whether Han was a threat or not. "Are you okay?" Han asked, extending his hand and offering to help Sean to his feet.

Sean chose to trust Han and accepted his help. The strangers hand revealed a lot to Sean from the look and feel of it. The fingertips were scarred, and there were calluses across the palm. Days' worth of dirt were layered beneath the fingernails and on the skin. Sean slowly made it to his feet and also noticed a terrible smell surrounding Han. There was no question that both he and Han shared the same course in life. They both traveled across endless miles of this deadly desert. Sean was sure that Han could smell something terrible off him as well. Neither man had showered for days.

"What are you doing here?" Sean asked.

"I saw smoke." Han pointed to the sky. "So I came closer to see what was causing the smoke, and I found you lying here. I thought you were dead. You didn't move at all. I gave you a nudge with my foot. I couldn't tell if you were breathing. That's when you moved your hand, and here we are now."

Sean was more worried about the mimic returning than how Han had appeared out of nowhere. "I was attacked when I made camp here. I thought I died," Sean said.

Han watched Sean grimace in pain as he lifted his shirt, revealing the wound across his stomach. There was more blood on his shoulder as well. "You're pretty banged up. Who did this to you?" Han asked, examining the wounds. He pointed to the jacket, and Sean allowed Han to carefully remove it. Han pulled out a thin long bandage wrap from a satchel on his belt. Han placed his fingers between the torn sections of the shirt over Sean's stomach, and he ripped it completely off Sean's body with ease. Certain sections of the wounds were reopened and started bleeding.

Sean felt vulnerable and didn't fully trust Han, but he didn't have much choice. He was already wounded, hungry, and tired. There wasn't much left in Sean at this point. Han could easily kill him without much of a fight if he had wanted to. Sean could only hope it wouldn't come to that. Sean then told Han what had happened. "Not *who* did this to me but *what*—a mimic attacked me last night."

Han didn't say a word; he continued examining Sean's shoulder for a few more seconds and then started to wrap it with the bandage. The word mimic didn't frighten him or cause any signs of panic. Sean was sure that being a traveler, Han had to know what a mimic was. If not, Sean at least had to warn him for all the help Han had given him so far. Sean gestured the best he could with his hands when describing the beast with every detail he remembered. Han circled around Sean, listening to him speak while tying the bandage around his chest for additional support.

"Very big animal, black hair, sharp teeth. It speaks what people say. Scary yellow eyes."

Finally, Sean got through to Han when he pointed to his eyes, describing that they were yellow. Han blurted a few words in Korean and stared in disbelief. Sean nodded in agreement, not needing to understand Korean because whenever anyone mentioned anything about a mimic, it was quickly followed by a curse or a plea to God.

"Yellow eyes! I heard stories about the yellow eyes. You say that you were attacked by yellow eyes?" He pointed to the wounds on Sean's body.

"Yes," Sean said regretfully. "Yellow eyes, we call—I mean, *I* call it a mimic."

Han gathered his thoughts, and so did Sean. Sean had survived a horror that had killed everyone up to this point. There wasn't anyone alive to tell about battling a mimic—except Sean. Sean didn't know how to feel. The mimic had so consumed his mind with worry and fear that Sean didn't realize he had found what he'd been searching for all this time. Han stood before him as the first person he'd come across, a person who came from somewhere with food and water. It didn't even occur to Sean that his journey was finally over and that he could return home with the news. He had saved Nova, and he hadn't even thanked Han yet. Sean let go of Junior's knife and wrapped his arms around Han, squeezing tightly, ignoring the pain in his shoulder. Sean pulled back, staring at Han, who was more confused than before.

Han saw tears of joy rise in Sean's eyes. Han gently pulled free from Sean, holding his hands up. "It's okay, Sean. I helped your shoulder. It is no problem. It looked worse than it really was. The wound is not that deep. Just give it some time, and try to keep it clean."

Sean gave a laugh at the misunderstanding. He would tell Han everything. "Please, Han. Behind me there is a village far from here that needs help."

"A village?" Han replied, seemingly with disbelief.

"Nova; the place is called Nova. We were running out of food, and our mayor picked four people to explore this land so we could find help or somewhere to get food."

Han stared over at the empty distance behind Sean, not knowing for sure whether Sean was telling the truth. Ever since he had found Sean, he had been acting strange. But to find a wanderer in the middle of nowhere was strange for Han as well.

"I can't," Han said.

Sean's heart sank as he heard the two words come from Han's lips. He couldn't believe his ears. Sean needed Han to help him. There was no way that he would last any longer in his condition. Without Han's help, Sean didn't need another mimic to kill him; the dessert would be enough to finish him off within a day or two. Sean's eyes fell to the ground. He saw that Han's mind was made up; he would not be the one to save Nova.

"But there is a place that might help," Han said. "I am just a scavenger. I can't save your village or give them food. I barely have food for me ... but over there might help." Han pointed straight ahead toward more miles of empty desert.

Sean clenched his fist in anger, and his knuckles turned dead white. He couldn't believe that he had to walk more. After all the countless miles he'd trekked to find an actual person, it was all just to tell him he had to walk some more. Sean struggled to believe that his salvation was still straight ahead and that he wasn't heading toward his grave. He strongly felt that it was a sick joke that would prolong his torture before death. Regardless, it didn't matter to him at all. All Sean could feel right now was complete exhaustion. His lips, tongue, skin, and even the air felt dry to him. The sweat inside his clothes was warm, and his body felt even hotter under the clothes than the outside temperature. Sean simply continued to stare at the ground as Han circled the camp and grabbed one of the bottles of moonshine from the ground.

"Payment for the bandage that you have," he said.

Han disappeared from Sean's view, but he could hear his footsteps walking back and forth in the camp. After a few minutes, he returned holding a jar filled with the blue thick substance. "Yellow-eye blood," he said, handing the jar to Sean. "Their blood is highly intoxicating. People use it as a pain reliever for injuries. It numbs the body completely, almost leaving it paralyzed. Others use it as a drug for a quick high." Han pointed at the several different shades of blue. "How potent the blood can be is based on how old it is. The darker the blue, the more potent it is and more addictive. If you were to use the light-color blood, you'd feel happy and relaxed. If you use the darker, thick dried blood, you could see hallucinations and maybe go crazy. Mimic blood is rare around here. So this is extremely valuable and a very good item to bargain with when you talk to him." Han finished sealing the jar and started to pack a small amount for himself.

Sean gathered his things that were scattered around the camp. "For him?" Sean asked.

Han patiently waited for Sean to gather his belongings before speaking. "He calls himself the Kid. He lives in the place over there." Han pointed to more endless desert. He saw Sean's disappointment. "About a half day's walk more in that direction, and you will see it. I promise, Sean. It is a pretty big place. I doubt you'll miss it." Han turned and began to head out toward the north.

"Where are you going?" Sean asked.

"I'm heading back to my hut. I was sidetracked by the smoke here, but I must hurry back before dark."

"Why can't I go with you?" Sean asked. But Han didn't respond. Sean wanted to follow Han regardless, just to be with and talk to someone, but Sean didn't see the point. Han couldn't help Sean, and a small hut wasn't enough to save Nova. Sean had no choice but to keep heading east as he had been doing.

"But before you go …" Han stopped and pointed to Sean's stomach. "You should treat that wound."

Sean looked down at his shirtless body and at the wounds on his stomach. There were four thick bloody lines across his abdomen. Three of the claw marks were only surface scratches, but the fourth was a deep cut.

"You need to clean and stitch the wound if you plan to keep on going," Han said.

"Can you stitch?" Sean asked.

Han seemed to be getting slightly annoyed with Sean's constant need of help. "Mr. Sean, I have to leave. I am already behind schedule, and being out here in the dark, with yellow eyes running around, is a bad idea. You will have to do it yourself."

Sean never had to stitch a thing in his life. Diane did all the family's stitching when it came to ripped clothes or toys.

"Please, Han. I will give you another bottle of moonshine," Sean pleaded.

Han paused and thought about the offer. "Okay, deal, but we have to be fast."

Sean nodded, relieved that Han would be helping him once more.

"I am going to need a needle and thread. Do you have one?" Han asked.

"Yes." Sean turned the knife over, twisting the cap off the handle, and poured the contents into his hand. He handed Han the needle and thread. Han grabbed the second bottle of moonshine and added it to his backpack.

"Grab one of those small, skinny sticks over there," Han told Sean.

"What for?" Sean said.

"To bite on. This will hurt quite a bit." Han grabbed a separate bottle of moonshine to disinfect the wound. Sean lay down on the ground, readying himself for what was about to happen. He knew what came next, and Han was right. It was going to be extremely painful. Sean waited nervously as Han counted down from three to one. Sean placed the wooden stick in his mouth between the count of two and one. Han poured the moonshine over Sean's wound. The wooden stick nearly cracked in half as Sean bit down hard, screaming at the top of his lungs. His entire stomach felt as if it were on fire, and the feeling lingered for several seconds. Sean rocked side to side, refusing to lie still.

"Lie back down." Han pushed and gently eased Sean back onto the ground. He took the needle and grabbed one of Sean's matches, striking it. Han sterilized the needle in the fire before beginning. "Okay, Sean. I need you to be very still from here on out."

"Okay, just give me a sec," Sean said, repositioning the badly bitten branch while taking a deep breath. Han wasted no time in sticking the needle into Sean. More pain shot from his stomach as Sean felt Han's hands begin to work with great speed and without gentleness. Sean tried not to watch. Each tug and push sewed a piece of the wound together.

"Ah!" Sean screamed. Han ignored the shouts and kept on stitching the wound. This wasn't the first time Han had showed his generosity for others.

Years ago he'd found a pregnant woman stranded in the desert. Her tattered clothes covered only half her body. She was a captive in a raider camp. They forced her to do work and other horrible acts for their pleasure. When she was found pregnant, the raiders couldn't afford another mouth to feed. So they all decided to let her leave and die from exposure. Han's heart nearly broke at the mere sight of her. He took her in and nourished her back to health. Weeks passed before she finally spoke her name— Loraine. Some nights, Loraine awoke screaming from nightmares of what the raiders had done to her. It wasn't until Han helped Loraine deliver her baby that she began to socialize and even be friends. Loraine ended up naming the baby after her younger brother, Ben. Each day after the birth was better than the last for Han. He had grown attached to Loraine and Ben, even accepting a small role as a father figure. Han found himself smiling every day, along with laughing, something he hadn't done for so long that he couldn't remember. Two wonderful years passed before things took a turn for the worse.

Ben showed signs of a sickness that Han didn't know how to cure. It began as a lingering cough that Ben could not shake for months. Then he started to become tired and weak. Ben would sleep nearly all day before waking up to play and eat. Soon the playing ended, and all Ben did was sleep and eat. Han caught Loraine crying over Ben, worrying for the worst. The next week, after a morning of hunting and fetching food, Han returned to find Loraine in tears again. She had been crying all day. Ben sat still; his back was to Han, and he was not moving or coughing. Han didn't need to see Ben to know. The tears spilled from his eyes as Loraine hugged him.

Over the dinner fire, Loraine told stories of her as a little girl. She laughed a few times throughout the night and thanked Han for everything he did. When Han awoke the next morning, he found Loraine was gone without a note or a trace. Han buried Ben near his hut and paid visits when he could. To this day Han didn't know what had become of Loraine. For Han, losing Ben and Loraine nearly took the last of his kindness. Han wondered if helping Sean was all he had left. Only time would tell.

Sean lifted his head to see how much more work Han had left—he was only halfway finished. Sean closed his eyes and laid his head back down. He dealt with the pain by thinking of the others in Nova. Each thought that crossed Sean's mind filled the empty tank of motivation. Sean was going to need every ounce to make it to the finish line that Han mentioned. He pictured Casey's dirty blonde hair and bright blue eyes as she smiled at him. Sean imagined Junior, sitting at the table with the guys, playing poker as usual. The final thought was his baby sister, Lucy, and how he would be able to watch her grow up to be a strong woman like Diane.

Han tapped Sean, bringing him back from Nova in his head. "Okay, I'm finished. You should be careful, though. You need time to heal."

"Thanks, Han," Sean said, carefully feeling the stitches across his stomach.

"Now I have to go. No more wasting time. Good luck, Sean. You will need it." Han didn't hesitate or look back as he started to walk at a fast pace.

Sean watched Han slowly grow smaller in the distance. It was time for Sean to leave when Han no longer could be seen. Sean grabbed his backpack, doing a final check of his things, making sure everything was counted for and not broken. On the side of the backpack, Sean grabbed the dirty, sweaty shirt he'd used to clean the wounds on his calf. Now he used the shirt to wipe off the remaining blood on his stomach, careful not to aggravate the already sensitive wound. With everything packed and as cleaned as Sean could be, he grabbed the final remaining clean shirt he had in his backpack and slowly slipped it on. The duster jacket felt heavy, along with the backpack. Before Sean took a single step, he rubbed Casey's bracelet, feeling the strands of her hair. His mind endlessly tried to convince him to turn around and head back to Nova, as it always did, but his heart kept pushing him to keep walking.

The barren land in front of him only paved more misery ahead. There wasn't any fight left in Sean. He was beyond exhausted. His muscles still were fatigued and sore, but it wasn't just for him. Sean needed to keep on fighting for them. He needed to make one final walk so he could end it and save them all.

CHAPTER 19

RUNNING OUT OF STEAM

The torturing sun took little time to reunite itself with Sean, who bore the heat overhead. The duster jacket, shirt, jeans, and socks were soaked with Sean's sweat. His inner thighs chafed, adding another source of pain. Each glance toward the empty plains tore away the little drive he had left. It was the same vicious cycle repeated over again. Sean looked over his shoulder, not able to tell he'd walked over a mile since camp. Everything around him was empty and looked the same. His mind angrily took in the madness of the desert. Any salvation that water could bring him only coaxed him into wanting to stop and drink every ounce he had left; because of it, Sean put the water away for good in his backpack.

After the second mile, Sean found himself feeling nauseated. His movement suffered as his feet stumbled, and he barely walked straight. The backpack teetered on his shoulders, almost pulling him to ground. Another mile passed by; still no sign of the place Han mentioned. Sean's irritation began to build. This was becoming too much for one person. Nothing within sight all around him, just as it had been before. Sean swore that Han had lied to him. His veins burned with the rage that sparked inside. This time the rage was aimed not at an enemy but toward the loved ones Sean felt had betrayed him. Nova did this to him. Casey, Junior, Lucy, and Diane all let him go through this.

Sean understood that Nova needed to be saved. The village needed food to survive. But he and the other three were the ones who had to go. All four were given a death sentence for a plan Reyes had no idea would work. The worst never seemed to be over. Sean endured only to suffer more. He made it through the scorpion, sandstorm, endless miles of barren land, and even a mimic. Sean lifted his head toward the bright sky and felt the sun on his face.

"Ahhhh! How much more, huh? Answer me!" Sean shouted, clenching his fists. His fingers dug deep into his palm, nearly breaking the skin. The words roared through him at an unknown target. Sean didn't know who to blame anymore—his father, mother, Casey, Junior, fate, or a God. It didn't matter in the end, for there was only silence in return. All Sean had left was to continue on. His body grudgingly began to walk again.

With no progress in sight, Sean started to sob. Feelings of sadness emerged where the rage disappeared, making its home behind the eyes. Tears poured down to his chin from the quiet sobbing. He walked mindlessly, no longer caring about the direction he was heading. Time passed by, and Sean's mind held empty thoughts; the world was trapped in a void of silence. His eyes stared at the ground for twenty minutes, not realizing that he'd stopped walking. Sean took another step and then fell to his knees. The long battle with the desert had come to an end, and Sean had lost. His lips parted, his breathing faint. The worst soon came for him. No longer did he have to battle his mind and body, but his eyes betrayed him too. Four hundred yards in front of him was a place that had appeared out of nowhere.

Sean knew how deadly hallucinations were, but he never had experienced it. His mind wanted the journey to be over from the moment he'd left Nova. Undoubtedly, this was the final effort from his mind. It was to convince him he made it and to no longer walk any farther. Han never spoke the name of the place or how big it was. Throughout generations, Nova slowly expanded its walls, growing into what Sean thought was a massive village—until now. The place before him was twice the size of Nova. Its walls reached twenty feet high and easily housed hundreds of people, possibly thousands.

"No, this isn't real. Don't do this to me. Not like this," Sean said, trying to break free from his mind's hold. He pounded the ground with his fists, trying to snap back into reality. He wanted the hallucination to be real. There still could be a chance that it was, but things didn't make sense, and Sean could feel his hope dwindling. The walls appeared to be made of sand, which could not be possible. Sean let out a crazed laugh. For a place that size, there was still silence in the air. No sound of children playing, livestock, or even workers. Nothing could be this silent, except for emptiness.

Sean hung his head, accepting the truth. There was no place. He was all alone. Still, his arms rose, and so did his feet. He drew closer; now it was only a hundred yards away, but it didn't matter. Everything would disappear the moment he touched the walls. Sean continued on, sobbing away more tears. A little farther ahead, Sean noticed something else that was strange and not possible. He kept staring at the ground, and the entire time he was moving, he noticed his feet were not walking at all but dragging. Something gently tugged Sean's arm, repositioning it. Sean lifted his head and found Junior walking with him. He held Sean's arm around his neck. Sean turned to his left and found Casey doing the same. Their faces were filled with concern and determination to save him. They were carrying him to salvation.

Sean glanced toward Junior, who gave Sean a smile behind his long hair and thick beard. Junior's loving face only pulled more tears from Sean. Sean had missed them both so very much.

Finally, the three of them approached the door, and Junior dropped Sean's arm and walked toward the tall metal entrance. Sean watched as Junior waved his hands in the air and pulled the metal door partly open. Sean's eyes ached from all the tears he'd cried. He shoved Casey away and lunged for the wall, slamming his hands into it. Sean pounded and rubbed the wall that wasn't real, but it didn't disappear as it should have. The wall remained there, burning Sean's hands from the heat. Sand caked the metal walls, giving the impression of a sandy hill or an oddly shaped mountain. Strong winds or sandstorms were enough to lift sand and dirt, causing it to stick to the hot metal and giving the illusion of giant walls made of sand. The place was becoming less of a hallucination; it was becoming more real. Han had been telling the truth all along.

"It's real," Sean told Casey. His words were weak and barely above a whisper. Sean wasn't ready to believe everything just yet. He didn't know how Junior and Casey had found him. Both of them hovered over Sean as he peered closely at them. Both Casey's and Junior's faces dissolved in the sunlight and were replaced by two men wearing helmets, with rags covering their mouths. They grabbed Sean with force, not pleased at all. Sean tried to speak as they dragged him through the doors, but they didn't respond. The doors closed behind him, and the sky disappeared. Sean heard sounds and muffled words as the two men shoved him in a room. They stood by, staring menacingly, until an elderly woman came in. They left her alone with Sean. She knelt next to him, peering over the battered boy. Her arms held a small bowl that she pressed against Sean's lips.

"Drink," she said. "You need to drink"

Sean opened his mouth and swallowed the ice-cold water. Sean never had felt water that cold in his life. Before Sean could speak a word, he fell into a deep sleep.

CHAPTER 20

THE ONE THAT HEADED NORTH

R*un!* A trail of footprints in the sand stretched across the desert. The footprints were spread apart, revealing a fast pace with a great amount of fear and panic. *Don't stop!*

Something deep within the dark was following the screams and footprints as they were made. It wouldn't stop or slow down; it continued to follow each footprint that had been pressed in the sand.

Keep running! Henry Collins screamed in his head. He had been followed ever since that morning, coming across the oddly shaped mountain.

****

To the north was a mountain that Henry had sworn was a giant hand, pointing to the sky. Stretching in the hot, blistering sun, the fingers curled inward in a palm-shaped base. The mountain/hand cast a tall shadow on the desert sand, providing shade for Henry to cool off. Henry enjoyed the view, taking several minutes to admire it as he approached it. He rubbed and felt its rough texture, and when he rounded the corner to keep walking, his eyes caught something in the distance. At first, the image was a little blurry and tough to fully see with the sun beating down. His eyes squinted, and Henry waited until he realized that imminent danger was ahead. Henry's average build doubled in size under the large clothes and the giant backpack. Out in the open, he would have surely been seen. Luckily, the mountain was there to hide behind.

Henry quietly stood behind the rough thumb-shaped piece of the mountain. His eyes stared in awe and disbelief. The beating of drums filled and pounded his ears as his hands trembled uncontrollably. His breath was short and unable to return easily. There was air all around him, but why was it so hard to breathe? The more Henry stared, the more the image reached and grabbed his soul, squeezing any remaining life from it. Three dead bodies lay on the ground, mutilated, butchered, and ripped apart. What had killed them was still there, still ripping them apart even more. Never in his life had he been as scared as he was now. The beating of drums that he heard before were louder now, increasing the more he stared. Henry grabbed his chest in pain, the heavy beating was not coming from drums—it was coming from his heart.

He closed his eyes; he had seen enough and couldn't take much more. Taking a step, Henry turned around and headed back to Nova. He wouldn't continue any farther to the north unless he wanted to end up on that pile of bodies. Carefully, trying not to make any loud noises, Henry walked south, thinking of what to say to Catherine, his wife, for why he'd returned empty-handed. His life would have been in danger, had he continued. He knew Catherine would understand. She had to understand. Henry, no matter what, would not tell her what he had seen today. Catherine was a tough woman, strong and loving, but even this would be too much for her. She would be just as scared as he was or even more. Henry wanted Catherine to stay the same as she was, melting him with her brown eyes. He would lie to her if he had to, just to feel safe again, holding her in his arms. Until then, he would not stop walking or looking over his shoulder.

Several hours passed as the sun moved from the sky above down to the west. Henry's pace was consistent and steady; he made great time crossing the desert. Before making camp, Henry turned around to look behind him for any signs of what he had seen. The desert was completely empty. Sighing with relief, Henry relaxed and began to set up camp.

The next morning, the sun's rays pierced through Henry's eyelids, waking him from his sleep. The ground was warm again, the air hot, and his mouth dry. Henry could smell the sweat on his clothes. He hadn't bathed in days and could smell his poor hygiene. It didn't matter anymore; he was going back home. All Henry could think about now was the long walk back—and Catherine. Later, he would hope for the others to succeed.

Gripping the jar of water, Henry drank nearly two-thirds and used the rest to clean his face. There was no need to save every last drop anymore. The same went for the food. He shoved handfuls of jerky into his mouth.

It had been several days since Henry had a full stomach, and it felt good. With a smile on his face, Henry continued, hoping to see Nova's walls again. Two more days would pass exactly the same, with a full stomach and a smile on his face.

The morning sun rose bright in the sky, peering down on him. Henry rubbed his eyes and yawned. Arching his back as he stretched, Henry caught a glimpse of the ground, and it sent him jerking to his feet.

Footprints.

The sand held several dozen prints, circling around him. Henry quickly spun around, searching for what could have made them. He found nothing. How could he have not seen or heard it walking around while he slept? His equipment, food, and weapon were not taken. Rubbing his chest and legs, Henry felt for any wounds or bites. He was perfectly fine.

Following the tracks, Henry circled around and away from his camp in a straight line. He found himself stopping about fifty feet from his camp. There, the tracks vanished, as if they had appeared out of thin air and walked toward him as he slept. Running back to the camp, he followed the tracks again, certain he must have made a mistake. He found himself back where he was before, fifty feet away from his camp.

Shaking his head in disbelief, the tracks did not continue in any other direction. Whatever came either had vanished into thin air or made sure to cover its tracks. Whether the impossible happened or he was being stalked, Henry knew he wasn't alone. He grabbed his belongings and made sure to have a full stomach before he started to walk. Over the past two days, Henry had not checked over his shoulder as often as on the day he came across that mountain. Now he had awakened to find something stalking him.

He wasn't going to make that mistake again. Every ten minutes or so, Henry glanced over his right shoulder and stared into the open desert; he found nothing. The empty scene of sand and sky gave little sense of safety to him, though, as that was exactly what he had seen before waking up today. Another ten minutes and nothing, then another ten minutes, and Henry still found empty desert behind him. Henry even walked to the top of a hill thirty feet high and looked all around him.

His pace quickened as the sun began to set. The sky over him blended with yellow, brown, and gold. The cool wind on his back changed the sweat-stained color of his coat and shirt. New life filled his lungs as the air grew cooler. The smile on his face returned as he looked over his shoulder yet again. There, in the far distance from where he stood on the hill, a dark figure stood exactly where he had stood before. It stared back at him; its shape and form was exactly what was tearing those dead bodies apart.

The smile on Henry's face collapsed to the ground, along with his hope and energy. After tumbling backward, Henry regained his balanced and began to run. The backpack swayed left to right and up and down, pulling him back. His breath grew tired and weak. The heavy weight was going to cause him to be caught and killed.

Nova has to be close now, he thought. Moving his arms, Henry let the backpack fall from his shoulders and crash into the ground. Water leaked from under the bag as his food and belongings spilled through the top.

His legs, now free from the weight, ran across the sand with great speed. The sky above turned dark. The sun was gone, and the night covered the land, hiding Henry's path. He couldn't see where he was going. Breathing heavily, Henry's fear surged through his veins as quickly the blood pumped through his heart. He had to keep going. He had to keep pushing himself to not stop. Nova had to be close now. Deep inside, Henry could almost feel Catherine near him. His legs plunged deep into the sand without a sense of direction.

He accidently stepped on his left shoestring that had come undone, and Henry's body collided with the sandy ground. Every ounce of air that was left in his lungs was ripped from him and disappeared. His hands stretched out, gripping the sand as hard as they could, while waiting for air to return to his lungs. The beating sound emerged again in his ears. Henry didn't bother looking back over his shoulder; nothing could be seen in this darkness. It was out there somewhere, getting closer.

The images of those bodies being mutilated filled his head over and over. His mind raced and tried to push away what he saw. Lying there in the darkness, he felt as if its breath was on the back of Henry's neck, as if it was waiting to grab and butcher him. Far ahead, small flickers of yellow appeared before him and then vanished. From his back, sheer terror crawled over his skin, stopping any air entering his lungs. His knees pushed against the sand, trying to stand as they trembled. Henry felt his body go numb and lose control. Warm yellow liquid trickled down his legs. Henry felt light-headed and about to faint.

Then, right at that moment, the air that was lost returned and lifted Henry to his feet, forcing his body forward. Some unexplainable force or will made Henry feel almost weightless. He could keep on running. He headed straight for that flickering yellow light. Due to the panic and fear, Henry didn't recognize the light at first until it outlined an image. It outlined Nova's walls. There was no mistaking it. Catherine was barely more than a mile away.

Henry crashed against the giant wall, banging as hard as he could. Screaming over to the tower's watch, he called out their names as he begged for the doors to open. He heard noises on the other side as people gathered to see what was going on. Henry banged louder until the doors began to slowly open. Squeezing into the opening crack, Henry's body tumbled into Nova.

Reyes and the rest of Nova stood around him. Catherine pushed through the crowd and rushed to Henry, who was lying on the ground, covered in sweat. Tears covered his face as he saw Catherine rush toward him. Clawing and grabbing her, Henry squeezed tighter, ripping the sleeves of her shirt. Everyone was speechless as they watched Catherine hold Henry in her arms. The two lay there cradling each other, in tears.

Henry never took his eyes off the door as it began to close. The darkness stared back at him, hiding what was coming. Lying in Catherine's arms, covered in sweat and urine, Henry only hoped that Nova's walls could protect him.

CHAPTER 21

A NEW PLACE

Sean awoke, staring at a ceiling. He'd slept through the night without any interruptions. His eyes scaled the room around him. All four walls held different pieces of scrap metal welded together. The room was surprisingly cold, much like the water he'd drunk. His hands still clutched the backpack he used as a pillow through the night. A green woven blanket lay over him, keeping him warm. The old woman had left hours prior to Sean's waking, leaving just the bowl of water behind for him to drink. Sean drank the remaining water and carefully placed the bowl on the floor, not wanting to break it. Across from him was the door the men had carried him through. There was light shining behind its frame. He approached the door slowly, trying to listen for any sounds of talking or movement behind it. He could hear soft chatter and commotion but could not make out the words. Sean stared nervously at the door, not knowing how he would be greeted or what he would see. With a deep breath, Sean grabbed the door's handle and pulled.

As the door cracked open, the sound of the soft chatter grew louder, and the light got brighter. Three steps out the door, Sean still looked around him in awe. Hundreds of people walked back and forth, socializing and bartering. Along the walls were dozens of merchant stands. They were selling clothes, food, and scavenged items. Nova was decades behind this, even generations. At each one of the corners stood a tower that extended beyond the twenty-foot walls. Inside was a guard who stood as a lookout. From such a height, the guard could easily see any possible wanderers or threats from miles out. Each one of the seven towers doubled the height of

Nova's. Sean wished Billy could see them all; Billy would be as speechless as he was right now. Different aromas filled the air, pulling Sean's attention from the tower and waking his stomach. There were a few stands cooking food near him. They held a range of different animals inside cages—cattleworms, birds, sheep, snakes, and creatures Sean had never seen before. They all had been safely locked away and fed.

Sean spotted the old woman from yesterday. She gestured for him to walk over. The old woman finished selling a beaded necklace to a teenage girl in a white dress. The dress was dirty and ripped at the shoulder from constant use. The girl waved at Sean, and he smiled at her. Her left sandal was missing a strap by her ankle. It flapped carelessly as she walked back into the massive crowd. As Sean watched her disappear, a loud whistle tore through the chatter. A group of soldiers burst from the crowd and ran toward Sean. They circled around strategically, cutting off all possible exits. Some were carrying sharpened wooden sticks; others held blades of metal filed down to short swords. None of the crowd seemed to panic, as they expected this to happen. Everyone left for their homes and stood against the walls. Only the soldiers and Sean were left in the open. Sean didn't know what to do or what was going on. He decided the best thing was for him to remain still.

From behind the soldiers, a tall, lanky man emerged. He was young. His face and jaw were well defined. He wore a military suit, well pressed and tailored. The awards on his chest were not military, but they seemed to hold some meaning here. The respect in the air was palpable from the soldiers and even the crowd. Without a doubt, Sean believed this was the Kid Han had mentioned. He approached Sean, standing upright with his chest out. Every step was filled with pride and strength. The crowd glanced at him and whispered to one another. They all watched from their homes, waiting to see what would happen. He stood three feet away from Sean with his head tilted, looking down at him. He held hands behind his back. His eyes stared with bright-blue hatred; his blond hair was neatly combed. With his jaw clenched, fighting back a look of disgust, he walked with a slow pace around Sean.

"What's your name?" His voice was just as cold as his eyes.

"My name is Sean."

There was no response, just silence. The man didn't care. Sean waited for another question. The man remained silent, examining Sean as if he was looking for something.

"Why are you here?" he asked.

No matter the answer, Sean thought it was pointless. The man wouldn't trust Sean or believe a single word. Sean had no choice but to speak the truth and hope that he would believe him. "My village is running out of food. I went to search in the east to find any signs of food or help. That is how I got here."

"It must have been a long walk ... since I know nothing of a village to the west of here." Every word held disdain and growing annoyance.

Sean nodded in agreement. He mentioned the days and miles the journey had already taken him and that he'd almost given up, until Han had found him almost dead and had told him of this place.

The blue eyes stared without blinking and then rested on the button that Billy had given Sean that he wore on his jacket. The man rubbed the button and flicked it with his index finger. "Is this the symbol of your village?" He didn't wait for a response. "This bird that you call the ram?"

"No, it's not. It was a gift from a friend before I was sent out. Look ... whatever you may think, it's not—"

The man raised his right hand, interrupting Sean. There was more silence. Sean stared at the black leather glove in his face. Still not speaking, the man lowered his head and turned his back to Sean. As he walked away, he said, "I've heard enough."

Sean wasn't surprised at the response, yet it still angered him. Clenching his fists, Sean stepped forward, forcing the soldiers to step closer to him with their weapons ready to strike. Every weapon pointed at a location on Sean's body that would fatally wound him.

Sean shouted with his hands in the air, "I want to speak with the Kid! I was told to ask for the Kid and that he would help me. So I want to speak with the Kid!"

The crowd looked at one another, seeming surprised. Sean took a step back as the man turned his head. His reaction to the name was far more noticeable than to anything Sean had said. Sean bit his lip, hoping that the man wasn't the one Han sent him to find, or Nova surely would be lost.

"Has he requested you?" the man asked, still not turning around.

"No."

"Has he met you before?" he asked, the agitation growing in his voice.

Sean was beginning to see where this was going. "No."

"Has he heard that you were coming?" the man shouted, throwing both his arms into the air and waving them impatiently.

Sean lowered his head in defeat. "No."

"Then why would he help you?"

Sean closed his eyes, trying to remain calm. He'd come all this way. This could not be the end, but Sean had no answer good enough to allow him to meet the Kid. He didn't know what the soldiers would do to him afterwards. They might cast him back outside in the desert or strike him down where he stood. But before it came to that, Sean wanted the man to know he would not be beaten by him.

"I'm not afraid of you," Sean said.

In an instant, the man spun around and lunged at Sean, grabbing his throat. The black leather glove squeezed tighter and tighter, pulling Sean's face close to him. Sean grabbed the man's arm, trying to force him off, which caused the soldiers to close in and press their weapons against Sean's skin. Struggling to breathe, Sean started to feel dizzy.

The man leaned over to Sean's ear and whispered, "You should be." With a quick motion, he struck Sean in the stomach, sending him to his knees, coughing and fighting for air. He watched Sean struggle for a few moments and then turned away. Sean reached for one of the black boots and grabbed it by the ankle. Sean would not give up on Nova, nor would he lose to this man. The man easily broke free and punched Sean square in the jaw. Its impact left Sean dazed and unaware of an oncoming kick. The force lifted Sean off the ground and into the air. Sean felt a stitch rip in his stomach wound. The man took a step back, adjusting his gloves and hair, repositioning himself for another strike. Sean closed his eyes and was ready for more pain.

"Enough!" A different voice roared from above. Sean opened his eyes and saw everyone step back, staring toward the second floor. The voice came from a hooded figure who stood on a balcony overlooking the entire place. "Step aside Rufus," he said, waving his hand. Sean stared at Rufus, who moved to the side, adjusting his blond hair with a troubled look on his face. The hooded figure moved closer to the edge of the balcony and spoke to Sean. "Get up," he said, raising his hand. Sean struggled to his feet; the pain throbbed with every turn and twist he made. "Why are you here?" the hooded figure asked. It was the same question Rufus asked earlier.

"To save my village!" Sean shouted, throwing up his hands in frustration.

The hooded figure's voice grew louder. "Don't get snotty with me ... boy."

"I came to ask for help." Sean got down on his knees and looked straight toward the hooded figure. "You can all laugh at me for begging, and I feel humiliated for it, but please take me to the Kid. I was told he could save my village. I beg you, please!"

Sean waited for a response. Everyone watched, unsure of what the hooded figure would say.

"There is nothing humiliating about a man sacrificing his pride to save his people. It's quite honorable, and as for the Kid you seek ... you're speaking to him." He leaned over the railing and signaled for Sean to come closer.

Sean grabbed his backpack and walked over. The soldiers moved with Sean in unison and so did Rufus. Rufus's look of resentment toward Sean spoke a thousand words. Sean hoped Rufus was in as much trouble as he looked to be.

The Kid asked another question. "Where is this village you speak of?"

"Nova is to the west of here. Far to the west."

The Kid shifted his body away from Sean, banging on the railing with his fist, nearly breaking one of the metal bars. "Stop lying to me, boy! There isn't anything to the west of here; nothing could survive out there!"

"Yes, there is!" Sean screamed. "Nova is real, and it needs your help. Why don't you believe me?"

"How could I? I don't know you. You appeared out of nowhere. If anything, you could be an assassin sent to kill me, and you wouldn't be the first either."

The soldiers approached closer from behind with their weapons inching closer to Sean's skin.

Sean looked back at them, accepting what would come next. "If you're going to kill me, then fine; do it already. I'm not scared to die."

"Neither am I." The Kid pulled back his hood and revealed his face for the first time. What Sean saw was beyond belief and crossed into the impossible. Sean might have fought a creature that could turn invisible, but nothing could prepare him for what he saw. The Kid's face was part machine and part human. The upper right part of his face held a metal plate with a glowing red eye. Half of his jaw was replaced with metal. Some of his flesh had been pulled over and held with screws to cover the metal. Sean couldn't believe it, but it was real. The Kid then said, "As you can see, I have survived many encounters."

"So have I." Sean reached into his backpack.

Once again, the soldiers raised their weapons, ready to attack. The Kid raised his hand, calming the soldiers, and waited for Sean to show him what was in the backpack.

Sean pulled out the mimic blood and unwrapped the cloth around it to reveal he wasn't lying. "Mimic blood. I was told you have uses for it. I am willing to trade it for your help."

The crowd gasped, and soon the place filled with commotion. The Kid's red eye glowed stronger as he stared at the jar and then pointed at Sean. "Did you kill the beast?" he asked.

"No, I didn't," Sean said, shaking his head without hesitation. "I injured it badly, causing it to run away, but not before it left a reminder for me." Sean lifted his shirt and showed his wound for everyone to see.

The Kid still held his hand in the air, keeping the soldiers at bay. Then he slowly closed his fingers, asking, "Who are you?" His words stretched slowly from his mouth.

"My name is Sean Anders."

The Kid cocked his head as if he had heard of the name before.

There was silence until Sean said, "I come from a place in the west called Nova; whether you believe me or not, it is there." Sean lifted the jar high in the air and screamed out to everyone. "Who here can help me for this?"

Hordes of people rushed toward Sean ignoring the soldiers and Rufus. They all offered a variety of goods and foods. The soldiers struggled to contain the crowd and eventually were overpowered.

The Kid gave out a roaring laugh, clapping his hands. The crowd was silenced in an instant. "Not bad, Sean. I must say I am impressed. All right, I will help you. Please follow me." He gestured for Sean to climb the steps to the left of him. As Sean walked toward the stairs, the Kid spoke again. "Forgive me, Sean. Where are my manners?" He spread his arms wide open, speaking with great pride. "Welcome ... to High Heaven."

At that moment every person clapped and shouted praise, throwing their clothes in the air and whistling loudly. The Kid watched Sean step by step with a smile on his face. He placed his arm over on Sean's shoulder and guided him to his chamber. "Please sit down and tell me more about this place you call ... Nova."

CHAPTER 22

THE KID

The Kid led Sean to a large room where important meetings took place. Inside, there was a large desk with pictures and many maps. Several chairs were folded and propped against the wall. Behind the desk was a large red-leather chair. Sean found it amazing. The red chair held auburn-shaded areas, showing great amounts of age and wear. A studded pattern on the chair's back went all the way down to the seat. There was a tear at the top right corner of the chair's back, with the cushion spilling out from underneath. Sean's eyes finally rested on the seat's cushion. It sat nearly flat and was at the end if its life. The entire chair spoke a single word in Sean's head: royalty.

A soft noise coming from the Kid broke Sean's trance. Sean couldn't hear it until the Kid closed the door behind him. It was the noise of a mechanical shift with every other step the Kid took. The Kid favored his right leg quite heavily, exposing a limp to his walk, which explained where the noise was coming from. He told Sean to sit down and grab one of the chairs against the wall. Sean sat down on the cold steel chair and wondered what it would be like to sit in the Kid's chair. The Kid grabbed the left arm of the red chair, using it as leverage, while he slowly placed himself in the seat. The task seemed to be a little painful for the Kid, but he finally fell into chair.

"So? Are you hungry? How about some food?" the Kid asked.

Sean nodded. He still had food in his backpack, but he couldn't muster the courage to eat any more beef jerky, no matter how hungry he was. Sean hoped to eat a warm meal for a change. He stared around the room, seeing all sorts of trinkets, flags, trophies, and even a sword, much like one held by a soldier who was guarding him.

"Were you a soldier once?" Sean pointed toward the sword hanging behind the red chair. The Kid's human eye rose to Sean's face and then fell back down to his desk. He didn't even look at the sword. He just shook his head and said no. The Kid stared at him with a weird gaze. Sean looked away, trapped in the uncomfortable silence and feeling awkward, until a small head propped itself on Sean's forearm. Small gray eyes looked at him with curiosity, and a tongue stuck out. To Sean's surprise, it was a black-and-white dog. He had only seen dogs in pictures in the old books, and this type of dog had a particular a name—Siberian husky.

Sean smiled as he rubbed its head and patted the fur. The dog barked excitedly, wagging its tail and pushing its head deeper into Sean's side. Sean patted down the dog's back, scratching up and down—and then he felt metal. Sean jumped at the very touch of it and noticed that some of the dog had been replaced with the metal, just like the Kid. The front left paw, two back legs, and the tip of the tail had been replaced with metal.

The Kid finally broke the eerie silence in the room. "Ah, no worries, Sean. That right there is my best friend. I've had him since I was eight years old. Rafa was only three months old when my parents gave him to me. We have been best friends ever since."

Sean caught a glimpse of the dog tag dangling under Rafa's neck. Its gold finish shined and captured his eye. Sean rubbed the engraving, saying the name. "Rafa."

Rafa barked at the sound of his name and placed his paws on Sean's lap. Sean turned the tag over and found more writing on the back. He read, "Welcome to the family. November 8, '22." Sean stared in confusion. The date didn't make sense as. He rubbed the engraving again, feeling every number as he read it again, just to make sure he wasn't mistaken. "Wait—this year is 2126. You said you were eight years old when you met Rafa, so that could only mean—"

The Kid nodded. "It was 2022. Exactly four months before the bombs fell."

"That's impossible," Sean said. "If that's true, then you have to be—"

"Yes," the Kid interrupted, and then he gave an answer that Sean did not expect. "Over a hundred years old."

Sean struggled to believe it, but the Kid's face was dead serious. Sean's mouth fell open, and his eyes showed his shock.

"It's true, Sean. Rafa and I are over a hundred years old. Yet we don't look as if we've aged."

The burning questions that piled inside Sean were endless and waiting to get out. Sean opened his mouth to ask the first of many questions but lost his train of thought. A tall, slender woman walked in, holding a platter of food, which took away all of Sean's words. Her tanned skin glowed under the ragged clothes that draped her body. Her hair was short, barely falling below her chin. Sean sat quietly as she placed the food in front of him. Everything was neatly organized on the table. Sean politely thanked her; it was clear this wasn't the first time she had brought food to someone.

The Kid pulled several coins from his pocket and gave them to her. Her face expressed her delight, as she had gotten more than she expected. The Kid thanked her, and she left the room. He then turned to Sean and extended his hand toward the food. "Please, Sean. Eat, and I'll explain."

As Sean began eating, the Kid told him that before the bombs fell, humankind was on the brink of a new breakthrough in science a field called advanced prosthetics. The breakthrough would allow anyone who had lost a limb or other body part to have it replaced with an artificial one. This had been done before, but now it could be pushed to new heights with artificial prosthetics that could move according to their own signals from the brain. The Kid showed Sean his left hand, exposing a scar around his wrist. His hand wasn't plated with metal but rather completely severed and attached to a fully metal prosthetic limb.

"Back then, Sean, humans could have only latex molds of limbs that couldn't move or bend at all. They simply held one position." He began to slowly move his fingers and his wrist. "But now, humans can have complete mobility, as if they've never lost a body part at all." It was quite the breakthrough, he explained, but unfortunately, the bombs fell before it could be made available to the public. "And like that, Sean"—he snapped his metal fingers—"it was lost … or so I thought. Then I met a man who claimed that it wasn't. He told me his father was the lead scientist on the project and that the knowledge had been handed down to him. I doubted him completely, but as you can see, Sean"—he pointed to his face—"I was wrong. Of course, the bombs created a problem by wiping nearly all the prototypes from existence. But a few remained intact, like my eye and jaw. As for other parts, we had to be a little more creative. They aren't as advanced as I would like them to be, but beggars can't be choosers."

The story was hard to believe, but Sean listened as he ate. He had to admit the Kid was a walking miracle of science. There could be no other possible explanation for it. Sean consumed everything on his plate—boiled potatoes, carrots, beans, and chunks of meat that Sean couldn't identify, but it tasted better than cattleworm. So far the story explained what Sean had seen of the Kid and Rafa, but it didn't explain how they could live for so long. A hundred years was unheard of and impossible in this new world. Sean had to ask.

The Kid smiled and lifted his shirt, revealing a metal hole in the middle of his chest. He gave it tap. "Artificial heart with a few slight modifications." He pulled his shirt back down. "Amazing what science can do without laws to confine its progress. How can Rafa or I die when both our hearts won't stop beating?"

An hour passed as the Kid talked about the scientist and where he was now. The Kid told Sean that they had gone their separate ways, and the last he'd heard of the scientist was that he ventured somewhere far to the north.

"Enough of about me, Sean. Please … tell me everything about Nova."

Now it was Sean's turn to tell the Kid everything. He did his best to include every bit of detail, from Mayor Reyes's meetings to Mr. Davis's class about the old world. The Kid laughed at how sheltered Nova truly was. He was amazed by how they had remained unnoticed by wanderers, traveling merchants, and the rest of the world for so long. Hours went by as Sean told him stories about Junior, Billy, Barry, Lucy, Casey, and everybody else in Nova. As Sean spoke, he got up and circled the room, glancing at the objects in front of him. He noticed a picture of the Kid and Rafa.

"That was taken in a park a week before the bombs fell," the Kid said, noticing Sean's interest. In the photo, the Kid had wrapped his arm around Rafa and was smiling at the camera. Another photo was of the Kid's father and mother, with the Kid standing between them. Sean then grabbed a photo that was hidden behind three others—a baby photo of the Kid and the only one with just him by himself. The picture didn't interest Sean as much as the frame did. Its white plastic border held a thick layer of dust over an engraving on the bottom. Sean cleaned off the dust and read it. The Kid's true name was exposed by Sean's fingertips.

"Charlie," Sean said.

Rafa barked loudly, jumping up and down, recognizing the name. He scurried over towards the Kid and sat next to him. The metal hand reached over and patted Rafa on the head. Sean tried to read the Kid's expression, wondering how he would react.

"It has been a long time since anyone has called me that." The Kid rose to his feet, wincing in pain. "Looks like we have talked long enough, Sean." Rafa slowly followed beside the Kid, not missing a step. "I have agreed to help, but there are certain rules you must agree to first." He guided Sean out of his room and led him around, showing Sean all of High Heaven. "You must understand that I just can't take in your village due to the amount of supplies we have. If they need food, they must pull their own weight. They need to provide something to trade and buy with; give us a reason to do business. We aren't a charity, Sean."

Sean agreed. He looked at the many houses and shops within High Heaven.

"Second, I'm sure you'll want to go back home with food and supplies as proof. But you must earn them first."

They continued on through a garden area with a greenhouse. The plant life alone could sustain everyone for weeks. Next was the farming area where animals lived and reproduced.

"You see, everyone has a role in High Heaven," the Kid explained. "You either help, or you create something from which we can prosper. After that, if you want to make extra money by trading with other vendors, feel free to do so."

Deep in the back, sectioned off from the vendors, was an area that Sean knew Junior would love the most. "Here is our gambling area," the Kid said. "We bet money, items, or goods here. There are card games, dice games, and even fights."

Sean circled around the tables, watching the people play. The Kid made his rounds, greeting anyone who approached him. After Sean finished seeing all the games available, they returned to the center of High Heaven. To the far right, near the middle, stood the biggest door that Sean had seen in High Heaven. The Kid steered Sean to it and stopped.

"Sean, you will have a job here, and this is how you will help." The Kid opened the door and revealed a large room with a vehicle inside. "This is our garage and your way back to Nova. You will help repair and build this dune buggy."

Sean stared in awe, reaching for the buggy. High Heaven was proving to be more than Sean could have dreamed or imagined. He already had seen so much that he'd thought wasn't possible. "I never thought I would see a car again or any vehicle that wasn't a picture in a book," Sean said.

"Yes, I'm beginning to see that. So take some time to acquaint yourself with it. But do know, Sean, that this will be your new job."

Still in shock from the sight, Sean mumbled, "How will I know what to do?"

The Kid tapped the buggy hard with his walking stick. A few seconds later, a woman slid out from underneath the buggy. She was covered in filth and wore a tattered tank top. The Kid introduced Sean to his new boss. "This is Amy."

Sean shook Amy's hand. She had a strong, firm grip, and she squeezed tightly as she said hello. She wore her bright-red hair in dreadlocks, and her tender, rich green eyes stared at him. There were freckles on her face, but they were hard to see, as her white skin was covered in grease and dirt. Amy took some time looking up and down Sean's body, judging his usefulness for the job. She didn't seem impressed.

"So you're the new guy."

"Yeah," Sean said, rubbing the back of his head.

Amy looked at the Kid, who nodded and pointed to the corner room. "All right, new guy. Your room is that corner. You will live and sleep here. There's plenty of work to be done. You will work until we say you are done for the day or if we take a break to eat. Do as I say, and we will be fine. Okay?"

Sean nodded in agreement. He stared at the corner that she'd called his room. After seeing all the wonders in High Heaven, Sean expected something different or a little more hospitable than what he was given. In the corner was a saggy pillow and a soiled blanket nearly worn through the cloth. Both were placed between two metal barrels. Despite Sean's disappointment, it was still better than sleeping outside with deadly predators lurking about.

"I'm done here, new guy, so rest up for tomorrow. We have a long day ahead of us," she said. Amy grabbed a towel and wiped her hands and face before hugging the Kid as she left the room. Sean realized there was something more to the Kid than he'd been led to believe. Unlike Rufus, Sean sensed an air of gratitude from everyone that the Kid was here in High Heaven. During their walk, Sean saw the people smile at the Kid with a glimmer in their eyes. Amy just had given the Kid a hug that he didn't expect. This was genuine. All of it was. The Kid seemed to be a hero to some, a protector to others, but to all, he was someone they loved.

"So we have an agreement, Sean?" the Kid asked, raising an eyebrow. Sean looked at the corner bed and nodded. "Good." He headed for the door, and the sounds of grinding metal from his right leg trailed behind him. Before he grabbed the handle, Sean asked him another question.

"Charlie …?"

The Kid stopped and turned. "Yes, Sean?" he said patiently.

"Why do they call you the Kid?"

He sighed and hung his head, reflecting on the words. The name was indeed an unusual one, but it was a glorified title in High Heaven that needed to be explained. "Because I was the youngest ever to win a tournament in the gladiator pit." The Kid's face held mixed emotions; his brown eye glistened in pain while the rest of his face struggled to reveal the pride that was underneath the piles of shame.

"What's the gladiator pit?" Sean asked.

"That's a story for another day." Turning back around, the Kid opened the door. As he stepped one foot over the threshold, the Kid stopped himself and said hesitantly. "Sean … you can keep calling me Charlie, if you like." The Kid looked hopefully at Sean.

"Okay, Charlie," Sean said.

Sean saw the pain, burden, and shame melt away from Charlie's face. The pride that had been buried underneath was all that was left. Sean couldn't imagine what he had gone through or why the nickname cast such heavy guilt. From seeing the picture of him as a baby and the one with Rafa, the name *Charlie* held a childlike innocence that must have been stripped or stolen from him. Everyone knew and recognized him as the Kid, except for Sean. For every time Sean called him Charlie, it gave the Kid a new beginning, an innocent past, and for that, Sean gained a friend.

The door closed behind him, leaving Sean in complete darkness. It was getting late, and half of High Heaven went in their homes to sleep. Sean felt a sense of security, yet he had a hard time sleeping. He was surrounded by strangers that he didn't know and soldiers who nearly had killed him. The soft yet ragged blanket provided little warmth, and the cold floor hurt his back. No matter how much Sean tossed and turned, there wasn't going to be a position that felt comfortable. Sean gave up and stood up, searching for a light. Near the buggy was a box of tools with a candle inside. Sean picked up the candle, returned to the bed, and grabbed one of his matches from the backpack. With the candle lit, Sean began to write for Casey and tell her the good news about today.

Casey,

> I finally did it. I saved Nova. I saved you all. I can't wait to see you and the others.

Sean scribbled the next sentence, laughing and agreeing that this was incredible. All the days and nights he'd spent alone had finally paid off. Slowly taking the time to imagine coming back to Nova with the great news, Sean practiced his celebratory act in the dark. He shook invisible hands, gave high-fives to himself, and smiled to the crowd in his head. Sean focused his attention back on writing.

> I better get a reward for this. I have been through hell and back. I even fought a mimic, Casey—a real-life mimic, like the one we heard stories about growing up. My God, when I see you, I want to kiss you again and again never stopping or ever let go of you. Out there in that outer

desert, I thought about you day and night. Especially the nights, thoughts of you kept me warm through the coldest times. There is more you need to know, but I will tell you when I see you. I am so happy, knowing that while I write this, I know that this will be the last entry of my journey. I know that very soon I will be placing this entire journal in your hands. Remember, Casey ...

He stopped writing and thought, *I love you*. Sean didn't write it on the paper. He had a plan. Sean's mind raced with the idea, looking for any flaws. There were none. She would read the journal on the tower under the stars. Then, at that moment when she read those final two words, she would turn to Sean and ask what he wanted her to remember. Then he would tell her that he loved her. They would kiss again and, he hoped, repeat that night on the tower once again.

"Perfect," Sean whispered. He folded the paper in half and placed it among the others that were neatly held together in the backpack. Sean returned the candle next to the buggy. He lay down, placing the severely worn blanket over him. Although it didn't seem possible, Sean actually found comfort. This would be the first time since leaving Nova that Sean would close his eyes and not fear opening them later. Whirling winds flowed through High Heaven, and the sounds of animals resonated through the walls. A familiar feeling stirred inside, spreading a smile across Sean's face. The metal walls, the sense of security, the animal sounds—all of it felt like home to him. A few minutes in, and Sean was already deep into sleep.

CHAPTER 23

LEARNING THE ROPES

Sean awoke the next day to Amy's gently kicking the side of his leg. Rubbing the sleep from his eyes, he stared at her blurry face, still dazed and tired.

"Hi," she said. Amy was holding breakfast in front of her. "The Kid bought you some food, but you have to earn the rest of your meals from now on. So hurry up and eat. There is much we have to do."

Sean reached out and received the metal tray from her hands. There was bread, water, meat, and some eggs. He quickly scarfed down the food as Amy suggested and was ready for his first day of work. They didn't speak much, as Sean hoped they would. He really wanted to get to know her and maybe become friends. Sean gave a final yawn when a new voice spoke from outside the door.

"So is this the new recruit I was hearing about?"

Sean turned and saw a heavyset man. His thick gray hair had a splotch of black above the forehead, which he brushed back. Sean's hand disappeared as the man engulfed it with his. The greeting was friendly, but Sean could feel the sheer power in his grasp, waiting to break every bone at will.

"Yup, that's the new guy." Amy shrugged, still not impressed with what she had been given.

Sean introduced himself and smiled, expressing as much kindness as he could.

"The name's Rick; nice to meet you." Rick's handshake nearly lifted Sean off the ground. His power was frightening. "I'm Amy's dad." Letting go, Sean was relieved that his hand was still there and not broken. "You got a long job ahead of you, and we appreciate the help."

"He didn't have much choice, Dad. It's not like he volunteered for it," Amy interrupted.

Rick turned and gave her a stern look. Sean saw it all the time back in Nova. With all the kids running around, screaming their heads off, someone had to keep them in line.

"Don't mind her," Rick said, "She gets like this whenever I have to leave. I have some business with the Kid that has me leaving here for several days." His scruffy black beard spread around a smile. "No need to worry, either of you. Usually, I go alone, but this one's pretty important, so the head honcho is giving me three guards as an escort." Rick pulled Sean off to the side and huddled over him, speaking softly. "Amy can be quite the handful when I'm gone, so try to bust your ass so she won't kill you before I come back. Okay?"

Sean nodded.

Rick moved toward the door, creating heavy, pounding thuds with every step. He gave one last look to Amy and yelled as he closed the door, "Love ya, princess!"

Amy didn't respond. Her arms were folded across her chest, like a child pouting after being denied a toy or candy. For a few minutes, neither of them spoke or moved. Sean didn't know what to do or say. With her back still facing him, he watched her wipe her eyes and turn to the buggy. They didn't talk about Rick or where he was going. They didn't talk about Charlie either. When Amy did speak, it was only about the buggy. She simply gave commands and told Sean to tighten certain screws or help her lift certain parts as she worked underneath. The day was indeed long, and the labor soon began to take its toll on Sean. When Sean wasn't lifting parts or tightening screws, he was eating or listening to Amy explain how to repair the buggy. She had little patience for mistakes, and she reminded Sean how much it delayed her.

The work ended with Amy giving her final command to wash up. At the back of the room, beyond the metal door, was a small private tub with a large bucket of room-temperature water. Amy had mentioned the area once before while tightening some screws in the driver's door. There was a small curtain hanging from a metal bar above the tub for some privacy. Grease, dirt, sand, and God-knew-what-else filth covered the tub's walls and lay inside the dark, murky, used water. It must have not been cleaned or changed for several days.

Tossing his clothes to the side, Sean stuck a toe in the murky water. He gagged at the possibility of what was living inside it. Sean quickly wet the rag that was placed beside it. He hurriedly scrubbed his body of any visible dirt. He was careful around his stomach, gently rubbing and splashing the wound. He didn't need to rip another stitch like before. After a few agonizing minutes, Sean leaped out of the grimy tub. Somewhat clean, Sean was better than he was before, and that was good enough for him. He peeked behind the curtain to see if Amy had left. She was gone, and Sean scampered naked across the room. He found several small coins on his pillow, which he guessed was payment for his work. Sean reached for some new clothes and slipped them on. He left the room in search of some food to purchase with the few coins he'd earned.

Outside in High Heaven, several of the shops had closed for the day, and Sean had no idea of the value of the coins. Not knowing what to do so late at night, he decided to ask Charlie for help. Charlie's door wasn't open, but there was light glowing from behind it. Approaching closer, Sean could hear an unpleasant conversation between Rufus and Charlie. Sean pressed his ear to the door and listened.

"How many times do I have to say this over again? You are putting all of us in great danger. You and I are well aware of the rumors about those things out there," Rufus barked.

"Relax, Rufus," Charlie said. "I am well aware of the possible consequence of keeping Sean here. But you must at least see this from my point of view." The door hung unevenly from its frame, a full inch off the ground. Sean knelt on his hands and knees, peering under the door. Rufus was sitting in the chair where Sean had sat the day before. His blond hair poked out from underneath a black beret. Charlie leaned forward, closer to Rufus, staring into his eyes. "What has you so worried are rumors that have swirled around. You have forgotten that they are exactly that— rumors, Rufus, mere rumors. You and I truly do not know if there is any truth to them at all. So I am keeping Sean here, and there will be no more debate on this. Are we clear?"

Rufus rose from the chair, and Sean could see him buttoning his jacket. He didn't say a word but acknowledged Charlie with a simple nod. Sean pulled back and quietly stepped away from the door. He made his way back to his room.

Rufus clearly was not happy with Sean's staying in High Heaven. Sean sat on the floor, wrapping the worn blanket around him. He thought about the conversation. Sean wondered how he could have put High Heaven in danger. He thought more about what the rumors could have been. He tried to think of the stories and warnings Alex told but couldn't remember. Sean twirled a bronze coin between his fingers. The face on the coin wasn't recognizable, and the back showed a coliseum-like structure.

Sean wanted to ask Charlie about the rumor and if there was a way he could make things safe again but that would mean he'd have to admit to eavesdropping. The last thing Sean needed was to anger the only possible friend he had. Sean closed his eyes. They were tired, and his back ached. The whole day slipped from his mind.

The next morning, Amy found Sean fast asleep in his bed. She kicked him as she had done before. "Let's get to work." She spoke firmly, ignoring his tired state.

Sean was awake for only a few seconds before his stomach growled, still waiting for food since last night. He interrupted Amy as she headed for the buggy to mention he hadn't eaten.

She looked back. "I don't believe a single word you said."

Sean begged to eat some food before working. Amy was annoyed but now could see Sean wasn't lying. She nodded her head and placed the tools that were in her hand back in the tool box. The two headed for the door and made their way to the center of High Heaven, where they looked at the variety of stands.

Each one offered food and goods found through scavenging and farming. They scanned fruits, animals, plants, clothes, broken toys, and weapons crafted from sharpened metal. Sean stopped in front of a stand that Amy said was her favorite.

"This is where I got your breakfast yesterday," Amy said, signaling for a plate.

"Coming right up!" the lady shouted. The dark-haired woman hovered over a large grill with a small fire inside. Sean watched her grab a metal pan from a rack. She tossed a thick slice of meat inside and began to work on the eggs. Sean turned to the lady and asked for a little extra meat and eggs, if she could. "We got hungry man here, ladies and gentlemen," she joked, laughing as she cracked two more eggs, to Sean's delight. The woman whistled and danced to a tune in her head as the food cooked. After several minutes, she finally placed the food on a metal tray.

"Three commons, please," she said.

She was asking for coins, but Sean didn't know which ones she meant. He pulled out two different colors from his pocket. Rolling them over, Sean looked for any indication of what she meant.

"Here." Amy reached over and grabbed the coins. She pointed to the five brown ones. "These are called commons. Their value is the lowest, and they're used the most around here." Then she pointed to the three silver coins "These are called slims. Their value is higher than the commons but not as much as the gold-looking ones."

"The gold-looking ones?" Sean repeated.

"Yeah, a gold one is called a rare. They are the highest in value around here. Now pay the nice lady so we can get back to work."

Sean did as he was told and then scarfed down the meal—with the two extra eggs and slice of meat—as fast as he could. He wondered about the coins that Amy called *rares* as he ripped the juicy meat between his teeth, satisfying his hunger. Sean returned the metal tray to the lady, who was impressed to see the tray had been licked clean. Sean thanked her for the wonderful food and headed back with Amy. His stomach was full, but he wasn't looking forward to another long day at work. He dreaded the idea as they walked back to the garage.

The day, however, ended like the day before, and the same went for tomorrow and every day after that.

CHAPTER 24

GUARD DUTY

All was quite in Nova. Nothing came past its walls since Henry had arrived several days ago. Billy leaned back on his chair, propping his feet on one of the tower windows. He gazed out on the desert terrain, wondering how the others were managing and, most of all, if they were okay. Ever since Henry's return, all Nova did was talk about how scared Henry looked that day, as if he had seen a ghost. Billy continued watching the setting sun move across the sky and dangle right below his boots. He worried about Casey and all the drama affecting her.

She'd become distant and quiet, not wanting any company, and she never talked. Casey kept climbing the tower and staring out onto the horizon. She no longer waited up there for a few hours; now it was the entire day. Her legs and arms were badly burned from the sun. Casey had stopped eating as well. Billy began delivering her food at the start of each shift; if he didn't Casey wouldn't eat for the day. He didn't mind at all. In his eyes, both Sean and Casey were destined to be with each other. He understood the worry and sadness that Casey was going through.

Below the tower, Jerry aimlessly walked around, pretending to know how to use Alex's machete. Reyes doubled security, taking able men to patrol Nova in shifts. It angered Billy to see Nova in such a panic, even though Henry wouldn't explain what he was running from. Reyes, Old Harrison, Catherine, and even he had tried to pull some kind of answer from Henry. But the village had gotten nothing out of him. Maybe that was the reason why everyone kept freaking out.

Henry simply stayed in his home, not speaking to anyone but

Catherine. When he did talk to her, Catherine tried to coax Henry into speaking about what he'd seen, but that would only result in his changing the conversation. Some nights, Billy watched Catherine leave her home in the middle of the night to cry on a nearby bench. In some way or form, Catherine lost a piece of her husband that night. All that Billy could do was watch and feel sorry for poor Catherine.

The local games that Junior held in his home had changed as well. The concern and uneasiness that surrounded everyone sucked any joy from regular activities. Even Old Harrison stopped making his moonshine. Nova was left in disarray. No one knew what they could do to help each other or comfort the families whose loved ones were out there, wandering alone. *Sean has to return*, Billy thought. *One of the three left has to come back with good news to lift Nova's spirits.*

The sun finally set, and the sky grew dark. Billy's shift was finally over. Tapping the tower's roof, Billy checked on Casey. "Hey, Casey, you all right up there?"

Casey sat upright with her legs crossed under her, staring out into the distance. Her blue eyes and freckled face showed no response at all. Billy grabbed a small ledge that jutted out from the tower's side and stuck his head out to get a better view.

Casey didn't move her eyes off the desert.

Billy waved his arms, bobbing his Mohawk up and down. "Hey, yoo-hoo!"

"I'm fine," Casey said.

"No, you're not," Billy said. "Hey, I know how you feel, okay? I miss Sean too."

"I know, Billy, but I need to be here when he comes back." Casey shifted her gaze toward Billy. Her eyes were red as her sunburned skin; she had been crying silently up there the entire time.

"Hell, I understand that, and I want to be here too when that happens. Who else jams with me out here in the middle of Nova?" Billy shrugged. "Remember that time when I was by myself in the middle of my air guitar solo, and Sean jumped in out of nowhere, playing his solo next to mine? That was pretty awesome, right?" Billy smiled as he finally saw Casey's face break from all the sadness to giggle.

"Yeah, it sure was. I could hear the two of you rock out and head bang all the way from my house."

Billy stuck his hand out, waiting for Casey to take hold. "So how 'bout we get you home to some food and a good night's rest? I'm sure I'll see you here bright and early tomorrow anyway."

Casey nodded and grabbed Billy's arm. He pulled her inside the tower. "Thanks, Billy. I appreciate it."

"Don't mention it," Billy replied.

The two lowered themselves down the ladder and onto the ground. Peter Campbell was waiting at the bottom to greet them as he waited for his shift to begin.

"I thought Danny was on guard duty tonight," Billy said.

"No, his wife wasn't feeling too well, so he asked if I could take his watch tonight, and he would take my watch tomorrow."

The two watched Peter nervously climb the ladder and almost stumble off. Casey shook her head at the pathetic scene, which made Billy burst out laughing.

"Be nice," Billy insisted, while still laughing at Peter.

Across from the tower, Junior peered out from his home, watching Billy and Casey walk by. He heard them talking about the good times they had with Sean. The mere mention of Sean's name almost made him cry. He walked over to his kitchen table and took a seat. The night's poker game wasn't the same. The mood was dead, and so were the cards. No one wanted to place a bet or talk about anything at all. Each hand was laid down without a fight. Moonshine wasn't lost but opened and shared among everyone.

Thoughts of taking Sean's place entered his mind daily. He knew Nicole needed him, but so did Sean. Junior wasn't getting any younger. He was fifty and had several problems of his own. His knees would hurt from time to time, and his back started to give. There was no chance at all he would survive a journey that severe. As hard as it was to accept, he knew Sean at least had a chance to make it. Junior reached over to one of the half-empty jugs of moonshine and popped the bottle opened. Taking heavy swigs, Junior tried to drown the horrible thoughts of Sean being out there alone. He had promised his brother, Jacob, he would look out for Sean as if he was his own son. Another swig swirled in his mouth and down his throat. He felt his chest burn inside, along with his feelings of guilt. Over and over in his head, Junior told himself that Sean was okay and would be back soon, but it was useless.

The bottle of moonshine was now empty, but the feelings of guilt and shame were still overpowering, forcing Junior to bury his face in his hands. He wept quietly, trying not to wake Nicole. He continued to cry, hoping that Jacob and Sean could somehow forgive him.

Diane struggled to cope with Sean's absence each day. She stopped eating. Her face and arms grew skinnier, and without knowing, she lost nine pounds. The nights were hard, as her dreams pictured Sean dying different horrible deaths every time. They kept her up late at night, tossing and turning. Sean was out there, somewhere deep within those sands. Before attempting to sleep, Diane rubbed her necklace and prayed that

Jacob was watching over Sean. She was never big on believing in a higher power, so religion wasn't a part of her life. But losing Jacob years ago and now seeing Sean leave made Diane need something to call to. She needed something to keep her from breaking further apart inside.

Eric held her close as he spooned next to her, squeezing tightly. His breath gently blew at the back of her neck. Diane followed her fingers across his forearm. Thick strands of hair were brushed aside, and some wrapped around her fingers. Eric was a hairy man. It was one of his few flaws, but it was his kind heart that won Diane over and made her overlook his "human fur," as she called it. Diane knew Eric loved her, and she loved him back, except for a small part, a special part. That part was forever locked away for Jacob.

Quiet in the corner, Lucy snored peacefully. The purple pacifier dangling from her lips eventually fell as she wiggled unexpectedly. Her soft baby face relaxed, as her dreams were soothing. Holding her necklace tight to her chest, Diane closed her eyes and tried to fall asleep. Before she would even dare to dream again, she prayed to Jacob to once again look after their child.

Casey made it home and waved goodbye to Billy. Right before closing the door, she saw Billy cuss out loud and walk back. She shook her head and smiled at how careless Billy could be at times. The door sealed shut, and a small candle provided little light inside. Her mom was in a deep sleep, unaffected by the kiss Casey gave her. Unlike her mom, there wasn't going to be a deep sleep for Casey. She planned on an early rise, ready to make another climb on the tower. There was a weird feeling that made her hair stand up on the back of her neck. She couldn't explain it or understand it, but she had a feeling that Sean would soon be on his way.

Billy had forgotten a book he'd borrowed from Mr. Davis. It was a science fiction novel that Sean had recommended to him several weeks back. Billy never cared for reading, but after the Henry incident, his shifts in the morning were longer through the day. After a while, he needed something else to help pass the time than humming the same songs. So he decided to try something new. Sean claimed the book was one of his favorites. It was called *The Exiles of the New World*. The story focused on a group of scientists who were unwillingly forced on a ship and hurled into space. Before escorting Casey back home, he was at page 169.

He wanted to read more before bed, as the story had reached a climactic turn. The ship was headed straight for a black hole in space, and before his starting shift tomorrow, he wanted to know if the ship would reach it. There was no way he could wait, and he didn't want Peter Campbell returning it or taking it to read for himself.

Old Harrison sat on his steel chair with his elbows on his knees. He watched Billy scamper and hurry past him. The rattles of chains and stretching of leather resonated off Billy as he moved. Old Harrison didn't care for the whole biker look. Maybe he was too old to understand it, or maybe it was the fact that he didn't care.

The middle portion of Nova burned brightly in the night. The bonfire's flames flickered with great warmth, resonating from its core. A surge of intense heat slapped Billy's face. He walked around, drawing closer than he expected. Billy felt the fire's fury on his back. The heat felt good, as the air went cold from the night. The watchtower was only a few more feet away. He was almost there, and then he'd hold the book in his hands; he was anxious to find out what happened next. His feet in their leather boots increased their pace and skidded along the ground. He placed one foot on the first step of the ladder. Pulling himself up, Billy suddenly stopped moving. In the corner of his eye, he caught something strange in the middle of Nova. Billy called out to see whether it was someone just strolling by. Normally, he would carry on as usual, but the dark silhouette became still and stared at him. Lowering himself, Billy called out again and began to approach the dark figure.

Still not moving or acknowledging Billy, the dark silhouette watched as he came closer. He could now see the flames of the bonfire flicker in its eyes. They were wide open and glowing with rage as Billy took each step closer. The darkness slowly pushed back, inch by inch, until the dark silhouette disappeared, revealing what it had been hiding.

Billy's eyes filled with utter shock and disbelief. His thoughts raced and fought with what to do next. He took a step back and felt a sharp pain in his stomach. Blood covered his hands as he fell to his knees. His stomach was slit wide open in an instant. Words couldn't free themselves from his mouth. They were trapped inside, unable to warn the others or cry for help. The raged-filled eyes lifted, and the dark silhouette gave a thunderous shout. All that Billy could do was watch more of the dark silhouettes climb over Nova's walls.

CHAPTER 25

GETTING READY

A full week passed since Sean was carried into High Heaven. Every day, piece by piece, the buggy came closer to being ready to drive. Sean learned so much and no longer was an annoyance to Amy. He was contributing more throughout his stay, and the work progressed greatly. The two no longer stayed silent while working. They talked about their childhoods and friends, and now they joked with one another. Some days they even competed to see who would finish first. Amy tried to hide the fun she was having, but Sean knew it. Today, they raced again to see who would win, and Amy loved it.

Sean stared at the buggy with a smirk on his face. He was ready for Amy to be impressed and finally admit it for once. "All done," he said.

Amy dropped her wrench and poked her head out from under the engine. Grease and oil was splattered across her face like war paint. She wiped her hands on a red towel, checking Sean's work. Her eyes scanned the wheel nuts as she tugged on the tires. "Not bad," she said. She walked to the driver's door. Yesterday the alignment was off and needed grinding on the sides to close properly. Now the door opened and closed with ease. Sean even greased the hinges, quieting the squeaking from before. She only nodded her head with a smile.

"Yes!" Sean said.

Amy rolled her eyes. "Relax, now! Just because you can put on a few tires and fix a few things doesn't make you an expert."

"Well, it does make me done for today," Sean said, crawling toward his bed. He plopped himself on the pad, closing his eyes. He listened to

Amy slide back under the engine. His mind reflected on the busy week he'd had with Charlie.

Charlie had stopped by a few nights ago, asking Sean to join him for dinner. They discussed more about Nova and the journey from there. Charlie sat in awe, listening to Sean describe the deadly sandstorm and the fight with the mimic. Sean asked about the currency in High Heaven and the items he gave to trade.

Charlie told Sean the coins were to keep order and balance. When High Heaven first opened, he spread the currency around to keep people civil and to make trading easier. It eliminated all the haggling and arguing. Charlie did emphasize that the coins did not have universal value throughout the desert, like metal did. Metal was the new gold. It provided weapons, shelter, tools, and endless possibilities. Each week, Charlie sent a team to scavenge and trade for whatever supplies High Heaven needed. If, by chance, the teams were unsuccessful, Charlie mentioned a place that always was available to use but only as a last resort—a place that Charlie refused to speak more about when Sean asked.

As for items that Sean gave Charlie to trade, Charlie assured him that he was working on it and was waiting to find the best value for them. A few days later, Charlie called for Sean, saying that he'd found a buyer. Jokingly, Sean asked if the merchant Han had taken the items. Charlie shook his head with a clear no. He didn't have to say anything. Sean saw pain and disgust layered over Charlie's face. It was that place he never spoke of. They bought everything—the jerky, the water, the moonshine, and all the mimic blood. A large pile of coins flew from Charlie's hand and landed in Sean's.

The black velvet pouch weighed three pounds and almost burst in his hands. Sean had to hold the bag with two hands for fear of dropping it. He loosened the string, peered inside, and found it full of silver slims. There wasn't a single brown common in the bag. The entire amount would have taken a year to earn, working on the buggy.

"Wow." Sean was speechless and struggling to say more.

"You don't have to say anything, Sean; it was my pleasure." Charlie leaned back into his chair. Rafa barked happily as Charlie gave him a good scratch on the chest.

"Thank you so much, Charlie." The words finally fell from Sean's mouth.

"You know, Sean, with the money you earned working on the buggy and from selling your items, you have enough here to hand a fair amount to each of your friends and family. You already know they can use this money to buy whatever they want here. Before you go, I need to ask you two things."

Charlie stopped and waited for Sean to look him in the eye. "First, try to bring someone back with you so they can start working here right away. It will make the transition easier and will help increase the amount of money earned to provide for Nova. Second ..." He rose from his chair, grimacing in pain. Charlie limped his way around the desk and sat on the center. Rafa loyally followed each step, propping himself beside his master. Charlie looked intently at Sean. "I know this might sound strange to you, but please do be careful, Sean. Nova's way of life is different. It's so young and innocent. These lands are harsh and cruel. They have taken and changed so many things. Everyone here gets along, for the most part. But I'm afraid that there will be a few disruptions when your people head over. Not everyone is so open to newcomers, especially in great numbers."

"Rufus, I'm sure," Sean replied.

"Yes, but not just him; others are not happy with this."

"But everyone seems so friendly around here. No one has given me a problem, other than Rufus."

"You are just one person to tolerate, not an entire village. These are good people, Sean. They just need someone to guide them along the way. That is why I asked you to bring someone back with you. I feel if we slowly move Nova into High Heaven, one at a time, it will help break the tension so everyone can get along. Make it back here safely and quickly. Because I do quite enjoy our talks in this room. I spend my day haggling over items with outside traders, fixing grievances among guards, and worrying about everyone's safety. It's nice to take a break from all that and simply just talk." Charlie's face fell to his hands as he sighed. "It makes time not seem so very long."

"Don't worry, Charlie. I'll be okay out there. Believe me; you are going to like my people, and so will High Heaven."

"Good. I'm looking forward to meeting them."

Sean opened his eyes. His thoughts were interrupted by Amy's banging and cursing from under the engine. He rose from the bed to pack his belongings. Sean changed shirts and carefully put away the three-pound bag of slims. He stopped midway through and thought about what Charlie had said about time being so long. Charlie had lived on the land for over a hundred years, and with the enhancements, he would live another hundred more, if he wanted. Immortality wasn't really that enticing, as Sean learned how Charlie spent it. All this time, Charlie made sure everyone was happy, fed, working, and protected. He even worked on improving High Heaven, expanding it year after year. It must be impossible to sleep with all that responsibility on his shoulders. Sean could see why Charlie's attachment to him grew every day. Perhaps he was the first real friend Charlie had in High Heaven.

"So are you done yet, master of the garage?" Sean said.

"Yup!" Amy shouted. She tossed the wrench and slid from under the buggy. Excitement filled her eyes. She skipped toward the back by the bathtub. More loud noised filled the garage as Amy sifted through random parts. She rolled out an object underneath a large beige curtain with a DO NOT REMOVE sign on it. "This is huge, new guy, so brace yourself. Dad found these bad boys while scavenging outside one day." Amy yanked back the curtain. "Behold!" she shouted. Two large blue panels sat before him. Underneath the blue screens were thick yellow wires sprouting out, circling the chair. "Sean, let me proudly introduce you to the first solar-powered buggy ever. Well … since the bombs fell, at least," she corrected.

"I'm sorry. I don't understand."

Amy rolled her eyes and pointed to the solar panels. "These suckers right here absorb the sun's rays and turn it into energy and then feed it to the buggy." She demonstrated the process with her finger. "You with me so far?"

Sean did not have the faintest clue of what Amy was talking about. He simply nodded, hoping it would get him into the driver's seat faster.

"Usually, you would need gas to power the buggy, but my Dad and I rigged it so you don't have to—unless you know where I can find several gallons of gasoline?"

Sean shook his head.

"Thought so. Anyway, you let the sun's ray's fall on these blue babes, and poof!" Amy slapped her hands, pushing one forward and the other one back. "You are off to the races, my friend." Amy's cheeks glowed with great accomplishment as she stared at a speechless Sean with a smirk.

Sean wasn't shocked at how truly amazing the machine was. He was in shock because he never had seen Amy so happy.

"Oh, and don't forget!" Her smirk fell, and her tone became serious. "If you break this wonderful beauty, my father and I will happily kill you. Do not get me started on what he had to go through to find these panels and a working frame. So no joyriding or jumping hills. Understand? Also …"

Sean clenched his fist, growing impatient.

"You better plan your time well, because this baby needs sunlight to move," she said. "If you see it's getting late in the day, you better find a good spot to make camp and wait 'til sunup. This baby will die on you when there is little light. It's not perfect, but we are working on it. Dad and

I didn't get enough time to fix that little problem, but we will when you come back. Okay?"

"Okay," Sean said.

"Just let me fasten them on top." For five minutes Amy worked on fastening the solar panels on the roof. Then she jumped down, saying, "You're all set. Now, tell me you will remember everything I told you."

"Yes, Amy, I will," Sean said.

"Good! You won't have any trouble finding your way back?"

Sean pulled out the compass from his pocket and showed Amy. "No, I won't have any trouble."

Amy walked around to the door in front of the buggy and began to pull the chain beside it. The door shifted up slowly, and light pierced underneath it. Gusts of wind pushed sand inside under the door. Sean lifted his hand, blocking the light as it filled the room.

Amy leaned forward behind the buggy, motioning with her hands to hurry up. "C'mon, Sean, I don't have all day. Help me push."

Sean sprinted next to her, pushing the buggy outside into the daylight. From the roof the panels gave a glistening shine as the sun reflected off them.

"Give it a few seconds, maybe even a minute!" Her voice was anxious.

Sean leaned over, touching the panels' surface softly. Their rectangular frame stretched across from the rear to the front. The surface was sleek and smooth. Each panel held hundreds of hexagons, absorbing the sun. A minute passed, and the buggy remained still. Sean looked over to Amy, who shook her head.

"Not yet," she said.

The hot sun burned in the sky, and the scorching heat traveled through Sean's clothes, bringing back that feeling of misery once again. A green light turned on from the back of the bumper. It beamed as bright as the sun. Another one appeared by the driver's dashboard.

"Bingo!" Amy swung her arm, slapping Sean's shoulder. "It's ready!" She rocked upright on her toes.

Sean opened the driver's door and stepped inside. His heart pounded, and his blood raced through his veins. Never did he imagine he would be driving. He was sure the buggy had died along with all the other vehicles in the old world that were waiting to be dug up for scrap. Sean took a deep breath and buckled the seat belt. The keys turned, and the engine roared. Amy motioned to Sean to shift gears, as she'd taught him several days ago. The wheels began to move on their own, slowly crawling across the desert. Sean's foot pressed the pedal, roaring the engine as the buggy drove farther out and deeper into the land. Sean popped his head out, staring at the turning wheels. The biggest smile stretched across his face as he waved to Amy.

She nodded and headed back into the garage. She was done for now and would wait for Sean to return before beginning a new project or repairs. Sean slammed his foot down and felt his head whip back. The buggy roared louder and rocketed farther into the desert, leaving High Heaven behind. Sean found himself traveling across the desert once again, only this time he wasn't trying to find hope. Instead, he was bringing it.

CHAPTER 26

SMOKE IN THE SKY

Sean sped through the desert with increasing speed. Puffs of sands lifted into the sky from under the tires, leaving a trail behind. Sean glanced at the speedometer, which read thirty miles per hour. The new goggles he'd bought from Charlie helped keep his vision clear. Sean spotted a small hill up ahead. Amy's voice echoed in his mind, telling him to stay away. He smiled and veered toward the hill. Amy's voice faded as he shifted gears and slammed the pedal. Sean gripped the steering wheel and braced himself. The buggy went over the edge and into the air. Time stood still as the soft wind brushed against his face. Sean closed his eyes and stretched his hands into the air. The buggy floated in the air for a second and then tilted toward the ground. Sean landed with a crashing sound that forced his eyes open. He laughed uproariously. He knew he had to listen to Amy about the reckless hill jumping, but he couldn't help it. The landing marked the fourth time he'd jumped a hill since leaving High Heaven.

Sean pulled the buggy over near another hill he was going to jump and shut off the engine. He reached for his bag and grabbed a sports bottle that was heavily wrapped with duct tape. One of the vendors in High Heaven, a balding fellow with bulging glasses, sold it for a single common. It had a nozzle cap that Sean liked very much. Sean practiced squirting the water into his mouth from a distance, each time farther and farther away. Not even remotely tired, Sean stretched his legs and back. He stared into the sky. Clouds slowly passed over, drifting aimlessly. A few more squirts from the bottle, and he was ready to drive again. Glancing at the back bumper and driver's dashboard, he saw both lights shone green. Sean tapped the buggy's hood with great appreciation. He couldn't believe how easy the journey was, thanks to this machine. *If only Nova had one of their own,* he thought. Sean closed the nozzle and tossed the bottle back into his bag. He climbed back in and started the engine.

The seat belt wrapped around him and fastened tight. Sean shifted into reverse and backed up the buggy thirty feet. His eyes glowed with the utmost lust for the thrill of jumping the hill. It beckoned him to do it; the hill needed to be jumped. The thoughts of Amy or Rick killing him later didn't even put up a fight against the urge. Sean's lips stretched into the most sinister smile he had ever given.

"Ahhhh!" Sean screamed, slamming the pedal down to the floor. The tires screeched and spewed more sand and dirt into the air. Sean's body jerked, nearly snapping his neck and slamming him into the seat.

"Yah-hoooo!" Sean screamed. The hill sent Sean flying higher than the previous ones. He felt like a bird in the air, spreading its wings to fly. His hands were off the wheel again, stretching for the sun. The buggy crashed to the ground, nearly toppling over upside down. For a moment, Sean could see Amy's and Rick's eyes widened and filled with unimaginable anger. Unlike them, Sean's eyes filled with unimaginable relief as he gained control of the buggy. A few left and right swerves shook Sean around before the buggy was back on track, heading west at thirty miles an hour.

Several miles ahead, Nova waited in the distance. Sean stared deeply at its faint outline. On the inside pocket of his dust jacket were the letters he wrote to Casey. They nestled neatly inside, half tied with a red ribbon. He planned to hand them to her after the celebration of his return. His mind spun with ideas on what to say and do as Nova slowly grew in size. *How is the village going to react? Who will hug me first—Casey, Junior, Mom? Am I the only one to have saved the town, or have the others done the same?* Sean would find out the answers soon, as it was only a matter of minutes before he would finally be home.

As Sean grew closer, he noticed smoke rising from the center of Nova. The timing was right, as Alex should be starting up the grill for dinner. The smell was fantastic, and his stomach rumbled with hunger. Finally, Sean had arrived. He shut off the engine and stepped out.

"Hey, everyone, I did it! I made it back! I found food and shelter!" Sean screamed at the top of his lungs. He walked over to the rear trunk, pulling free the straps that held his supplies and backpack. Sean grabbed some food to bring with him. Looking up at the watchtower, he called out to Billy, but there was no answer. He couldn't see Billy or anyone in the tower. Sean stepped back, trying to find Casey on the roof. There were no signs of her either.

Sean didn't understand what was happening. It was strange to leave the tower unattended, and Casey had promised she would be waiting for him every day on the tower until his return. Sean shook the eerie feeling and rushed for the entrance. Nova was quieter than it ever had been. Not a single sound filled the sky—no Old Harrison screaming strange obscenities, no children crying or playing, no animals making sounds. It was extremely odd.

Sean pounded on the metal door, yelling for anyone to open up. The smoke had an acrid odor, as if something had been roasting for quite a while and was now being burned. It wasn't like Alex to overcook meat, let alone ruin it. The eerie feeling returned, creeping along the back of his head, and Sean couldn't shake it. He pounded again and felt the giant door give. Moving back, Sean gained a running start and slammed his weight into the door, pushing it farther open. *Why isn't anyone answering me? Where is everybody?* The giant metal door was almost wide enough for Sean to slide through. *Why is the door unlocked? This door is never unlocked.*

Sean's heart sank as he kept pushing. Something was definitely wrong here. Sean desperately kept slamming his shoulder against the door, moving it inch by inch. With all his might, Sean pushed the door, sliding it a few more inches open and stepped inside. He bent over his knees, exhausted and sore, trying to catch his breath—only to have it taken away the moment he looked up. Sean's eyes fell, confirming the strange feeling as true. Nova was in ruins.

Paralyzed from shock, Sean slowly turned and gazed at the destruction that had befallen his village. The homes had been broken into and ransacked, with their belongings tossed outside. Blood was splattered across the homes and on the ground. The tables were flipped upside down, chairs were broken into pieces, and the bulletin board had been smashed into rubble. Clothes dangled off the debris, torn and ripped. All the live cattle were gone. There wasn't anyone in the tower. Sean didn't know what to say or do. His eyes rapidly searched for any signs of survivors. He raced inside his home, hoping to find someone alive.

"Mom! Mom!" Sean shouted. He searched around but found no one. His bed had been lifted on its side, and Lucy's crib was smashed and broken. His mother's clothes were like the ones outside, torn and ripped. There was blood everywhere but no bodies. Sean hoped that it was a sign that they might still be alive. *Oh man, this can't be happening; this has to be a dream. Right now I'm still sleeping in the garage. I have to be.* Sean turned around and headed out the door to search for Junior. He ran past house after house but still with no signs of anyone. Ahead, Sean came across the source of the smoke that filled the sky. His steps slowed as he came face-to-face with the horrible nightmare that couldn't be real.

Nova's bonfire that lit the night no longer burned with salvaged wood.

It now burned with its creators, its residents, its founders, piled on each other like unwanted spare parts thrown in a corner. Most of the bodies lay on their backs, while a small few were huddled together holding each other, showing that some were still alive as they burned. Blackened holes where their eyes used to be held images of sheer agony, sorrow, and suffering that was still on their faces. The pile rose over Sean's head and was wider than a house. It filled the center of Nova completely, like a giant monument of death. Sean's strength left him as he fell to his knees and cried. He could see the bodies of children, their skeletons reaching for their parents in pain, only to join them in the fire.

"No, please, no." Sean whispered as the tears spilled down his face. He felt the unspeakable sorrow fall upon him as he realized that Lucy and his mother were in that pile somewhere, holding each other, screaming in pain. The thought nearly killed him, right then and there. Tears flooded his face, and his heart screamed as if it were being ripped from his chest by some invisible force. Sean reached over and held a small hand that extended from somewhere under the pile. The child's hand was still warm from the flames that faintly burned inside. *What could have done this? Who could have killed so many innocent people?* Sean squeezed the hand, hoping to somehow comfort the child's lost soul. The hand collapsed from its arm and fell through Sean's hand like sand. As he wiped the tears from his eyes, Sean's hands were still covered with the ashes of the child, leaving streaks of dark gray across his face.

He wasn't going to give up. If anybody was alive, it would be his uncle. The man was as smart as he was strong. "Junior! Junior!" Sean yelled, rising to his feet, stumbling toward his uncle's house. His door was kicked opened. His home too was ransacked, as Sean expected. "Nicole!" Sean screamed, looking for any signs of life. Sean only found more blood on the walls and furniture. No matter how long or how hard Sean kept looking, Junior and Nicole were gone. They too were in the burning pile somewhere. Sean's heart again felt the unknown force grabbing at it, squeezing and turning, bringing crushing pain deep inside.

His whole world crashed to a speeding halt. Sean couldn't stand it any longer. His trembling legs could barely hold him upright. He sat on the only chair that wasn't broken in the house and again began to cry. Weeping, with his head down, he couldn't hear a single sound, except for the crackling flames that still filled the sky with the odor of burning flesh.

With no more tears to cry, Sean stared at the ground, motionless and without blinking. His mind was lost in the pain and sorrow. He finally accepted that they were all gone. Everyone here was gone. His entire family and friends were left to burn in a pile like garbage. Junior's lucky deck of cards (his only deck of cards) lay scattered across his entire home, revealing a story of panic, chaos, and murder, all rolled into one. A little more than a week ago, he was sitting here, talking with Junior, who had said he was proud of Sean. Sean had met with Casey on the tower that night, with an ending that was so special. Sean kicked the table farther away in anger. *They were supposed to be here. All of them were supposed to be here.*

Sean couldn't stay any longer; the memories filled his head, reminding him of what he'd lost and could never get back. Sean walked over to Junior's front door with fists clenched. Recklessly, Sean punched the metal door as hard as he could. He did it again, slowly increasing the speed. A flicker of rage ignited inside him. His teeth ground on each other as he clenched his jaw tightly shut. He listened to his banging on the door.

"Ahhhh!" Sean screamed, still punching until the pain washed his thoughts away, pushing them deeper into the blackened void, hiding their faces somewhere far in the back of his head. It had worked. His mind was numb; like a switch being turned off, their voices, faces, and laughter were all gone, and so was the pain. Sean leaned down to grab the two closest playing cards from Junior's lucky deck. He didn't care which two he grabbed; Sean just needed something more personal than a knife to remember Junior. Sean left the house clutching a king of spades and a nine of hearts before shoving the cards into his pocket. He would search for Casey, but judging on his success here so far, he knew she was gone too—but maybe the lucky cards would change that.

Mr. Davis's classroom was on the way to Casey's house. Sean feared what he would find inside, and he was right. Desks, chalkboards, and Mr. Davis's podium were all broken rubble and debris. Blood spattered the desk and walls. He assumed it was Mr. Davis's blood; who else could the blood be from? *Children.* Sean turned around, ready to head back outside toward Casey's house, and then he heard it.

Thud!

Sean spun around toward the noise. *Can it be? Is it even possible? A survivor?* Sean ran toward the sound that came from the back of the room. He pulled several desks away, tossing them in random directions. Sean was right. Someone did survive this horrible massacre. Before him lay a shaking and scared Mr. Davis.

"No! Get away!" he screamed, flailing his arms back and forth and landing a few strikes against Sean's face. Sean managed to grab and pin Mr. Davis down to calm him.

"It's okay, Mr. Davis. It's me. Please, Mr. Davis. It's me, Sean Anders. It's okay." With Sean still holding his arms down, Mr. Davis resisted every second until their eyes finally met. Mr. Davis seemed in disbelief, as if Sean was some sort of illusion, a cruel trick his mind was playing against him.

Sean's face curled from the pungent smell that Mr. Davis gave off. Sean would learn that the man had been hiding here for days, never leaving or making a sound. There wasn't an area on his body that wasn't covered in dirt, sweat, tears, and the unique smell of very unpleasant things.

Mr. Davis finally spoke. "Are they gone?" His words were blanketed with fear that lay deep within his eyes.

"Who?" Sean asked. "What happened?"

"It was Henry."

Henry?

The word was barely above a whisper that trailed from his mouth, trying to remain hidden from something or someone. "Henry came back." Still shaking in Sean's arms, Mr. Davis's words were short. "He ran all the way back. Came through the doors, covered in sweat, terrified beyond belief. He saw something, Sean."

Saw something?

"He wouldn't tell us why he was so scared. He didn't speak to anyone but Catherine the entire time he was here. Even then, Catherine couldn't get the information from him."

Now his eyes rapidly searched the room, making sure that he was still safe and that Sean was the only one still in the room with him. "We didn't know. They came from everywhere."

They …? In a calming voice, Sean asked him, "Who came?"

He ignored the question. "They hid in the night." His eyes seemed to relive that day. "Climbed over our front door. I could hear screams." Mr. Davis began to cry, and his words slowly increased in volume. "I was home when it happened. The parents told the children to come here to this room. That they would be safe in here."

Sean pulled his hands free from Mr. Davis's grip to wipe his tears.

"I saw them fight," Mr. Davis said. "There was no chance at all. We were all being slaughtered. We couldn't kill a single one before we were gathered to that pile outside." He pointed at the door into the classroom. "They came through here, grabbing all the children."

Sean followed the blood-stained walls, picturing the children being murdered.

"I could hear screams from everywhere," Mr. Davis said.

So could I.

"I hid as they came looking for me." His sobbing grew more intense, and his words were barely understandable as he continued. "I hid as the children screamed for help. I hid as the children were grabbed."

Now Sean squeezed Mr. Davis as hard as he could. "Who did this? What came that night?"

His eyes shifted back toward Sean. "Didn't you see the sign?"

Sign? "What sign? What are you talking about?" Sean shook Mr. Davis as if the answers would tumble from his mouth and onto the floor.

"They made him watch as they burned them. I could hear him plead for them to stop. But they didn't. The screams, Sean, the screams in the fire—they made Reyes watch them all burn."

Still without an answer to who had done this, Sean was beginning to lose patience with Mr. Davis. *"Who,* dammit? Who did this to us?" Sean finally got through to him.

His body, his face, and his eyes—everything was telling Sean that he was going to say the answer. "I don't know who. Some tribe. They were barely clothed, marks on their body, and had evil in their eyes. That's all I know. I'm sorry."

"I'll be back." Sean got up and went outside, leaving Mr. Davis in the room alone, still crying, while he went to search for Mayor Reyes. *They made him watch.* The notion swirled around in his head. *Maybe they let him live. Maybe he could tell me more about what happened here if he's still alive.* Outside, Sean couldn't see Mayor Reyes anywhere. Perhaps they had moved him elsewhere, or maybe he was hiding in a room, like Mr. Davis.

Sean then noticed that a deep, thick line in the ground reached a little more than halfway into Nova, as if something had been dragged away. Sean followed the trail all the way to the back of Nova. It was there he found Reyes. He had been tied to the top of a giant metal pole that overlooked Nova. Reyes didn't acknowledge Sean or react that something was approaching him. At first, the sunlight made Sean's eyes blurry and unable to fully see him as he came closer. When he used his hand to partly block the sun from his eyes, it became clear that Reyes wasn't alive. He was untouched, except for a spear plunged deep into his chest.

Flapping wildly in the small gusts of wind was a small piece of leather that hung from the spear. There was an image on it. Sean gathered a few items from the houses that he could use to stand on and get a better look. Sean climbed close enough to grab the leather piece on the spear.

He ripped off what he now saw was apparently a flag and stared at the image that had massacred his village. The image was drawn in blood. Sean's knuckles cracked as he clenched the flag tightly, burying the image within his fingertips. Whatever this could be, whatever it meant, all Sean knew was that he held both a symbol and a message. The three lines—this symbol—represented someone. And the message was plain and simple. *This is what they do.* Sean returned to Mr. Davis, finding him in the exact place he had been earlier.

"Did you see him? Is he ...?" He spoke curiously and a little hopeful, but there in his tone, somewhere within the words, he already knew the answer.

"He's dead. Looks like he's been like that for a while," Sean said. Sean didn't tell him about the flag that he found or the symbol that was drawn on it. He couldn't. The rage inside him stirred again, filling his veins. All his friends and family's faces began to reveal themselves. Sean fought to push them back. But the rage took over. Sean felt helpless, like a shadow was following him around with no control of what he was doing. Sean watched as he grabbed Mr. Davis, violently shaking him, asking why he hadn't fought back like the rest of his family and friends. Why had he sat there like a coward and hid as their screams echoed through Nova?

"The others fought back," Sean said. "Junior, Billy, Alex, and the rest fought back!"

"Because I would have died!" Mr. Davis screamed, pushing himself free from Sean's grasp. He sobbed as he had before, but this time with a difference. The tears weren't from fear or from reliving the horror that took place here. No, these tears that poured down his face were from guilt. It finally found him, and its punishment was far worse than any yelling or shaking Sean could ever give him.

"Please, Sean. Please leave me."

And so Sean did. There was no reason to talk to him anymore. The guilt wouldn't let him. This was his punishment, and Sean was going to leave him to it. Slamming the door closed, Sean took the flag out from his pocket and stared at the symbol. He lowered his head in shame, still clenching the flag as tightly as he could. Sean blamed himself for what had happened. *I should have stayed. I should have never left.*

Unlike Mr. Davis, there was no guilt waiting to surround or consume Sean. He didn't save them, but it wasn't because he hid but because he wasn't there. Which one was worse? He didn't know. But if there was no guilt to surround him, then he would create it from somewhere within these walls. He would attach it to the faces of those he lost.

Placing the flag back in his pocket, Sean remembered that he hadn't checked Casey's house yet, but his hopes were far from high. Even though he trekked back and forth between Reyes and Mr. Davis without finding any other signs of survivors, Sean still kept a sharp eye, hoping to find someone.

Casey's door hung halfway off its hinges. The ground was like the rest, covered in debris and blood. Sean closed his eyes and ran his hand through his hair, not wanting to check Casey's corner. Blindly, he walked over and stood where Casey, on any other day, would be sleeping. She was missing. All her clothes, blankets, and pictures of her family were ripped or torn like the others. He sat down on her bed, stroking the blanket she would be under. Every rip on her blanket was a reminder that Sean wouldn't get another kiss on that tower. Pulling the blanket to his chest, he sat there for some time, pressing it against his nose, trying to smell her sweet, warm scent. More tears emerged and trickled down his face. Sean pictured Casey screaming in that fire. The image tore at his heart like a wild animal. Reaching in his jacket, Sean pulled out the letters he'd written and gently placed them on her pillow. His heart needed more time, but his head knew what needed to be said.

"Goodbye, Casey."

Sean headed back home, but not before placing all of Casey's belongings back where they belonged and in the way he had remembered them. Each piece was filled with memories and joys that occurred there; mostly it was when they were kids, playing inside. The last thing Sean placed back was the table he used to sleep under during their sleepovers. He knew it was silly, but the table created some sort of comfort that made him feel safe in what had been a stranger's home.

He was all done and had relived all he could handle for now.

Sean stepped outside, accepting that there were no more survivors, no more signs of family or friends. There were only two things left to do before Sean left Nova for good to begin another journey that likely would end with him dead.

CHAPTER 27

BURYING THE DEAD

The sun was setting, and Sean needed to hurry before it became too dark for him to see. He returned to the smoldering pile of what was left of his people. He took off his dust jacket and his shirt and threw them on the ground. The cold air brushed against his chest and wound. Sean remembered that Alex stored several tools in his home. He would search there for anything that would be helpful. He returned with a shovel, tightly gripped in his left hand. He was lucky the tool remained undamaged. It was behind a dresser on the floor. Sean began digging a hole a few feet away from the smoldering remains. The little light made the task difficult, but Sean kept digging. His palms blistered, and his back began to tire. Halfway down, each shovelful of dirt felt twice as heavy. Sean's breathing quickened, and his hands burned. The pain had little effect on Sean; he only dug faster. The hole was massive. He didn't know how wide to make it or how deep, but it was more than enough.

Sean climbed out, taking a moment to catch his breath. He grabbed his shirt and wiped the sweat off his face. The bodies were next. Blackened arms stretched from the pile. Sean didn't know which one to grab. He reached for the closet body and pulled. The skin was still hot, and the blood burned as it dripped on his body. He placed the body in the hole as gently as he could and then grabbed another one. Sean couldn't identify any of the bodies. There was no way of telling which were his family or friends.

Tears poured down his face as the bodies became more difficult to remove. Limbs cracked and fell apart. Some of the skin peeled off, and organs fell to the ground. Each body became more fragile than the next as Sean came closer to the center. Every corpse that Sean could carry now lay in the grave. Sean bent over, grabbing Alex's shovel. There was no choice but to scoop up the ashes next.

Mayor Reyes's body still remained to be buried. Sean climbed up towards Reyes, carefully loosening the restraints. His body collapsed over Sean's shoulder. The weight made Sean's thighs tremble on the way down. Sean was too tired to carry Reyes all the way. He dragged Reyes by the arms. The lifeless eyes stared at Sean with horror. Sean gently laid Reyes down to close his eyes and then proceeded on. With everyone now buried, Sean realized that he had carried Junior into that grave at some point. It broke his heart that he couldn't dig Junior a special grave for him and Nicole.

Words needed to be said, and some peace needed to be made. Sean took a few minutes to find them both. *He should be here.* Even though Sean hated Mr. Davis for his cowardice, he still needed to be here to make his peace as well. Sean wasn't the only one in pain. Nova was stolen from both of them.

Walking back through the classroom door, Sean spoke loudly to grab Mr. Davis's attention. He didn't respond or make the slightest movement. A trail of blood spilled from behind the desks. Sean slowly approached, calling for Mr. Davis.

Mr. Davis stared back with emptiness. His right hand clutched a sharp piece of broken metal he'd used to slit his throat. The guilt evidently had been too much for him. Sean guessed he couldn't bear the thought of what he'd done. Sean stared in disgust and anger. He took his own life rather than die trying to protect Nova. Mr. Davis was a coward for hiding, and now he had died as one. Leaving him there to rot was what Sean wanted, but he knew it was wrong. It wasn't his place to decide, nor was it his right. Mr. Davis was a part of Nova, just as much as Sean was. If he was dead, then he needed to be buried like the others.

Sean reluctantly carried Mr. Davis's body across the village, feeling his cowardly blood crawl down his bare chest and back. Sean didn't bother closing Mr. Davis's eyes. His cold body flew and dangled like a ragdoll in the air as Sean threw it onto the pile. Sean wasn't careful or respectful. He gave Mr. Davis the dignity of being buried with the rest of Nova, but how he would be buried was on Sean's terms. That he knew was at least his right.

Night grew quickly as Sean finished covering the hole. Tapping the filled grave, Sean let go of the shovel and watched it fall, bouncing twice off the ground. The first part was done. Before he began the next part,

Sean wanted to clean his home. He didn't take his time to clean as he had done with Casey's, but he placed all the beds and stored the clothes away. Sean gathered all the pieces of the broken crib and placed them in a corner. He thought of Lucy in a better place and cried a few more tears. Sean flipped over a broken picture frame that held a photo of his great-grandparents on their wedding day. He turned toward the back wall, as he remembered his mother had mentioned a secret compartment. His father built it a year before Sean was born. It kept their valuables safe, in case of an attack like this. Sean tossed the picture on his mother's bed and felt for the loosened metal plate. Diane would put all her jewelry there. Sean was sure she would have hidden it during the attack. Sean slid the metal plate aside—he was right. He found the necklace she wore all the time. It also held the wedding ring her grandparents handed down to her and his father's ring too which didn't fit him anymore deciding to give it to Diane for safe keeping.

Sean put on the gold necklace and rubbed the rings between his fingers. Diane's diamond shined brightly, and Jacob's band still looked new. He slid the plate back, blending it with the others. It was time to leave. He walked outside, closing the door, sealing it like a tomb forever. Sean sat on a bench and waited for the stars to appear. His fingers rubbed the rings over and over again as he stared at the mass grave. An hour passed before the moon hung overhead, and the stars filled the sky. Sean looked up at the tower's roof. There was one last thing he needed to do.

CHAPTER 28

A PAST TO REMEMBER

N ight fell over High Heaven, leaving a peaceful air around it. Charlie leaned back in his red-leather chair. His left eye slept, while the right dimmed in the low-power mode. Occasionally, it would flicker from worn-out wires, but tonight it worked fine, lighting the darkened room with a soft glow of red. He tossed and shifted, sinking his body deeper and deeper within the chair. No matter the position or how soft the chair was, Charlie couldn't sleep full nights. Placing his elbows on the desk, he moved his fingers through his hair. It was frustrating. There was no use in trying anymore; it had been like this nearly all of his life. The dreams that waited for him in his head wouldn't leave him in peace. They haunted him, cursing him every night. The worst ones left him soaking in sweat from terror.

Rafa lay curled up, fast asleep next to the chair. His furry face slept pleasantly under his metal paw. *At least Rafa's dreams don't keep him up at night.* Moving silently, Charlie left his chair the best he could. A shot of pain fired through his leg, pulsating within his knee. Rubbing to ease his suffering, the metal fingers tried to soothe the skin and bone. It had been decades since he had any cartilage left in that knee. Things would have been far worse for him, if it hadn't been for Dr. Christopher Alchemius, widely known as Dr. Chaos. The doctor fixed Charlie the best he could with what was left of him. Limping to the door, Charlie turned the handle and quietly pushed it open.

Before he could step out, Rafa was awake, watching him. Charlie was proud to know that Rafa was still as sharp as ever.

"You still got it, huh?" Charlie said.

Rafa barked and walked on through the door.

Why do I ever doubt that dog? They made their way down the stairs and rounded behind them. Rafa already knew where his best friend was headed, and he led the way. Off to the far corner was a secret hidden door. Rafa pawed at the fake tiles as Charlie slid it open. A thin set of stairs trailed down under the ground. At the bottom, Charlie approached a vault door. He reached for the handle, feeling the cold metal in his palm. The door opened, and Rafa strolled inside, grabbing one of his toys from the ground. In the pitch-black darkness, Charlie reached over for a small, thin shaft he'd memorized long ago. His metal fingers followed straight up until they reached a switch. Turning it clockwise, a sphere of light emerged, sparkling and then fading away.

Charlie limped to an old gold lamp and tapped the bulb several times before the light returned. The lamp's cord connected to a solar panel generator that he'd bought off a merchant several years ago. Whenever the generator ran out of power, Charlie would sneak out during the night and place it in the sand outside the walls. By the end of the day, he had a fully charged battery for whatever he needed. Their value was beyond any price, and this was the sole reason why Charlie used every resource he had to find more of these panels outside in the desert. He was extremely lucky that the merchant cared more about getting drunk than finding out what the panels could do. He had hoped that Rick wouldn't come back empty-handed like he did several times before.

Next to the lamp on the floor was a wooden foot locker, filled with Charlie's childhood things—photos, toys, old bedtime books that his father used to read to him. That was a time when he could sleep without nightmares. Somewhere inside was a golden-brown teddy bear. It was his best friend before meeting Rafa. Blue buttons for eyes, with one missing now; several red stitches across the back that his mother had sewn after Rafa chewed on it as a puppy. There were even pajama pants of his father's favorite sports team. They lasted for only two months before being tossed next to the unused clothes he had out grown. Charlie recalled the memory of his father poking fun at him that he was growing faster than they could buy clothes.

Charlie proceeded farther into the room to a silver-colored locker. Lifting the handle, the door opened, revealing small circular containers. Strips of tape ran across each cover with thick black words. *Christmas '21. Halloween '22. Charlie's first days '14. Third birthday '17. At the park '23.* The writing went on all the way to the bottom, the containers neatly stacked on one another. Even then, it wasn't enough. Charlie had shoved more into the locker's corners on their sides. When the locker couldn't hold any more, Charlie created piles next to the walls. He had eight long, neat towers, stacked twenty rolls high. On the top of the locker stood a small reel-to-reel projector, his father's favorite possession.

It was all about antiques with him. No matter what device, car, camera, or movie seemed newer or better, nothing could beat the classics. But this was it—his *baby*, he called it—the Super 8 projector held cradled in his arms. The spools waited for another roll of film to be placed inside for the thousandth time. With everything set up and the cord plugged into the generator, Charlie grabbed the roll that read *At the park '23*. It was the last roll of film his dad ever used. Charlie turned the knob, and the spools began to turn. The sound of the film rolling throughout the Super 8 was indeed unique. There was something special that words couldn't describe. It wasn't a sound that filled his ears; it was a feeling that flowed through him. A feeling that his father was right after all, and his mother just couldn't understand.

She was embarrassed by his father's obsession. Watching him walk around the house and outside with that machine drove her crazy. Their neighbors and friends were embarrassed to be seen near such outdated technology. Charlie's father couldn't wait to add another roll of film to watch on his *baby*. Her face was the first one staring back at Charlie off the metal wall. Bright and filled with life, she smiled, and her brown eyes matched her hair. Her small, curvy nose was an adorable feature. The camera zoomed in closer and captured his father leaning in from the side, planting a kiss on her soft lips. Rose-colored cheeks shined in the sun, expressing her awkwardness with kissing in public. She was a good girl, raised to appreciate a skirt that hung below her knees. A classy woman was rare to find, an *antique* in the eyes of his father.

Now the camera spun around, focusing on a little boy playing with his favorite friend. Rafa barked, recognizing his younger self running around, chasing after a ball and playing with an even younger Charlie. The little boy laughed as his friend tackled him to the ground. With a mechanical heart beating in his chest, Charlie knew that machines couldn't understand or feel these moments, yet there was a warm feeling in his heart that ached to turn back time. He waited for his father to hand over the camera to the younger boy, so he could film the two hugging and posing. Charlie stopped the film at that exact point—with his father and mother both smiling at him with loving eyes. He remembered that day so very clearly because two days later … the bombs fell.

It was a scary time for everyone. A new world was created, a world without laughter or smiles, except for hers. No matter how terrible things had gotten out there, no matter how much his father worried, the bombs couldn't take that away from her. The loving, motherly smile that would bring joy and soothe any whimpering baby was always there—until the radiation finally found a way to take that from her. Charlie began to shed a tear as he continued to stare at his mother. There was no film for that last time she had smiled back at him; this was the closest time he could get. Tears fell from his eye as the feelings of guilt and shame stirred inside him. *What would they think of me now? Would they still be proud? All the things I have done—could I ever be forgiven?* He looked at his father's blue eyes. *Would he love the newer, better version of me—this metal on flesh—or would he have preferred the original version?* That one would have wrinkly skin now, weak muscles too tired to lift themselves, and bones too old to stay unbroken. He would be a shell of himself, waiting to break and be buried underneath the desert, just like an *antique.*

Charlie walked to the wall, and his metal hand traced his mother's smile. His eye poured back undying love for her. He shifted, trying to feel his father's face. Charlie's lips curled in sorrow as he wept uncontrollably.

"I'm … so … sorry."

The words took turns in between the tear-filled breaths. His father's face reflected off the back of his metal hand. Charlie hung his head, no longer having the strength to look at his father.

"I'll make things right. I promise."

Rafa's ears flickered from the sound of tears hitting the ground. He spat out his toy, rising to his feet. The back right leg needed oil, as it started to squeak again. He hung his head as he approached. His best friend was in pain. Rafa plopped next to Charlie, whimpering gently. He wasn't going to let Charlie be sad alone.

CHAPTER 29

ONE LAST TIME

Step by step, Sean climbed the ladder, his eyes locked on the stars above. They glistened like diamonds across a black sheet. Every step stretched his aching muscles and worsened the fatigue that had set in. Sean reached the tower, exhausted and out of breath. The tower was untouched and free from blood. Everything was just as he had left it that day. Sean stepped forward, reaching for a coverless book left on a desk. "Well, I'll be damned," Sean said as he held *The Exiles of the New World* tightly in his hands. The pages flipped across his fingers, opening to Billy's comb. *Did you like it, Billy?* Sean set the book down, hoping the answer was yes. He pulled himself on the roof, struggling a few times before reaching the top. *They are beautiful,* he thought. They always were to Sean. This was the last thing he needed to do. See the stars for one last time up there. From the special spot that belonged to Casey and him. Soon, it would belong to no one. For Sean wasn't coming back; there was no reason to anymore.

Sean watched the moon's glow fade and stars slowly slip behind the blue sky, while the sun peeked from the horizon. He watched it, all while rubbing Casey's bracelet. The heat slipped in under Sean, raising the temperature closer to the bane he was familiar with. It was time to go. Sean climbed back down the tower and prepared to leave. Without the burning pile in view, Nova held a small glimpse of its original self. Sean shook the image from his head and gathered mementos of his family and friends to take with him. He closed the entrance the best he could, leaving only a small crack. Sean tossed his backpack and supplies in the back of the buggy. He checked the front dashboard and rear bumper for green lights.

They remained off, as the solar panels needed more time. Sean looked back at Nova. Without anyone else to run around, play, laugh, work, and live inside there, Nova was a shell of the home Sean once knew and a place that couldn't survive in the new world. Charlie did say how cruel the new world could be at times, but Sean never expected anything like this.

A spark of rage flickered inside again. Sean turned back toward the buggy and retied all the food and belongings. He checked the gauges and tires and adjusted the seat belt, looking for any signs of wear that should be fixed. Then he waited again. *What about the others, Sam and Jason?* Sean contemplated whether or not he should leave a sign if one of them should return. *What if they're both dead, and I really am the only one left?*

C'mon. The light wasn't turning green, and Sean was growing impatient. Sean walked over to the solar panels, wiping away any sand or debris. His fingers checked the wires for disconnections, but everything checked out fine. Sean began to worry. The buggy was taking longer than usual to turn on. He contemplated whether the joyriding had anything to do with why the buggy wasn't working. Sean paced back and forth, holding his hands on his head. He refused to accept the buggy could be broken. There was no way he had it in him to head back by foot. Sean was already exhausted from earlier, and if the desert didn't kill him on the way back, Amy surely would finish the job. There were no signs of any damage from the exterior. Sean crawled under the buggy. He stared at the engine and several parts—he had no idea what they were for. Everything seemed to be connected down there, but Sean didn't know what to look for.

He pulled himself back up and walked around to the rear bumper. On his knees, he stared at the green bulb closely. He held his breath and tapped the bulb several times.

Bingo.

The light gave a brief flicker and then shined brightly in his face. Probably a loose wire that needed to be fixed, but Sean would keep that a secret for now. He didn't want Amy to start asking any questions. She had a way of seeing through the lies that people gave her. That was one of the many skills Sean noticed she had. He ran around and grabbed two items from his backpack. He decided that he would leave a note after all.

Sean fastened his seat belt and turned the ignition. The engine kicked to life. He was *ready to rock*, as Billy would have said. Slamming the pedal down, Sean left Nova behind. The wheels spun and kicked the sand into the air. Lifting his head out from the window, Sean stared back at the small piece of paper he'd neatly folded under a metal panel, with half of it flapping in the wind. Inside, he'd written:

Sam, Jason,

If you are reading this, then you will find out that Nova is lost. No one is left here. They are all dead. I buried them and marked the grave. There is no home here anymore, but if you have the strength to walk a few more days, there is a place to the east. But I won't be there for long. I am going to find out who did this to us, and I am going to kill them.

—Sean

Never looking back, Sean headed straight toward High Heaven. Feeling the torn flag in his hand, he realized there were so many answers he needed to know. So many questions he had to ask, and maybe Charlie could help him with it. As Nova shrunk in the distance, Sean still wasn't happy with having buried Mr. Davis with his friends and family. He was in there next to them, the ones who had cried for help as he hid and ignored their screams. There was no use in still holding on to the idea, but Sean couldn't let it go. For his sake, Mr. Davis better hope that they could forgive him for what he had done because Sean sure as hell wasn't going to.

CHAPTER 30

ANSWERS

S ean drove toward High Heaven like a bat out of hell, never lifting his foot from the pedal. He wove left and right, avoiding any rocks, ditches, and hills. Sean still had plenty of time before reaching High Heaven. It was enough time for him to mourn and come to terms with what had happened, but he chose not to; instead, he thought of Christmas in Nova. The memory shot through him, locking his mind with the images.

Every year Nova celebrated Christmas within its walls. Everyone gathered in the middle of the village as Reyes gave a speech. He commented on family values, friendships, love, and prosperity. It was a time of extreme joy and happiness. Sean remembered reading about families huddled around each other under a Christmas tree, opening gifts and sharing stories over a table filled with food. The pictures showed a jolly fat man riding a sleigh pulled by reindeers; kids opening presents; and houses decorated with lights in the snow. Nova didn't have lights to decorate their homes, or trees on which to hang ornaments, or cool winters filled with snow, but they did have plenty of food and gifts to open. Diane would say it was more of a "Christmas in July" than the traditional one. The men would tell jokes and drink their moonshine. Junior hosted his card games with pans of chili for everyone to enjoy. The women talked about their kids, husbands, and even embarrassing moments. The kids ran about, ecstatic; they knew they were getting presents—and a lot of them.

When Sean was old enough, Diane forced him to help influence the kids to behave by telling them that some magical fat man was going to ride in the sky and drop off presents. But if they misbehaved, he would fly over, ignoring Nova until next year.

All the children anxiously waited for the fat man. Looking back at it now, Sean found it quite stupid, really, but the kids loved it. He'd loved it too when he was their age. When the fat man did arrive, they screamed with joy, hugging and squeezing the magic man, not knowing it was one of their parents in disguise. The costume had been sewn together with patches of red from torn dresses and suits. They stuffed pillows under the layers to help whichever parent was chosen to look fatter and lovable. Sean found himself laughing at the mere thought of how hot it must have been under the suit. The kids circled around the fat man as he handed out the gifts for all the good children. They were all good children and got presents, regardless of whether they had been bad; in this case, they were always good.

Grabbing the toys that were handed to them, their eyes would always light up with the greatest excitement, followed by another scream. Some ran around, already lost in their own world, with their new toy. Others ran straight to their parents, showing off what the fat man brought them. The toys were usually old ones rewrapped and passed on to other kids. They were so young they didn't even notice. Sean laughed, rocking his head back, remembering Timmy jumping with joy after receiving a new wooden train. He'd forgotten that it was the same train he made quite a scene and cried for when he'd lost it several weeks earlier.

Last Christmas, Casey handed Sean a scavenging kit filled with rope, a Band-Aid, a sifter, a small blanket, a shiv, and other items, including a small portion of dried food. It was one of the best presents he ever got for Christmas. As Sean shook away the memories, he could see High Heaven. There was no more time left to reflect. He was glad to be back and tired of thinking about the past. Sean slammed the brakes, stopping the buggy out in front of the garage. He shut off the engine and hurled himself from the driver's seat. Sean banged on the garage door fiercely. He could hear Amy tell him to hang on. She lifted the door, and Sean walked right past her, not saying a word.

"Whoa, new guy, you forgot your stuff."

Sean left Amy there in the garage, shocked and confused. He ran upstairs, straight for Charlie's office.

"Charlie!" Sean screamed, slamming his shoulder into the door and swinging it violently open. He found Rufus inside, talking to Charlie once again.

Rufus walked over, with his hand reaching for Sean. "Not now. We're busy."

Sean swatted the hand away as the other one reached for his throat. Leaning back, Sean swung his fist straight for Rufus's jaw. Rufus countered the punch, grabbing Sean's arm and twisting it behind Sean's back, and then slammed him against the wall. Trying to break free, Sean tried to hit Rufus with the other hand. It only angered Rufus more as he twisted Sean's arm harder and farther up, nearly breaking it.

"I'm quickly growing tired of you." Rufus emphasized the words with more twists and jerks of the arm. Charlie rose from his seat and slammed his walking stick onto his desk.

"Enough, both of you! Stop it right now!" Charlie's red eye beamed with intensity as he shouted.

"They're dead! All of them! They're dead!"

Rufus let go of his hold, shocked by what Sean had said. "What?" Rufus asked.

"Sean?" The redness in Charlie's eye calmed and faintly glowed.

"They're dead, I said. I arrived there and found them all dead. One of our villagers, Henry, came back scared out of his mind. He saw something out there, and it followed him home." Sean explained what he saw that day and the extent of the damage. He mentioned the bodies piled up and set on fire, and that Mayor Reyes was tied to a metal pole and forced to watch his people burn and scream, and how he had dug a mass grave to bury them all.

Charlie fell back in his chair, at a loss for words.

"I'm so sorry, Sean," Rufus said, trying to console Sean by placing his hand on his shoulder. Sean's reaction was to try to punch Rufus again, but he didn't. Rufus held his hands up. "Easy, Sean. I know what it is like to bury someone you love." Rufus was sincere, but he and Sean were far from friends.

Sean hated his guts, and Rufus felt the same. Rufus might have put his hatred aside for now, but Sean didn't. "Do you, Rufus? Unlike you, I'm not man who had to bury a loved one. I'm a man who had to bury an entire village."

Rufus stared at Sean, who wasn't calming down or accepting his pity. "Do you know who did this, Sean?"

Sean shook his head in failure. "But I did find this attached to a spear." Sean handed the folded flag to Rufus.

His black gloves squeaked as the leather stretched for it and unfolded it. Rufus stared at the symbol deeply and turned his gaze toward Charlie. He lifted the flag for Charlie to see.

In an instant, Charlie recognized the symbol and spoke the name that took everything from Sean. "Dragus!" Charlie leaped out of the chair as if the news couldn't be true.

"Who's Dragus?" Sean asked. Neither spoke as they stared at the flag and back at one another. Growing impatient, Sean asked again. "Who is Dragus?"

"Dagus is a barbarian and the worst one at that. His tribe roams these lands, randomly attacking shipments that carry food, metal, and clothing. He only takes the food and leaves the rest to burn." Charlie pointed to the image on the flag. "This is the symbol of his tribe."

Rufus handed the flag back to Sean. "He kills the guards escorting the shipments. He never stays in one place, so we can't find him." Charlie pulled opened a drawer in his desk and reached inside. "Dragus is as ruthless as he is cunning. He strikes fear in everyone. Some even say he cannot be killed."

"Well, I'm going to kill Dragus for what he did," Sean said, looking first at Charlie and then Rufus.

Charlie grabbed what he had been looking for from the drawer and walked toward Sean. "Many have tried, Sean, and so have I." He handed Sean an item wrapped in cloth.

"What's this?" Sean asked.

"That is a reminder of the last time I sent the best mercenaries to kill Dragus." The cloth in Sean's hand was soaked in dried blood. Inside was the exact symbol Sean had found in Nova. "I found that symbol underneath the heads of the three men I paid to hunt Dragus … on a spike."

"I thought you said that Dragus never stays in one place and that he can't be found."

"He did say that," Rufus said, finally joining in the conversation, "and the Kid is right. Judging by the massacre, the men didn't find Dragus. Dragus found them." Rufus's words were serious and grim.

Sean was scared, and he wasn't going to lie to himself and say he wasn't. "Then what do you expect me to do?" Sean heard no answer. "I'm not going to stand here and let Dragus get away with this."

Charlie stared at Sean not wanting to say what followed. "Nothing. You must do nothing, Sean," Charlie said.

Sean couldn't believe Charlie's words. "Nothing? You're telling me that there is nothing I can do? You weren't there, Charlie! You didn't see them burning like firewood. Dragus took them from me!" Sean felt the rage grow inside him again. His eyes were wet with tears of anger. "And I wasn't there to protect them. I wasn't there to save them!"

Charlie pulled Sean in and gave him a hug. "You can't blame yourself for what happened. There was no way you could know. I know this might sound horrible, but I am happy you weren't there. Dragus knows more ways to break a man than to kill one, especially one who has something to lose."

Gently pulling free from Charlie, Sean headed for the door. "All I care about now is killing Dragus for what he did and for what he took from me. I will make him suffer. I will make him bleed."

"Sean, wait!" Charlie reached out, but Sean ignored his plea. Halfway down the stairs towards the garage, Sean heard Charlie scream after him. "I won't let you!" Sean grabbed the garage door handle and began to pull. "You will die, Sean!" Charlie said. Sean kept ignoring every word. "Guards!"

Sean stopped and turned. In an instant, all the guards had cornered him by the door. Their weapons were drawn and pointed at his chest, throat, and stomach, ready to attack. He watched Charlie walk down the stairs toward him. They stood face-to-face in silence. Charlie's red eye beamed brightly and then quieted to a soft glow.

"I'm not going to stay here, Charlie. So if you're going to kill me, then get on it with." Sean was ready to die and held his arms open. The weapons drew closer now, touching the skin.

Charlie was shocked and hurt. He looked down, trying to find the right words to say. "You're going to die, Sean, not by me but by him!" Charlie pointed toward the outside. "I'm sorry, Sean, but I have seen how you defend yourself. Dragus wouldn't even raise his heart rate killing you."

"I thought—"

"You thought I would kill you, Sean? After taking you in, feeding you, giving you shelter. That I would raise my hand against you? You wouldn't last a day out there."

Sean shook his head. "I don't care. I'm still going."

"I can see that, and I will not stop you anymore." Charlie signaled the guards to put down their weapons. "But please let me help you. Let me teach you how to defend yourself." All the guards gave a quick look to the Kid in disbelief. "Let me train you to survive an attack by a skilled opponent. Then maybe you can achieve what no man has done."

"And what's that?" Sean asked.

"Kill Dragus."

"So you know how to fight?" Sean asked.

Charlie smiled with accomplishment. "I may know a thing or two."

Sean took a moment to think about it and then said, "Okay. I'll let you train me."

Charlie smiled and nodded his head with relief. "Get some rest. We will train tomorrow, first thing in the morning." He waved off the guards, and they all returned to their posts, whispering among themselves, not believing what they had heard.

Charlie went back to his room, and so did Sean. Amy was in the garage, working on the buggy, when he closed the door. She was upset by the way he had treated her earlier. She quickly slid out from under the engine and stood in front of him, squeezing the wrench in her hands. She imagined beating him over the head with it. She watched him walk over to her with apologetic eyes.

"Okay. You are probably mad at me, and I'm sorry. I disrespected you earlier, and it won't happen again. I promise. I'm going through a lot right now, and I hope you can understand. My entire vill—"

"I heard you screaming about what happened to your village, all the way from here," Amy interrupted. Her hand flew out, slapping Sean's face with great force, almost knocking him off his feet. Sean regained his balance, only to receive another slap across the face that sent him falling onto the uncomfortable bed. "First one was for how you treated me earlier. The second was for how you treated the buggy. I know you had a joyride and jumped off those hills because the suspension looks like it has been through hell."

Rubbing his face, Sean felt immense heat coming off it in the shape of Amy's hand.

"Also, I accept your apology. I'll see you in the morning." Amy turned and closed the metal door behind her, leaving Sean in the dark.

Today had been a long day for Sean, and, according to Charlie, he was going to need some rest for the next one. Pulling the blanket over him, Sean closed his eyes and tried to dream about killing the man they called Dragus.

CHAPTER 31

TRAINING

The next day Sean awakened to the noise of metal hitting metal. He rubbed the sleep from his eyes and ran toward the door. Pushing through, he saw a sea of soldiers practicing their stances and attacks with one another. Charlie stood in the middle, quietly watching and correcting the soldiers' mistakes. Rafa sat right beside Charlie, watching for mistakes as well. At times, Sean was frightened by how Rafa mirrored the intelligence of a human. He almost seemed to understand and read others incredibly well. Sean made his way to Charlie, carefully avoiding any contact with the soldiers. Sean watched Charlie correct any mistakes with a swift poke of his walking stick.

"Bend more with the knees. You, over there—keep your back straight!" Charlie sidestepped left and right, moving with the soldiers. "Keep your eyes on the enemy."

Sean waited for Charlie to turn around.

"Ah. Sean. Good morning, and welcome to the first day of your training. Now come here and face me."

Sean listened and stood tall, staring into his eyes.

"If you are to defend yourself, you must learn how to control your own weight." Charlie circled around slowly, looking for any faults in Sean's posture. His stick slowly slid down the side of the right leg and stopped at Sean's knee. "Bend with your knees to help keep balance. A fighter without a sense of balance will find himself on his back and suffer a quick death."

Sean bent his knees and lowered into a squat.

"Too much bend," Charlie said. "A little less now."

Sean loosened his stance, comfortably finding the balance.

"Good. Second, you never fight with your body fully exposed. Turn it a little, and hide half of it, like a boxer."

"A boxer?" Sean never heard the word before.

"Never mind that. I'll tell you later. Now turn your body." Charlie waited to see which side of the body Sean chose to hide.

Sean's right leg stepped forward and the left one shifted slightly back. The right shoulder leaned ahead of the left. Sean's right fist stuck out in front while keeping the left one close behind and away.

Charlie's eye opened wide as he smiled in amazement. "Very good, Sean. Looks like we have a southpaw, Rafa,"

"What's a southpaw?" Sean asked. Another word he'd never heard before.

Charlie bellowed a strong laugh. "It means you are unique. You show that your dominant hand is your left instead of the commonly chosen right. This means most fighters will not have as much experience in fighting someone like you. You will have an edge that will annoy and frustrate their minds." Charlie moved in front of Sean and took same stance. "You see, when both fighters have the same stance, there are no secrets between them. You move the same and you attack the same. Your attacks come from the same angles that they are used to seeing." Charlie shifted to what he called the common right-handed stance.

He lifted his cane and shouted to three guards. "Randy, Paul, and Willie, come here and show me your stance."

Rafa barked as well, supporting the commands. The three guards ran and stood in a straight line. Their bodies were positioned in the same stance as one another. Sean could see what Charlie was talking about.

"You're different, though," Charlie whispered in Sean's ear. "Now you see their stance; they don't fight like you. Your body is turned differently and hides your left hand. The hand that is in front of you is the weakest, and the hand you hide close to your chest is the strongest. Everything is backward for them now. Your attacks are different, and movements are opposite. They have learned to fear the right hand, which is your weakest, and ignore the left hand, which is your strongest. Their strategy has to change into something that they are not used to, but yours doesn't. Nearly all the fighters you will meet will fight this way." Charlie lifted his hands. "Second lesson is how to attack."

Sean spent the rest of the day learning how to attack with punches and kicks. Next was to learn how to defend himself from attacks. They worked over and over again on how to properly move with the feet. After the day was over, Sean was exhausted, drenched in sweat, and out of breath. Thankfully, Charlie left half a day for Sean to rest and work with Amy on the buggy.

The next day Sean expected the same routine as yesterday, but he was in for a big surprise. There were no soldiers practicing their stances or giving shouts as they sparred with each other. All the soldiers were at their posts, patrolling High Heaven and keeping an eye on its residents. All that waited for Sean was Charlie, Rafa, a pile of huge rocks, and a metal bucket.

With each step Sean took, a small fraction of a smile seemed to creep over Charlie's face, almost to say that Sean had no idea what he was in for. And by the end of the day, Charlie was right. Rafa, no doubt, was replicating that exact smirk.

"Today we are weight training," Charlie said, pointing toward the items on the ground. "Now, judging by your physique and muscle tone, you are in some shape, but I'm going to make you better." Charlie told Sean to do a push-up.

Sean positioned himself on the floor accordingly, with hands shoulder-width apart.

"Now begin," Charlie instructed.

Sean began the push-up.

"Head facing up, Sean." Charlie counted twenty-five push-ups in a row.

Sean's chest burned, and his arms hurt at the wrist. He could feel his heart beating faster and the blood rushing through his body.

"Good. Now stand up. You are now going to do some squats."

Sean followed the motions that Charlie signaled with his stick. Sean knew how to keep his back straight and knees bent perfectly after being struck with Charlie's stick eleven times.

"And ... twenty-five. Very good. Now do another twenty-five push-ups."

Sean gave Charlie an evil glare as he got into position. He was waiting for Charlie to start counting when he felt a heavy rock placed on his back between shoulder blades.

"Begin."

"What the hell is this?" Sean said, feeling his arms tremble under the weight and barely managing to get through one push-up.

"That is probably fifty, maybe sixty, pounds on your back. Trust me; after a few weeks of training, you will being doing a hundred of these without any trouble."

Sean stopped doing the push-up and shifted the rock off his back. "A few weeks?" Sean said, standing eye level with Charlie. "How long do you plan on training me here? You know that Dragus is out there somewhere, and I should be killing him at this very second."

"Don't worry about Dragus. No one has ever laid a scratch on him, and no one will. Your training will last as long as it takes, Sean." Charlie's face gave no sign that he was joking. He was dead serious.

Impatiently, Sean shook his head at the thought of waiting to kill Dragus. "How long does what take?"

"For you to be skilled enough and not be killed in less than five seconds," Charlie said.

"You know, I really think that both you and Rufus are full of crap." Sean clenched his fist.

Charlie leaned back, surprised at Sean's rudeness. "How so, Sean?"

"I think you two are making Dragus out to be this unstoppable killing machine, when he isn't. Just because he ambushed some mercenaries doesn't make him unkillable." When Charlie didn't respond, Sean thanked Charlie for the day's lesson and said that he would be leaving soon.

"Okay, but can I see something first?" Charlie said.

"See what, Charlie?" Sean spoke each word in an irritated tone.

"See if you can hit me." Charlie spread his arms wide open, waiting for a punch to land on his half-metal jaw. "Here." He tossed his cane over to Sean, who caught it in midair.

Sean looked at the cane, then at Charlie, and then at the cane once more. Shrugging his shoulders, Sean gave in and readied his stance. He relaxed his arms, cocking the cane, and was ready to attack. Charlie waited with the exact smile he had before, when Sean was in for a surprise. As fast as he could, Sean swung the cane, aiming dead center on Charlie's face.

Charlie turned and evaded the attack.

Sean was impressed by Charlie's speed. He lifted the cane, preparing for another strike. Charlie tilted his head, ask if to ask Sean if that was all he had. Rage fueled Sean, who swung violently twice in opposite directions. Charlie evaded each strike with ease. Taking three steps back, Sean paced back and forth, twirling the cane around, trying to figure out what Charlie was trying to prove. Sean wasn't going to let Charlie get in his head again. Sean took a deep breath and focused. He just needed to think clearly and find Charlie's weakness. *The leg.* Sean would aim for Charlie's bad leg and would the win the challenge.

Charlie lifted his metal hand and gave Sean the *C'mon* wave with his wrist. Sean smiled; his attack was planned out. Digging his feet deeper into the ground, Sean gained a better grip on the cane and was ready to unleash a fury of strikes on Charlie. Sean screamed as he pushed off the ground, gaining a small sprint toward Charlie and swinging his cane with all the strength and speed he had. Up, down, left, right, up, left, right, and left—the cane hurled past, leaving a whirling noise following every swing.

All the swings were just a distraction, a trick, but had they hit Charlie, Sean would have been happy nonetheless. No, the real strike was for his leg. Spinning gracefully, Sean whipped his head around with eyes locked on the knee.

Heaving the cane around as fast as he could, Sean created a blurred image of the cane, which came to sudden stop. *Impossible!* Sean couldn't believe it. Gathering his breath, Sean noticed he'd missed Charlie completely. Charlie dodged all the swings without trouble or loss of balance, and the cane that came to a sudden stop missed as well. Sean's hand was near Charlie's right leg, and if things had gone accordingly to how he had planned, the cane should have been lodged in Charlie's right leg—but it wasn't.

Sean saw Charlie's right foot standing on the cane. He timed it perfectly, stomping on the cane right before Sean made contact with his leg. Speechless and in awe, Sean watched Charlie cock his right shoulder and then drive it deep into Sean's chest.

To the naked eye, the amount of room Charlie had to drive his shoulder into Sean would hurt as much as being hit with a pillow, but that wasn't the case. Sean was sent flying backward and onto his back. All the wind was knocked out of Sean. Dazed and confused, Sean stared at the blue sky, wondering what just happened. *How did I miss him? How did he do that?*

Rafa stood over Sean, licking his face, breaking Sean's daze. Sean batted away Rafa as he heard Charlie speak.

"Are you okay, Sean? I hope you aren't seriously hurt," he said with some concern.

"Yeah, thanks for asking." Sean was being sarcastic, still sore from two things—not being able to strike a one-hundred-year-old man, and his back, which absorbed most of the impact coming down.

"I'm sorry about the hit, but I felt it would be the exclamation mark to the point I was trying to make."

"Which is what, exactly?" Sean replied, dusting off the dirt from his shirt and pants.

"That if you couldn't land a single strike on an old man, who, by the way, just beat you with a single hit, then what makes you think you will be any match for Dragus? I admit that even I am no match for him. As a matter of fact, while I'm thinking about it, even in my prime I think I was no match for him. Maybe …" The maybe wasn't like any other maybe. There was something more to it. Charlie reflected on the idea of being in his twenties again, challenging Dragus to a fight. He imagined the fight in his head, waiting to see who would win.

No matter how awful waiting to kill Dragus sounded to Sean, Charlie was right. He wouldn't last five seconds with Dragus. Sean needed to avenge his friends and family, but he wasn't ready to do so. The wound on his stomach also needed time to heal. It still was sensitive, and it hurt like hell. Killing Dragus would require Sean to be 100 percent healthy and ready. Sean lowered his head and accepted staying, no matter how long it took.

Charlie placed his hands on his cane and waited to see if Sean was going to continue the training. Sean's disappointed face said everything Charlie wanted to hear. "Good!" he shouted, wasting little time in placing the heavy rock on Sean. They continued as if their little argument and sparring lesson never happened. "Again!" Charlie said, with Rafa barking along. After reaching another set of twenty-five push-ups, Charlie told Sean to stop.

Sean saw the pattern in the workout and guessed squats were next. Unfortunately, Sean was right. Charlie told Sean to hold the rock tightly to his chest. Up and down Sean went, with thighs burning and shaking. Beads of sweat poured down his cheeks, chin, and lips. Sean even felt some fall into his eyes. "Ugh!" The sweat burned, and he closed his eyes for the remainder of the squats. "Twenty-five!" Sean screamed, letting go of the rock. It crashed to the ground with a heavy thud. Sean collapsed to the ground, aching and sweating. Rubbing his eyes, Sean tried to remove more sweat.

Charlie stood over Sean, smiling at his discomfort.

CHAPTER 32

A NEW MAN

As he promised himself, Sean did stay as long as it took for him to be ready. Days, weeks, and months went by, with every morning starting with a lesson or workout. Each session grew in difficulty, challenging Sean, often pushing him to the brink. Sean tried to cheat through a few mornings, but Charlie saw through it and pushed Sean to exhaustion. Sean quickly noticed results in the training. He became faster, stronger, and more resilient to pain with each passing day. The rock on his back during the push-ups was replaced with a bigger one. It kept being replaced until Sean easily did the sets with the biggest one they could find. Without heavier rocks to find, Charlie began to use his feet. His strength pushing against Sean's was awful and extremely difficult, but Sean passed that challenge too.

By the time Charlie was convinced that Sean was ready to fight Dragus, three years had passed. Sean's wound had healed, leaving a long scar across his stomach. Some nights he would run his fingers across the smooth line and reflect on him nearly being killed. It was indeed a miracle that the mimic hadn't killed him then and there.

Amy and Sean spent a lot of time together, both changing through the years. Sean grew stronger, while Amy became more attached to him and less hostile. Sean listened and learned more about the buggy and other side projects. He became quite the mechanic, almost as good as Amy, but she just called it being *handy*.

They finished their projects and repairs faster each day, leaving room to talk afterward for a while. Sean got to learn about Amy's childhood and past.

Like his, it too was rough and cruel. Amy grew up on the surface but never got to know her own mother. She died during childbirth and never held Amy in her arms. To this day, Rick cried alone outside on his wife's birthday. Before finding High Heaven, he visited her grave daily, speaking to it about Amy. Rick didn't find another woman to share his love, so he gave it all to Amy.

Amy didn't have to tell Sean how close she and her father were. They were nearly joined at the hip, always working as if they were reading each other's minds or understanding what they were feeling without asking. They shared the same dislikes and interests. She was indeed a daddy's girl. But if Sean ever said it, Amy would pulverize him into oblivion, no matter how strong he became.

At times, Sean accepted Amy's increasing connection toward him, but it became difficult to ignore his feelings for Casey. He still thought about her daily, and at nights he fell asleep still rubbing her bracelet. Three years was plenty of time to grieve and let Casey go, but his schedule was grueling. Sean barely had any energy left to properly mourn her. He needed more time when he wasn't exhausted or working on a new project. Perhaps he would find the time while searching for Dragus. Then and only then would Sean tell Amy how he truly felt for her. But for now, they would remain friends.

Sean wasn't the only one who noticed Amy's connection with him. Rick wasn't blind; Rick was a father. Fathers know these things and dread the day that their daughters show signs of falling in love. When Rick approached Sean, asking for a word in private, Sean knew exactly what Rick wanted to talk about. He only feared that Rick would be angry. To Sean's surprise, it wasn't the case at all. Rick didn't want to give Sean the talk about staying away from his daughter or about killing him if he ever broke his daughter's heart. No, in fact Rick just wanted to talk and get to know more about the man who made his daughter laugh and be happy. These talks later became a common thing throughout the three years and were always over a game of cards.

Rick's family, unfortunately, grew up poor. Without enough money to afford a bomb shelter, they were forced to stay on the surface and endure the bombs that fell far away but were enough to destroy most life. Buildings crumbled, fires burned fields of crops, and screams of terrified children filled the air. Sean had heard the story countless of times, thanks to Mr. Davis, who he hoped was in hell somewhere. But to hear the version of it from someone whose family actually lived to see it—that part was new.

Rick's father, Steven, was only seven when he met Mary, Rick's mother, one summer morning. She wandered up to their door and begged for help. She suffered from severe dehydration and collapsed in Steven's arm as he opened the door. His family took her in, nourishing her back to full health. Since that time, Steven and Mary were inseparable. They scavenged the wastelands together and eventually gave birth to Rick, twenty years later. They taught Rick how to hunt for food and scavenge the land. They witnessed his marriage and lived long enough for Rick to tell them they were going to be grandparents before burying them. As the cycle of life continued, Rick would have Amy to bury him one day.

"Sean?" Rick said.

"Yes?" Sean replied, not looking away from the cards in his hand—a five of diamonds and a three of clubs. The board held a two, a four, a king, and a nine. The last card flipped over was an ace. Sean made a straight. Rick reached for his chips to bet, staring at the last card. Sean knew Rick was holding a pair of aces.

"I need you to promise me something." Rick threw several red and blue plastic chips on the table.

Sean raised the bet again and threw double the amount. "Sure, Rick. What is it?" Sean waited to see if he would call or push all in.

Rick simply called the bet. "I want you to promise me that you will look after Amy if something should happen to me." His eyes revealed the seriousness of the matter, as did his tone.

"Of course, Rick. I will," Sean said.

"Promise me. Say you promise." The sound of his voice raised to just below a shout.

"I promise, Rick. I promise to look after Amy if anything should happen to you."

Rick's face lost the look of worry and fear that Amy might be in danger or not be protected when he was gone. With a sigh of relief, Rick gently placed his pair of aces down on the table, as if he'd just outplayed the greatest poker player there ever was.

Sean smiled, giving Rick the nod, a nonverbal indication that meant "nice hand." He looked down at the unbeaten straight he held, which begged him to wipe that smirk from Rick's face. Without delay, Sean tossed the cards face down onto the table and let Rick take the pot.

CHAPTER 33

THE SCARS ON HIS BACK

Sean's three years with Charlie changed both of them in a way. With Sean, it was more of a physical and an endurance change, but for Charlie, it was spiritual. A sense of happiness fell over him, as if he was finally doing things right by someone's standards. The guilt that once lay nestled under his face slowly disappeared throughout Sean's stay. Each lesson that he taught and physical challenge he made Sean endure sparked a fire inside him, like a man creating an invention that one day could save the world.

"Charlie?" Sean asked, taking a rest after reaching the halfway point of the lesson for the day.

"Yes, Sean?" Charlie replied, petting Rafa's head.

"Who was your teacher?"

"What do you mean?"

"You know, in fighting, like you are to me. Who taught you how to fight and defend yourself?"

Charlie cocked his head and thought of a way to answer the question.

Sipping water from the bucket, Sean waited patiently. Sean could see Charlie lost in thought, going back in time in his mind, looking for the name or face that was his teacher.

Rafa barked, pulling his friend back to reality.

"Thank you, Rafa," Charlie whispered, acknowledging the help from his long-trusted companion. Rafa turned to Sean, as if to apologize for Charlie's behavior. Charlie only spoke a single word. It wasn't a name or a place but just a simple two-letter word: "Me." That was it and nothing else. Charlie dropped his left hand over the right that gently cupped the top of his cane. He raised the only eyebrow he had, looking back at Sean and wondering why it was too hard to believe.

"How … did you just pull a technique out of thin air, and it happened to be the best one?" Sean said.

"Well, I did have some help … sort of," Charlie admitted.

"I knew it! So who was it then?" Sean asked.

"It still wasn't anybody," Charlie said.

Sean was confused, unsure of what Charlie was trying to say. Sean looked to Rafa for help, trying to see if he needed to pull back Charlie from being lost in his head again. But Rafa didn't bark or do anything at all.

Charlie nodded to himself with the answer. "My mistakes taught me." Sean still was lost by the words. Charlie loosened the straps of his clothing. First, his jacket fell to the ground, revealing a loose, tattered shirt. His thick arms had muscles that were still large and somewhat defined. The right metal hand was fully visible, and so were the scars that trailed up his arm from the surgery. Lifting the shirt that was neatly tucked into his pants, Charlie slowly turned and threw the shirt on the ground. "Each line is a reminder on how I made a mistake, either in my stance or my way of attack."

Sean's jaw dropped, seemingly almost flopping to the floor. Charlie's back was riddled with these lines. But they weren't lines at all; they were scars. Running all across his back, they slashed and piled on top of each other, like roads on a map, not leaving a single patch of natural skin.

"Every moment I left myself defenseless or whenever I missed my target, my opponent was given an opportunity to land a strike." Charlie stretched his left arm around his back and traced one of the lines with his finger. "Sometimes they would miss, but those fighters weren't skilled at all; they were rookies, fresh from the cage. That was never the case with veterans who survived several matches. They never missed their opportunity." He turned around, reaching for his shirt and jacket. His bare chest was chiseled in definition from countless push-ups and sit-ups. Scars ran across his chest as well. But Sean couldn't tell which were from the surgery by the mad doctor and which were from the battles.

Somehow and in some way, Sean broke through the wall Charlie built surrounding the topic about the place he called the Gladiator Pit.

"Was there ever a time when you thought you would lose or even die?" Sean asked.

Charlie put on his tattered shirt and the jacket again and tugged on the shoulders, making sure it was nestled back in its prior position.

"There is no losing in the Gladiator Pit. Every fight is to the death. Only twice did I ever feel I was going to die. The first came when I was dragged from my cell and thrown into the arena for the first time, fresh from the cage. With arms shaking from terror, I could barely hold my weapon. The second time …." Charlie went silent again, lost in a past Sean was sure Charlie desperately wanted to change.

Rafa turned to Sean again, cocking his head, as if to say, "You did it now." Rafa barked, just has he had before. This time it didn't work. Charlie couldn't hear him; he was too far gone. Rafa walked over and stood before Charlie, tugging his jacket with his mouth. Charlie's body rocked and began to teeter a little back and forth, until he realized he was back in High Heaven.

"The second time was when I was much older, and it would eventually be my last fight. That fight left me with … souvenirs … to remind me of my victory." Charlie tapped all the parts that weren't really him, all the parts that the doctor gave him.

"Who did that to you?" Sean asked, desperately wanting to know the one person who could have killed the unbeatable Charlie in his prime, the same Charlie who was known across the lands as The Kid for being the youngest person ever to have won a tournament in the gladiator pit. High Heaven was built with the money won from all the matches and tournaments Charlie completed. Sean had to know who was good enough to nearly have beaten the unbeatable.

"Besides Rafa … I had another friend, a good one. She and I were close." Rafa barked displeased with what Charlie said. Charlie turned to Rafa and corrected himself. "I mean we all became close." Rafa barked and wagged his tail.

"So what happened?" Sean asked.

"I won." And that was that. That was all Charlie said. Just by the tone in his voice and the way he said it, there was no mistaking that more needed to be told, but it wouldn't be. This "close friend" likely was more to Charlie than what he was indicating. His mouth might be able to hold back his feelings, but his face couldn't. The small glimmer in his eye spoke for him and told a tale that love and pain were woven together. Rafa gave a sad howl and lowered his head.

Charlie cut the lesson short for the day, asking Sean to help Amy in the garage. Sean left Charlie there, patting Rafa, both consoling each other over the sad memory of their friend.

While walking back, Sean ran what Charlie said over and over again in his head. *I won.* Sean never had heard someone say those two words with so much contempt and sadness as Charlie had just then.

Reaching the giant door, Sean grabbed its handle and twisted it with ease, thanks to his new well-earned muscles. Sean cracked it open and followed through. Before he saw Amy or even had a foot inside the garage, Sean said to himself, *Survival of the fittest. What a price to pay.*

CHAPTER 34

TAGGING ALONG

A few hours after Sean's lesson with Charlie, Rick came bursting through the garage door, calling for Sean. His bold voice pounded off the walls, overpowering the sound of tools.

Amy and Sean were working on the buggy, better equipping the frame with a sturdier and less heavy metal. The suspension was replaced, and the alignment of the buggy had been reset. The buggy was better than ever. On her personal time, Amy worked on trying to add certain defenses to the wheels and driver area in case of hostile attacks. She was in the early development stage, still drawing out the schematics on paper.

"Hey, Rick, what's up?" Sean said, still hearing Amy's banging away, lost in her work. Amy never wanted to stop fixing things. It wasn't her job anymore; it was her passion. Amy always found something to fix for Charlie or worked on creating something new from which High Heaven could prosper.

"Come with me," Rick said.

"Is everything okay?" The timing was rather inconvenient and too early to have one of his *talks* with Sean. Sean was not in the mood to play cards either.

"Everything is fine, my boy. We're just going on a trip; that's all."

Amy's tools stopped banging from the back of the buggy. She made her way around to Rick, slowly pulling off her gloves.

"The Kid thinks he may have found a location with some valuable stuff to salvage. No one knows about it besides the scouts and The Kid. He doesn't know how long it will stay that way and wants me to recover it as soon as possible, before word gets out. I want you to tag along, Sean. The Kid said it would be okay. I think it would be good for you to step outside these walls for a while. You know, it has been three years since you came back from your home."

Sean heard Rick say *home* very carefully, the way someone would mention a loved one who had passed away, not wanting to cause any tears. "Yes, I know," Sean said.

Rick's sensitivity with regard to Nova didn't work. The word still gripped Sean's heart, strangling as much life as it could. Sean swallowed down all the feelings that were crawling their way up from inside and fought back the tears. Rick's bulbous hand fell on Sean's shoulder for comfort. The hand alone weighed half as much as the backpack Sean had carried across the desert. Sean regained his composure, but three years was something he kept forgetting. Time passed without notice in High Heaven. If it weren't for Charlie and Amy wishing Sean a happy birthday, he would still think it had been only a year.

"So what do you say?" Rick asked.

Amy stared at Rick and then at Sean, waiting for the answer.

"Yeah, why not? Let's go," Sean said, placing his tools back.

Rick smiled and told Sean to pack heavy; the trip would take several days. Amy didn't say a word. She stared through Sean and watched him pack every piece of clothing without making so much as a sound.

After a few minutes, Rick came back, ready to go. He thanked Sean for tagging along. "Scavenging trips can get a bit lonely when I'm out for that amount of time," he said.

Sean nodded. "I know the feeling all too well."

"Ha, that's right, my boy. You do, don't you!" Rick laughed, patting Sean on the back. Each tap nearly sent Sean face down on the ground. "All right, let's hit the road." Rick headed for the door.

Sean looked back, wishing he could take the buggy, but there was no way that Rick could fit into it. He was twice the size of the machine and three times the size of the average man. So there was only one way they were doing this; they were going by foot.

Sean followed Rick through the door, and when they reached the middle of High Heaven, Amy came chasing after them. "Wait, Dad! Dad!" She plunged into Rick, her face buried deep into his arms, her chin just above his round belly. She shifted her head to the side, still halfway buried in him, with tears in her eyes. "You didn't say bye."

Rick always said, "See you later, princess," just before he left on a trip. This time, for some reason, he didn't.

Sean was shocked that Rick had forgotten, and judging by the expression on Rick's face, he was too.

"I'm so sorry, princess. I completely forgot." He lifted his arms and hugged her. Amy disappeared within his arms. "See you later, princess." Rick gently placed a soft kiss on her head between the dreadlocks and onto her skin.

Sean stood patiently waiting. This was a tough time for Amy. She never acted the same when Rick was gone on his trips. Each day, she barely spoke or ate. They would never spend any time outside of the garage or goof around inside it. Things only returned to normal when Rick came back through those doors.

Today would be the first of many things. Sean would find himself outside of High Heaven after three years. Rick had forgotten his special goodbye to Amy. And Amy gave Sean a hug. Sean didn't expect a single thing while waiting. Rick and Amy let go of each other, signaling Sean to get moving. He lifted the backpack onto his shoulders just as Amy shoved herself right into him. Both arms naturally fell around her, holding her securely. She didn't say single word to Sean. Sean's eyes were open wide at Rick, who smiled, happy to see the moment. The hug only lasted a few seconds before she let go and left; it was nowhere near as long as her father's, but that was okay with Sean. He could still feel her within his arms, still holding her in some way. There was a small stirring inside him. His feelings for Amy began to grow again, settling right next to Casey's.

Casey.

Sean shook the feelings away for another time. The door slammed shut, and Amy was back in the garage. Rick walked straight toward Sean, wrapping one arm around his shoulder as they walked to the front doors of High Heaven. A soldier shouted from ground level, creating a chain reaction from one soldier to another. It continued its way higher and higher until it reached all the way to the top of the tower. The last soldier shouted, and a few seconds later, the doors began to slide open. Gusts of winds whirled through the small crack of the door that slowly expanded. The sun greeted them both with blinding rays. Taking a step forward, they both lifted their hands into sky, blocking as much sun as they could. A dog's bark sounded from the right; Charlie and Rafa were waiting outside.

"Thank you for doing this," Charlie said, shaking both Sean's and Rick's hands. "I happened to come across some information regarding some goods that we can salvage." Charlie pointed southeast from their position. The sight was familiar to Sean, nothing but empty desert. "There is a landfill that's need a good picking. We might just get lucky." Charlie was referring to the blue babes he so desperately wanted.

"Anything for The Kid," Rick said. He marched ahead with ease, unaffected by the sun's rays.

"Don't worry, Charlie. We will be fine. I've tackled this desert once before, and I'm even stronger now than I ever was. We will be back in no time." Sean cocked his head, along with his ego.

"Good. I expect my training to pay off. This will be a good test of your endurance," Charlie said. Sean agreed and said goodbye. Rafa barked, lifting his paw into the air, signaling a goodbye wave. Charlie and Rafa watched over them until they disappeared into the desert, and then they went back into High Heaven.

CHAPTER 35

SOMETHING IS WRONG

Summer had ended a few weeks ago; it was well into fall. No more blistering heat to worry about, which was a godsend to Sean. The dust jacket wasn't a bother anymore. It didn't trap additional heat like it used to and became more useful against the cold nights. The trip started slowly, with nothing much to see. Both Sean and Rick tried to enjoy what little they could of the scenery, but they kept on walking. Sean stretched his arms out, breathing in the fresh air. He smiled gratefully for the opportunity to leave High Heaven for a while.

Rick stayed quiet, focused on what was ahead. He kept a steady pace while thinking about Mary. While pregnant, she worried about him just as much as Amy did. Mary gave Rick plenty of grief for scavenging over long periods at a time. He didn't know whether or not the pregnancy had anything to do with her crying when he was gone, but she did a lot of it. It became exhausting at times, forcing him to hurry for supplies and food. Rick worried about not being as careful from all the rushing he did to hurry back. Mary was a handful, but he loved her more than anything before Amy.

A day and a half later, they finally reached the landfill that Charlie mentioned. The smell was unpleasant—garbage mixed with metal, sitting under the sun for God knows how long. Without hesitation, Rick walked right through without any reaction to the smell.

"You get used to it," he said.

Sean followed with one hand covering his nose. Sean's stomach turned as they walked through the rows of garbage. Rick's eyes circled every pile, leaning his body in and out to get a better look. Several items were pulled free that appeared to be rusty pipes and chunks of metal scraps. Sean wasn't having any luck finding any blue babes, but he still kept searching. The picking lasted for a good hour, leaving them with twenty pounds of scrap metal. There wasn't a single trace of any blue babes. They carried as much as they could fit in their backpacks.

"Let's go," Rick said.

"But we just got here," Sean said, not sure what was going on.

"This place is dry. Everything here isn't special. It's a good pick for metal, but that's it. We'll let The Kid know to send more men for the rest." Rick took off his goggles, cleaning them as he went on. "I figured we still give it a try, though. We might have gotten lucky. Who knows?"

"Dammit. I was looking forward to bringing back a blue babe," Sean said.

Rick went silent but finally said, "So you know about that, huh?"

"Yeah, Amy told me what Charlie sends you out for and what the buggy can do already because of them. I can see why."

"It's true; they are extremely valuable, Sean. With enough of those babies, we can actually turn High Heaven into a real paradise. I mean, a real place to spend the rest of our lives. Electricity, warm and cold water, and who else knows what we can accomplish." Rick stared off into space, picturing the future of High Heaven in front of him. "I've been doing this for a while, so I guess you can say that I have a nose for these things. With a single glance, I can tell you if a pile or fill has been picked through. This fill was picked a long time ago. It was hard to see at first, and maybe that's why it fooled Charlie's scouts but not me. Anyway, there is a spot I saw nearby that I want to check out."

"What spot? I didn't see any spot."

"I recognized this area. I traveled across here when Amy was just a baby. See those two hills down there?" The hills that Rick pointed to were the size of coins in the distance. "If I remember correctly, there is a bit of a dip underneath, and down there might be something worth looking into."

Sean thought Rick was a little crazy. The deserts were filled with small hills that all looked the same—until thirty minutes later, they were looking down at the small dip in the land.

"Told ya," Rick said with a sly smirk. He was right. There was salvage, but it was partly buried. Strong gusts of wind pushed against their clothes, cooling their skin under the jackets. They were careful with each step toward the bottom. Scattered piles lay across the ground, half submerged. Rick nodded his head with excitement. He wasn't as glad to see the piles as much as he was to see them untouched.

There was no sign of this salvage being spotted by anyone or being touched at all. Rick and Sean split up, moving through the piles. Rick took the higher ground and picked through what he could. Sean ventured deeper toward a strange bump in the sand. A large, thick, metal piece stuck out from underneath. Sean gently tapped the metal with his fingers.

Hot.

The metal had been here a while, a long while. The sun heated it beyond tolerable levels. Sean had to open his backpack and wrap his hands with cloth to keep them safe. He carefully dusted as much sand as possible, revealing a metal corner. Swipe after swipe, the corner's edge kept trailing to the left. Following the edge, Sean took several steps to fully reveal the outline. Whatever it was, it was going to be big—even bigger than the buggy.

"Hey, I might have something here!" Sean shouted. Rick had disappeared somewhere above. Sean managed to remove enough sand to identify what was submerged underneath. A giant truck—the sand nearly swallowed it whole over time, leaving only the small back corner bumper. Sean flung handfuls of sand over his shoulder as he kept digging near the front of the truck. The driver's window slowly came forth as Sean kept scooping.

A layer of sweat covered Sean's face, forcing him to wipe his forehead and around his eyes in order to continue. Taking a few seconds to rest, Sean built enough strength and plunged his hand into the center of where the window would be. His fist pushed through the thick wall of sand hitting something stiff and soft. Sean pulled his hand back to see if it was bitten or hurt in any way; it wasn't. Continuing, Sean removed armfuls of sand, as much as he could, until a human body burst through the sand.

"*Ahhhh!*" Sean screamed, falling back. He searched for Rick, who was still gone. Sean couldn't see him anywhere. Two black holes where the eyes had been stared at him. The body leaned forward, held in place by the truck's seat belt. A name tag sewn on the chest read *Bob* in bold cursive. He was from the old world. Bob's skin had rotted away, along with segments of his clothes and hair. His brown and yellow teeth filled what was left of his jaw. Bob's hands clutched outward, trying to escape his fate. Sean covered his nose, checking the front pocket of the shirt. *Nothing.* His fingers tapped Bob's pants and found a pen and loose change. He then flipped the driver's visor down. A Polaroid picture dangled behind the mirror's corner. Sean pulled down the photo and wiped away the sand. Bob smiled back, alive and well, with his family. His twin daughters sat on his lap, with his wife behind him. Sean placed the photo back, ignoring their ugly sweaters. He moved Bob aside, reaching for the glove compartment. The truck's downward angle made it difficult. Sean leaned over on his toes, pressing against Bob's chest. Farther in, the smell worsened, Sean yanked on the rusted handle a few times before it opened. Nothing inside except for a map and dead insects.

"Whoa! Hey!" Sean shouted. His body lifted and floated backward out of the truck before dropping onto the ground. Rick stood over him, looking at Sean with dreadful eyes. "What is it? What is wrong, Rick?" He looked around for any trouble or signs why Rick was acting weird.

"We have to go," Rick said.

"What … what's going on?" Sean asked.

"There's no time to explain. Get up."

"Rick, what is—"

"Leave your backpack behind. Move!" Rick shouted.

Sean wasn't going to leave his backpack, even if Rick wanted him to. He quickly grabbed his things without saying a word and followed Rick up the hill. Rick's pace quickened nearly to a run, leaving Sean behind. The backpack flopped up and down and finally nestled on Sean's shoulders as he tightened the straps. Sean gave a final glance behind him, trying to see if anything was chasing them. There was nothing except for the desert. Sean's heart pounded within his chest, not from the running but from fear.

Rick's colossal size alone intimidated everyone he met. His strength equaled that of three men. No one would dare challenge Rick, let alone threaten him. To see him scared of something or someone should never happen, but it did. Rick turned white as ghost in front of Sean. Whatever had Rick running was more than just dangerous; it was death.

CHAPTER 36

LISTENING IN

Out of breath, Sean collapsed to the ground and couldn't continue. Rick hadn't stopped running since leaving the landfill, and it was three hours into nightfall. Gripping the canister of water, Sean swallowed the remaining mouthful.

"We need to stop!" Sean yelled.

Rick continued running as if Sean was still right behind him. He turned and looked, disappointed, almost angry for stopping. They hadn't said a word to each other since they left.

"We can't stop; we need to get back to High Heaven as soon as possible," Rick said.

"Why? What are you afraid of?"

Rick didn't respond. He struggled to explain why he was scared. "Sean, we just need to get to High Heaven. We are in danger."

Danger? Danger from what? Sean's mouth was dry again, wanting more water, but he had carelessly used it all. The landfill added fifty pounds of scrap metal to his back. Sean's legs were sore and extremely tired. The soles of his feet ached with every step. Rick didn't want to stop to rest before High Heaven, but Sean had to.

"Okay, go ahead; I'll meet you there tomorrow. I need to rest. My legs are killing me."

Rick gave a heavy sigh of acceptance of what needed to be done. He nodded at Sean, who waited for Rick to leave him behind but didn't. Rick shrugged the backpack off his shoulders and sat on the ground with his legs crossed.

"We'll make camp here, but we leave first thing at sunrise. Agreed?"

There was no room for debate on this one. He was at least letting Sean rest, and Sean didn't dare ask for more time. "Yes, thanks. You want first watch, or should I take it?" Sean asked.

"No, I'll take first watch, and I'll wake you when it's your turn."

Sean was amazed that Rick wasn't even tired or slightly fatigued. Maybe it was the fear that was pushing him this far. Sean still couldn't grasp the idea that Rick was actually scared of something. It was completely unnatural, like a cat being afraid of a mouse. Sean laid the backpack down sideways and used it as a pillow. A giant blanket of relief fell over him as the running ended. They left a trail of footprints across the sand twenty miles long without stopping. Lying down with his eyes closed, Sean could still feel his feet moving. Before Sean could even get comfortable, he had already fallen asleep.

Rick tapped Sean on the foot, waking him. Sean rolled over onto his knees and wiped the sleep from his eyes. He was ready to stand watch, but it was morning. Rick had stood watch all the through the night. His eyes were bloodshot, and his body finally showed signs of fatigue.

"Why didn't you wake me last night?" Sean asked.

"Never mind that; just pack your things, and let's get going."

Sean did as he was told, and they quickly headed for High Heaven. The good news was that they had run most of the way yesterday. The bad news, though, was that Rick was tired and in no shape to defend himself. Without even asking, Sean knew they were going to walk the rest of the way. High Heaven was still fifteen miles away. Both Sean and Rick continued on, but there was no talking. Sean's legs were still sore, but they arrived in High Heaven in one piece. The doors split open, and both walked in. Sean could only imagine how they looked to everyone. Everyone was shocked to see them so early and then it turned to worry, as Rick and Sean barely could stand.

A crowd began to surround them, following their every move. Sean was glad to be home and wanted to find out what had Rick so spooked over at the landfill. Strands of red dreadlocks pushed through the crowd. Shoulder to shoulder, no one noticed Amy pushing them aside.

"Hi, Amy," Sean said.

"What happened? Why did you guys come back so early? It usually takes longer than this."

Sean shifted his eyes toward Rick's, which were telling him to stay quiet. Sean agreed that worrying Amy wouldn't help in any way.

"Nothing happened; the place had been picked clean. There was hardly anything more to be salvaged." Before she could ask another question,

Sean began to answer it. "Your dad wanted to get home as soon as possible, so we hurried back."

Amy let go of Sean's hands, which he didn't even noticed she was holding. "Dad? Is everything okay?" Amy looked over at Rick.

At least Sean hadn't lied to her, and he wasn't going to start any time soon. Rick wrapped his arm around Amy, and she disappeared under him again. They walked through together, with Sean following closely behind.

"No worries, princess. I just wanted to get back. I had a bad feeling about something, and it really might be nothing at all. I missed you so much," Rick said carefully.

Sean lowered his eyes and focused on carrying the heavy backpack. Up ahead, Charlie stood over the balcony with his hands on the railing, watching them with deep curiosity. Rick might be able to dodge and avoid certain truths with Amy, but Charlie would see through it and pull it out of him. It wouldn't matter, though. Sean felt Rick wanted to tell Charlie what he saw anyway. Sean continued to follow Rick and Amy toward the garage. He would keep everything predictable.

He would unpack his things, make his bed, eat some food, and look even more tired than he was. The plan was to sneak to Charlie's door and listen to what Rick had to say. For the next two hours, Rick and Sean ate a big meal with Amy and finished unpacking. Amy left to help clean the dishes as Sean lay on his bed. He angled himself to have full view of the stairs. When Rick crept up the stairs, closing Charlie's door behind him, Sean quickly followed, checking for anyone on the second floor. No one was around to see Sean as he listened in.

"Are you sure that is what you saw?" Charlie's voice was filled with concern.

"Yes, I found them all over the landfill. We were lucky it wasn't around, or we might have been dead before we could even leave," Rick said.

"Does Sean know?" Charlie asked.

"No, I didn't tell him what I saw, but he knows I'm scared of something."

"That's fine; it's better if he doesn't know. Anyway, it's probably long gone by now."

There was a sniff near the door and then a soft bark. Rafa's paw pressed against the steel door and scratched away at it. He smelled Sean's scent, soaking with sweat. Rick and Charlie stopped talking. Sean had to leave and was sure that one of them would open the door. Leaping down the stairs, Sean made his way back to bed as quickly and quietly as possible. He glanced over his shoulder; the door was still shut when he entered the garage.

Plopping onto the bed, Sean nestled in, tossing the blanket over him.

He plunged his face into the pillow, frustrated with Rafa. He was so close to finding out what had happened. *What were they talking about?* If only he had been there a few seconds longer or earlier, the answer would be twirling around his head by now. A heavy yawn unexpectedly came over him; he was still tired from today. Maybe a nap would shut up his tired muscles for a while. Sean fell asleep, but not before saying to himself, *That damn dog.*

CHAPTER 37

SOMETHING WICKED THIS WAY COMES

creams.

Sean awakened to screams and shouts. Bells rang across High Heaven as he heard the sound of footsteps running outside the garage. *What the hell is going on?* Sean jumped out of bed and propped the door opened. He could see a giant crowd in the middle of High Heaven, like the one that greeted them earlier for returning so unexpectedly.

Soldiers ran past, shouting about the front gate. Then another scream came, but it wasn't of fright. This was worse; it was of a man dying. High Heaven was under attack.

Dragus!

It had to be Dragus. He must have found Sean like he had found the other soldiers that were hired to kill him. Now, it was Sean's turn to be beheaded and placed on a spike. Sean might end up dying, but he was going to do it fighting, like Junior, like the others. Rushing toward the gate, Sean searched for Charlie, who he knew would be fighting with Rafa, along with the soldiers. A loud bang came from behind the door, leaving a dent in the wall. Something was pushing its way through.

My God! Dragus is strong.

Guards shouted from the watchtower and began to climb down. More soldiers ran past Sean, carrying staffs and swords made of metal. The door shook again, bending back. It couldn't take much more. Dragus was coming. His people were about to enter and begin slaughtering like they did in Nova. A sword pressed against Sean's chest, held by a soldier. It was Willie, one of Charlie's men from the first day of Sean's training.

"Here, take this; you're going to need it," he said.

"Thanks," Sean replied. The long metal blade shined in his hands. He had practiced with one like it countless of times. It was now a natural extension of his arm. That's what Charlie wanted Sean to achieve, for it to feel as if it was a part of him. With a final push, the door burst open, and the open desert was in wide view. Dawn had recently passed, leaving the sun peeking out behind the far horizon. Sean hesitated, unsure of what was going on. There was no clan, no rushing mob wielding spikes and blades, ready to slaughter them. There was no Dragus.

How's that possible?

All the soldiers stood still, with their weapons drawn and their stances ready. Their eyes focused on the nothing that was before them. Each arm held a blade firmly and without fear. Charlie's leadership and their undying loyalty to him provided a shield of great confidence over them. Not a single soldier showed any type of hesitation or act of cowardice. They were ready to die for Charlie, no matter how brutal or inevitable the outcome would be.

"It's broken through!" the guard shouted from the watchtower above. That didn't make any sense because there was nothing there at all. Then a yellow eye appeared, floating in the air. Within an instant, it vanished, and there was the open desert again, staring back in everyone's faces. Sean's heart sank down to the blackest depth of his soul, far below his very feet, and deep into the ground. The air around him grew cold as his breath shortened.

Oh, no.

Something was there, pounding at the door, and it had broken through. It may not have been Dragus himself, but it was just as bad. It was a mimic. Sheer terror burned through Sean's veins, taking any movement away. The sword stood still at his side, not lifting at all, not wanting to defend or attack. Whatever power of invisibility the mimic could control disappeared, revealing its size. Any pride Sean had of surviving a mimic disappeared along with its coat of invisibility. He realized that the mimic that attacked him at the fire wasn't a true mimic at all. It was only a mere pup. That was nothing compared to what came through the door. A monstrous demon, the mimic's black fur towered over all the men.

The paws could cover an entire man's upper body easily. The massive frame would need twenty men to hold it down. Jagged, sharp teeth opened wide, dripping with the blood of the fallen soldier Sean heard screaming earlier. It turned and faced Sean, recognizing him as Sean did it. The scar over its missing eye was a reminder of their encounter on that dreadful night. Now there would be a rematch between it and Sean, but this time it was fully grown.

CHAPTER 38

THE REMATCH

Face-to-face, Sean found the strength to raise his weapon. The mimic's jaws spread wide, growling toward him. Sean widened his stance and prepared to attack. With all his strength, Sean charged forward, screaming. All the soldiers began their attack as well, slashing and plunging their weapons into the mimic. They surrounded it, cutting off Sean's way of attack. The air filled with more screams as bodies began to fly and were ripped opened by the mimic. Blood splattered across the sky, walls, and onto faces. Sean jerked backward as he was pulled back by someone.

"This is not your fight. We need to get to a safe place." Rick stood behind Sean, not taking his eyes off the mimic.

"No! I have to help the guards!" Sean shouted.

"They can handle themselves. We need to leave," Rick said.

"I'm not going to let them die." Sean tried to pull free from Rick.

Rick grabbed Sean by the other arm and looked him in the eye. The fighting and the screams were behind them. "You promised me, remember? You better not break it." Rick was referring to the promise of looking after Amy if anything happened to him. Sean nodded as they ran toward the back, near the garage. Amy cracked opened the garage door and peeked from inside. "I had Amy gather your things; we are leaving as soon as we can."

Amy waved at them to move faster. She quickly slammed the door shut as soon as they got inside.

"How are we going to get out, Dad? We all can't fit in the buggy, and its twelve hours 'til sunrise."

"By then, there will be nothing left of High Heaven," Sean said.

Amy looked away, quivering at the sounds of dying men.

"We will have to go by foot," Sean insisted, "and head north behind these walls. If we head south, it will see us. Even if we made it out, we don't have enough food to survive. We don't stand a chance with outrunning it either. I'm sorry, but we have to fight." Sean looked to Rick, hoping he would agree or have a better plan. They didn't have much time to think things over either. More screams were coming from outside the walls. "The only way to make sure we can survive this is to kill that damn thing for good this time." Sean cracked opened the door and readied himself for the mimic.

Black leather gloves grabbed his throat, squeezing out all the air. "You killed us all. Your scent drove it mad, and it finally found you. It won't stop until you're dead." Rufus's blue eyes filled with rage as his grip tightened even more. "So I will give it what it wants to save my people."

Sean had been no match for Rufus when he first entered High Heaven. But now, Sean surpassed him in technique and in strength. Sean swung his arm as Rufus leaned back, defending his face, but that wasn't what Sean aimed for. Rather, he came crashing down on Rufus's arm, breaking the grip he had around his throat. Rufus retaliated with a straight punch, dead aimed for Sean, but that was countered with a block and a kick into the shin. Rufus fell on his knee, staring up at Sean, who landed a punch square on his jaw.

"What the hell are you talking about? I had no idea it was following me," Sean said, still keeping his hands up, ready for more fighting.

Rufus wiped a small amount of blood away from his lip and spoke down to Sean, even while lying on the floor, defeated. "You stupid fool; the stories are true. If a mimic tastes the blood of its victim and it doesn't kill it, it will go insane searching for it until it finds it. You survived it before, and now, for three years it searched for you across this desert until it finally found you. I warned Charlie about this, but he didn't believe me. It's all your fault that my people are dying."

It all made sense now. The tracks that Rick mentioned to Charlie were that of a mimic. That's why he was so scared. A mimic would be the only thing that could threaten Rick. And that day had strong gusts of wind that greeted their every move. It must have carried Sean's scent across the desert. That was how it found them.

"It's true." Charlie appeared from behind Rufus. "But it is not your fault; it's mine. I didn't think the stories were true." Charlie lifted Rufus to his feet. Rufus readjusted his clothing before thanking Charlie. Charlie's eye beamed bright as he threw Rufus against the wall like a rag doll. "I will deal with you later. Go now, and help my men!"

Rufus ran out the door without saying a word.

"Charlie ..." Sean said.

"There's no more time. We need to get everyone out of here. Listen to me; we will gather everyone we can and head through the back. I have a few soldiers waiting for us outside. Once we've saved all we can, then we will deal with the mimic. I have a plan."

Everyone followed Charlie to a small hole that he broke open in the back of High Heaven. They escorted as many of the people as they could who had hidden in their homes. The soldiers were buying them time but at a great cost. One by one, they slowly were being picked off and ripped apart.

Charlie successfully escorted two-thirds of High Heaven out to safety, and the other third were his men, keeping the mimic busy. Sean returned after saving the last resident he could. He watched Rufus fly through the air, landing on his back. He'd caught a vicious hit by the mimic and lay there on the ground, holding his arm. Writhing in pain, he stared back at the mimic, not giving up. His sword lay flat on the ground next to him. The mimic ignored the other soldiers and focused on Rufus, ready for a finishing attack. Sean ran toward him, waving his arms in the air, breaking the mimic's attention.

Roaring with anger, it found Sean again and released an uncontrollable rage from inside. It spared Rufus and charged straight for Sean. Sean dodged the razor-sharp claws and swung his blade at its mouth, locking the sword with its teeth in a stalemate. With both of Sean's hands holding on for dear life, its mouth was merely inches away from devouring the upper half of Sean's body. Saliva poured onto Sean, soaking his clothes. The breath of the beast smelled of hundreds of its fallen victims.

"Sean!" Rick's voice followed after him. Sean could feel Rick's heavy feet come closer, and he hoped Rick could deliver the killing blow to the mimic and save everyone, including him. But Rick didn't have a weapon. Sean watched Rick rush toward the beast and jump onto its back, wrapping his heavy arms around its neck, squeezing as hard as he could. Any man would have been crushed by Rick's sheer size and strength. "Don't worry. I got him!" Rick shouted. The mimic paid no attention to Rick or to the loss of air to its lungs. It was dead-set on killing Sean more than anything in the world, even breathing.

"I know you will keep your promise, Sean. Take care of Amy for me!" Rick shouted as the mimic finally accepted the fact of needing air and let Sean go. Sean ran over, grabbing Rufus off the ground. Rick swirled around in the air as the mimic tried to buck off its choker, but Rick still held on. He was actually doing it. The mimic was choking to death. Sean told Rufus to head toward the back with the others.

Charlie shouted at Sean from the stairs. "C'mon, Sean! Rick will be fine!"

Sean headed over, asking Charlie about his plan for dealing with the mimic if Rick failed. He led Sean to the secret passage he made while building High Heaven. They walked inside, and Sean recognized what it was—a fallout shelter, like the ones used before Nova. Rafa greeted them from inside, as Charlie had locked him in there for safety. There were items everywhere, pictures of a man and a woman.

Charlie's parents.

The pictures showed them hugging each other, smiling, blowing birthday candles, posing at special landmarks, and even with a mountain that had faces on them.

"What is this place?" Sean asked.

"My home," Charlie said, facing a set of stairs that led to the ceiling.

"Yeah, I know High Heaven is your home. I meant what is—"

"No, I mean this is my real home," Charlie interrupted, still not turning around. "My dad built this very shelter in the backyard for when the bombs fell. My house was destroyed, and nothing was left of my neighborhood. But I found this room when I came back many years later. So I built High Heaven exactly on top of where my home used to be." Charlie turned around. "Sean, you are ready now, and after this, you will need to go find Dragus." His red eye glowed brighter with every word. "There is a place to the northeast of here, a terrible, terrible place. And there you will meet a man named Marcus." Charlie grabbed both of Sean's arms, just as Rick had done before. "You cannot trust him, Sean! He will help you find Dragus but only if it will help him. He tells lies with the truth and will show you terrible things."

Charlie let Sean go and headed for the double doors on the ceiling. He climbed the stairs and slid the lock open. Charlie gestured for Sean to help him push. Mountains of sand and dirt tossed into the air as Sean found himself in the middle of High Heaven. The mimic roared, still alive, fighting the remaining soldiers, but Rick was missing.

No, no, no, don't let this happen! Sean scanned dozens of corpses that spread throughout the battlefield. His eyes stopped on a large mangled body on the floor, a body that was three times that of regular man. It stared back at Sean, not moving or breathing. *Rick.*

"Sean, look out!" Charlie screamed as he saw the mimic rush toward him, lunging straight for the fallout shelter. Sean would have been swallowed whole, had Charlie not pulled him out of the way in the nick of time. The mimic's body slid across the floor, banging against the wall, knocking shelves, pictures, and books over. Its raged-filled yellow eye fell upon Charlie. Charlie got into his fighting stance and readied himself. Before the mimic could attack, Rafa leaped forward, protecting his best friend.

"Rafa, no!" Charlie shouted. But it was too late. Rafa paid no attention to the command and instinct took over. He was doing what he was born to do—protect Charlie, his best friend, at all costs. Barks and yelps filled the room as the two beasts dueled. Rafa was no match for the mimic; he could only buy time for Charlie to escape.

"Lock the doors, and we'll trap the mimic in here!" Sean grabbed Charlie's shoulder and tugged him up the stairs.

Charlie resisted. "Take this, Sean." Charlie shoved a solid gold key into Sean's hands. "It's the key to High Heaven. She is yours now; take good care of her for me."

"Charlie, let's go!" Sean screamed, tugging and trying to pull him up the stairs.

"No! Where Rafa goes, I go!" There was no convincing Charlie. All the white parts of Rafa's fur were covered in blood. He was losing, but Charlie was still in danger, so Rafa continued fighting the best he could. "Please forgive me, Sean. One day you will learn a terrible truth that I have not told you."

"What the hell are you talking about, Charlie?" Sean said.

"I didn't know, Sean. I am so sorry," Charlie said, lowering his face in shame.

"I can save you. C'mon!" Sean shouted.

"You already have, Sean. Remember about Marcus. He is never to be trusted."

"What if I can't convince him to help me?" Sean said.

Charlie took a second and then shouted, "Win the crowd, Sean, and you will win Marcus! Now go!" Charlie pushed Sean away.

Running to the top of the stairs, Sean turned around. Charlie stood between the mimic and him, not letting anything pass. The mimic took a final swallow, moving Rafa's body from its mouth to its stomach. Charlie twisted his cane in a specific order, popping the head, revealing a red button underneath.

"Charlie!" Sean screamed again, but he didn't reply.

Charlie's eyes were fixated on the stomach of the great beast. Somewhere inside was his best friend. Charlie's metal finger pressed the button, triggering Rafa's body to glow with a pulsating light.

"I taught my best friend a new trick," Charlie said to the mimic, watching it turn to him. Mouth open and dripping with Rafa's blood, it pounced, taking Charlie right off the ground and shaking him violently in its teeth. Charlie screamed in pain, stabbing and punching whatever he could. The sharp, jagged teeth ripped Charlie's skin and scraped the metal. Blood and oil spewed in all direction, marking the walls and floor.

Charlie gave a loud shout, not in pain but in pride, a pride that takes nearly a century to earn, a century of seeing the happiest days and the worst of days together at each other's side. He raised Rafa, and Rafa raised him. There was only one way this journey was going to end. He and Rafa were going to die together. Fate would have it no other way.

"That's my boy!" Charlie shouted, with tears falling down his face. Rafa's pulsating glow increased faster and faster until it held a constant beam inside the mimic's stomach. A soft hum surged through the air, growing louder as Sean tried slamming the double doors as fast as he could. Past memories flashed across Charlie's eye. He watched a younger Rafa chase after his toy. The trees were still green, and the birds chirped in the sky. His dad looked through the Super 8, holding hands with his mom. She waved, giving Charlie her lost smile. Charlie smiled and closed his eyes. The doors slammed shut for a half second before a deafening explosion sent them flying off their hinges, taking Sean with it. The explosion burst through the shelter's ceiling and into High Heaven, sending giant boulders of sand and dirt toward the sky. For a moment, Sean floated in the air, defying gravity.

Without any control, Sean was at the mercy of the explosion. Even his very thoughts were out of reach, except for one. It wasn't death that crossed his mind, gripping him, forcing Sean to accept the idea of not surviving. No, the thought came with a devastating realization and a feeling Sean hadn't felt in three years. It was the same feeling of heartache that surged through him when Nova was destroyed, ripping all the happiness from his very core. All Sean could think of was that Charlie was dead. The very heart of High Heaven was gone.

CHAPTER 39

AFTERMATH

Sean crashed onto the ground, with the three-inch metal door following on top of him as he held the handle for dear life. Flames and smoke flew past Sean, dispersing into the air and then disappearing slowly afterward. Screams of chaos and panic came as soft whispers to him. Blood trickled from his ears as they pulsated in pain.

Charlie

The heavy door slowly slid off him, taking with it every amount of strength Sean had left. Halfway off his body, the door still pinned Sean underneath it. Sean shouted for help, but that too sounded as a whisper.

The ringing.

The loud, constant ringing filled his ears and head. All he could do was lie back down and wait until his strength returned.

Footsteps.

Sean felt footsteps pound the ground, running toward him. It was Willie. He was covered in sweat, blood, and dirt. Sean was shocked to see him still alive. The mimic had killed so many before following him and Charlie into the cellar. Willie tapped Sean's shoulder, and he knelt beside him. Blood trailed down his arm and dripped rapidly on the floor. The mimic left a deep scratch from his bicep to his wrist. Willie spoke, but no words came out. Sean tried to focus, ignoring the ringing in his head. Willie waited for a response and then spoke slowly again, moving his mouth, pronouncing every syllable thoroughly.

"Are you okay?" he asked.

"Yeah," Sean said.

Willie moved, positioning his shoulder under the door. Sean inhaled, trying to summon whatever strength he had left. When ready, Sean gave a nod and read Willie's lips.

"Push!" he mouthed.

Sean pushed as hard as he could. The door shifted, moving past his waist, down to his knees. After two more attempts, Sean was free at last. Willie helped Sean to his feet, happy to see he didn't sustain any serious injuries. Sean insisted that Willie should find the others outside to get his wounds treated.

High Heaven.

There was hardly anything left. The explosion collapsed the stairs to the second floor. The marketplace was completely destroyed. None of the stands remained. They were knocked over and crushed. Dead soldiers lay covered in their blood. Sean stepped toward Charlie's shelter. He looked inside, praying that he somehow lived. Everything was pitch black, burned from the explosion. Mimic blood stained the floor and walls blue. There wasn't a single trace of anything that resembled a mimic's body, Rafa, or even Charlie. Sean turned away, not wanting to look anymore. To the far corner, Sean noticed a body lying face down. Sean couldn't believe he'd forgotten. Everything happened so fast that he didn't remember.

Oh, no.

Sean ran as fast as he could, falling to his knees besides the body. "Rick … Rick …" Shaking him, Sean hoped it would snap him awake. He still didn't move. His giant frame rolled as Sean pressed his weight, trying to lift him. Rick stared back at Sean. Sean wiped the blood off of Rick's face, cradling him in his arms. He waited for Rick to give him the "I'm okay" smile. There was none. His face lay frozen in pain. Four giant claw marks trailed from his neck, having severed an artery, and down across his belly. The wounds were beyond fatal; even if Rick was still alive, it wouldn't be for long. Sean lowered his head, touching cheek to cheek as he wept over Rick. Rick saved his life without hesitation.

"Thank you, Rick," Sean said. If it weren't for him, Rick would have been turning him over and seeing Sean's face frozen in pain. Charlie as well; they all had. High Heaven saved his life at one time or another. Sean just didn't owe it to Charlie to rebuild High Heaven; he owed everyone who lived there too. They were his responsibility now, an oath he must fulfill. "I promise to take care of Amy," Sean whispered, so Rick could rest in peace.

Sean walked back through the hole where everyone had escaped. They all stood huddled near each other, waiting for more to follow behind. Rufus, Amy, Willie, and the rest waited for Sean to say something. Sean looked at everyone, their faces still trying to comprehend the terror that had happened. In that very moment, Sean would say the worst news they could ever expect. Looking down, Sean couldn't even bear to look them in the eyes. He gave a heavy sigh and softly spoke.

"I'm the only one left."

Gasps, moans, and shouts of *no* rained among them. Then cries of pain and anguish began flooding tears down their faces. Amy struggled to step closer to the hole. She wanted to see her father, but Sean grabbed her arm, not letting her in. "You don't one to see him this way," Sean said.

Amy shook her head in disbelief and collapsed into his arms. Her tears poured relentlessly down her face. Sean squeezed her tight, not saying a word. He couldn't, there was nothing to say that could make the pain go away.

Sean watched everyone cry in anger, refusing to accept the news. Now they held each other for comfort. Sean's vision blurred as the tears soaked his eyes. Amy tugged and pulled on Sean's shirt in anger. Her screams were muffled by his arms. He rested his head on Amy's soft hair, hugging her without end. Rufus, Willie, and the rest of the surviving guards cried for their fallen soldiers, their brothers in arms. Amy cried for her dad. The crowd cried for their loved ones who died fighting and especially for Charlie. As for Sean … he cried for everyone.

CHAPTER 40

SEPARATE WAYS

C louds passed overhead, leaving the sun alone. Amy was still shaking, not saying a word. Her hands repeatedly wiped away more tears from her eyes. Everyone waited in silence to hear what came next.

"What do we do?" a gray-haired woman shouted from inside the crowd.

"Yeah! Where do we go?" a man shouted from behind.

The soldiers turned to Rufus for orders as he pondered the idea. The danger was over; the mimic was dead because of Charlie and Rafa. Would they go back to High Heaven, or would they leave and try to find new shelter elsewhere? It was a question Sean waited for Rufus to answer. Their shouts roared across the soldiers, demanding an answer.

"Please! Please, everyone, calm down," Rufus said, raising both hands slowly and waving them in the air. The crowd noise soothed to a low murmur. "I know everyone is still shaken up; we all are. So let's just slowly relax so we can think about what to do next." For several minutes, Rufus talked among his men and threw around ideas on what they could possibly do. An elderly woman approached, offering Amy the last bowl of food she had left. Amy shook her head and walked away.

"To the north!" Rufus shouted out. Amy and Sean looked up toward Rufus, who stood with confidence. "There is a small refuge where merchants gather and stop to trade. Over there we can find food and trade for supplies. I don't know how long we can stay there, but we can at least buy ourselves a couple of days."

Amy walked over to Rufus, clenching her fists. "Why can't we stay in

High Heaven?" "It's stupi—" Rufus stopped to clear his throat. His blue eyes glared at her but soon calmed as he noticed Sean closely watching what he was about to stay. "It would be a bad idea to stay here. We can't defend such an area after sustaining such losses. We need a neutral area, where we won't be attacked. The merchants in the north have their own guards to help defend. We'll be safe there. Besides, a lot of people here might be uncomfortable sleeping near the ..."

"The dead!" Amy yelled, in tears. "With my dead father in there!"

Sean wrapped his arm around her, ending the conversation, allowing Rufus to continue.

"My men and I will gather all the food and any goods we can trade to keep ourselves well fed." The crowd grew quiet, watching Rufus pace back and forth. "We will need to carry our share of weight, and understand that if you have any valuables, it will be up to you to carry them, along with your share of food and supplies."

Cries of outrage and anger stirred, but it was understandable. It was a tough decision but indeed a necessity. They were being told to haul heavy loads of weight across the desert. If anyone knew how difficult it could be, it was Sean. He agreed with Rufus's plan but wasn't happy about it.

"I need to grab a few things," Amy said, whimpering in Sean's ear.

"Okay. Me too," he said. The crowd reentered High Heaven, one by one, not making a sound, as if trying to avoid being heard by the already dead mimic. Amy and Sean stood thirty feet from Rick's body. His grip tightened around her.

I'm sorry, Rick. I know you don't want her to see you this way. I wouldn't want her to see me like that either.

Amy resisted Sean, wanting to reach for her dad. Sean guided her though the garage door. They gathered the bags that were prepared earlier and any extra metal that could be valuable. Sean wasn't going to tag along, so he gave Amy everything she could use to trade. Sean made a promise to Rick, but Dragus came first, before anything. Back outside, Amy stood close, still sobbing, with sore red eyes, almost as red as her hair.

"I need to talk to Rufus for a minute or two. I'll be right back," Sean said. Amy nodded, rubbing her throbbing eyes. Rufus watched each step Sean took closer to him. Sean's feet sunk in the sand, and he looked straight into Rufus's eyes. There was an uncomfortable silence between them. Rufus was the first one to speak. Sean knew Rufus was going to thank him for saving his life.

"I just want to say—"

"I know," Sean said. They both didn't want to say any more. Sean didn't want to dwell on it any longer for fear it would turn into regret. "You know I can't com—"

"I know," Rufus said. He wasn't stupid, and word got around that Charlie was training Sean to leave soon before the attack. Sean sighed as he turned to look at Amy, who waited for him.

"I expect you to watch over Amy and make sure nothing happens to her," Sean said.

"I will." Rufus nodded.

Sean left Rufus there and took him at his word. Normally, he wouldn't believe him, but Rufus owed Sean his life. Rufus would rather pay Sean back through someone else than return the favor directly. Sean walked away, knowing Amy would be safe until he returned after killing Dragus. Sean's journey was far from over; the road ahead held a long path. If Sean did kill Dragus without dying in the process, he would have another promise to keep. Sean could only hope that he would keep his word. If not, Sean would have to answer Rick in the afterlife. Heaven or hell, he knew Rick would find him. Grabbing Amy's hand, Sean looked at her with guilt.

"You're leaving me too, aren't you?" she said.

"Yes." Sean wouldn't lie to her. He wouldn't ever lie to her.

Her green eyes sparkled under the tears. She squeezed Sean's hands tightly, and she gently tugged for him to follow. "C'mon, then. You're going to need the buggy."

The blue babes gleamed with joy, excited to head outside. With all the other projects that needed fixing or building, the buggy was often left unused and pushed aside. Sean missed the joyrides and the wind across his face. Now he would have that again for a short while.

"So you got everything you need, right?" she asked. He gave her a nod. "Remember to take it easy on the suspension." He nodded again. "Bring her back in one piece."

Sean quietly thought how hard that was going to be. He didn't know anything about the Gladiator Pit, so he prepared for the worst. A giant beam of light crawled across the floor, making its way up Sean's leg and onto his face.

Amy lifted the garage door and waited for Sean to return from his thoughts. "Help me push," she said.

The buggy shifted slightly as it leaned forward and rolled outside. Sean felt the heat rise from the ground, as the sand was hotter than the air around him. They waited in silence as time grew closer before the lights turned green. They glanced at each other while they waited. Amy longed for Sean to change his mind, but he wasn't going to. Green lights flickered, breaking the silence, as Amy reached out, holding Sean's hand.

"Be careful." She pulled him close, kissing him on the lips. A warm blur of buried emotions spilled from Sean's heart through his lips. He couldn't stop kissing Amy, and the kisses became longer and more passionate. Their arms locked around each other, not wanting to let go. Sean's hands moved along her body, feeling every curve. The last kiss ended with his hand pressed against her dreadlocks, holding her closer to him.

"Now go." Amy pushed Sean toward the buggy and watched him jump in. She double-checked all the supplies and made sure that they were all safely secured.

Sean turned the ignition and felt the buggy shake with power. He looked over his shoulder, not knowing when he would see Amy again. He hoped it would be soon, while his heart hoped it would be sooner. Slamming the pedal down, the tires spun, kicking dirt and sand, turning it into a thick, massive cloud.

Amy waved, deciding not to say goodbye. The words were too much for her. She had lost her father, and where Sean was headed, she might lose him too.

CHAPTER 41

RIDE

Northeast—that was where Charlie told Sean to go. Tires sped through the desert as he checked the compass to confirm his direction. Sean drove for hours and still saw nothing. He lifted a canteen, taking the final swig. Out here, he had time to think, time to heal a big wound in his heart. The faces returned, fighting back, but Sean kept them down, deep into the abyss. One at a time, Sean let one of the faces emerge into his thoughts, and he began to tear.

Sean went through all the faces he'd lost in Nova and now was on Charlie's when a small hump in sand caught his eye. This wasn't a normal hill as he'd seen before.

An entrance? The gladiator pit? Unsure whether or not he'd arrived, Sean eased his foot off the throttle. The buggy slowed to a stop, humming with power. Sean turned off the engine and jumped out. Walking over, the small hump grew larger as the sand dipped farther down. It was a small cave, barely large enough for a family. Sean lowered himself inside and stepped farther in. A crack sounded at his feet. He lifted them to find he'd stepped on bones. Examining closely, Sean feared they were human, but they belonged to an animal. A mountain lion, Sean was certain.

The cave must have been its home before the food ran out. Sean checked his surroundings; the whole area was barren. He didn't even think sand could survive out here. He chuckled at the fact. Eyeing its size, Sean thought of an idea.

The buggy! It was perfect. The hill was barely noticeable from view, and with a little help, it could almost be invisible. Amy kept a large tarp that she used on the buggy while working on other projects to protect it from spills, damage, and other debris. Sean ran back, searching the buggy high and low, until he pulled the tarp from under a few supplies.

Yes! Beige—the color wasn't perfect, but it was pretty damn close. Sean started the buggy and slowly entered the cave. About halfway in, he jumped out and shut off the engine. He pushed the rest in and looked around for what he could hang the tarp with. The walls around him weren't soft; some had a few jagged curves, enough to puncture the tarp. Near the back of the driver's seat was an emergency kit that Rick had installed, just in case something broke down on the buggy that needed to be fixed.

Sean searched inside for any heavy-duty tape. There was none. But he did find electrical tape, enough to fasten the tarp the securely. After an hour, Sean had perfectly hid the buggy from any unwanted guests. Before sealing the tarp all the way, he grabbed all the supplies he was willing to carry, especially the food. Sean had to make Marcus believe he stumbled across the gladiator pit while walking the desert. If he showed up without any food, water, or supplies to trade with, Marcus would know something was wrong. Sean didn't want Marcus to know of any connections with High Heaven and him.

Charlie had told Sean not to trust Marcus, and he sure as hell wasn't going to. Sean took a few extra minutes to erase any signs of tire tracks around the hill. After being sure no one could possibly know anything was near, Sean was ready for the worst part of his plan—the walking.

Alone walking the endless desert, Sean found himself as he had been when first leaving Nova. Back then, he wasn't as strong as he was now. There was plenty of daylight left, giving him time to reflect again. The faces returned and continued on with Rafa, Rick, and the rest of High Heaven. He had lost so many people on this journey, but he wouldn't give up. He would see Dragus dead at all costs. Dragus had to pay for what he did. Sean was going to do whatever it took to avenge them all.

Far ahead, a metal spike peeked from the horizon and grew taller with each passing step. Closer and closer, a heap of strategically placed metal formed an image of what Sean had seen in one of Mr. Davis's books. His eyes stared at a sickening yet marvelous sight. In the old world, the Gladiator Pit would have been a horrible accomplishment, impressing no one. But in the new world, the Gladiator Pit was magnificent; a symbol of power. Sean stared at a massive coliseum. It replicated pictures inside Mr. Davis's book titled *Roman Architecture and Engineering.*

Just like High Heaven, pieces of cars, pipes, signs, and anything worth salvaging was used to build the coliseum. Without a doubt, the Gladiator

Pit easily was five times the size of High Heaven. Sean approached the entrance, examining its massive doors. In no way could the mimic break through this one. Sean heart's pounded. What hid behind those doors scared Sean, forcing the hairs on his neck to stand on end. Charlie hated the Gladiator Pit, and he hated talking about it even more. Sean couldn't help but reflect on Charlie's death. He was gone, dead with all the others. They were all gone, taken from him, but he still had piece of them:

Mom—the rings he wore around his neck.

Dad—the pocket watch in his jacket.

Casey—the bracelet of hair wrapped around his wrist.

Bad Boy Bill—the button on his jacket.

Junior—the two playing cards tucked away in his pocket.

Charlie—the golden key stashed away in the backpack.

Sean had finished the first step of his journey by completing Charlie's training. Now the next one was here, at the Gladiator Pit. There would be only one more after that. The last step would be face-to-face with Dragus. As Sean softly rubbed the rings on his necklace, a gust of wind lifted the sand, swirling it around him. The ends of his jacket lifted and flapped in the air. Sean stared at the Gladiator Pit as its doors began to open.

ACKNOWLEDGEMENTS

I would like to thank the Escorcia family for all their support and love. I have been blessed with the greatest Godfather a boy could have. You were always there for me.

To the Sunday crew where we shared memories, food, and laughs over a game of cards. Junior Escorcia, Jorge Echeverria, Cesar Echeverria, Stanley Castro, Edwin Castro, Joe Vaughan, Jose Mora, David Guinan, Dan McDonough, thank you all for everything.

To my aunts and uncles, Louie, Carlos, Paul, Theresa, Marisela, Crystal, much love and thanks.

For my cousins, Julia, Summer, Adrian, Rene, and Benny.

Special thanks to Conor Dempsey. If you hadn't walked this road first I would have never believed it was possible. Thank you so much my friend.